Free Bird

PAMELA DEAN

ISBN 979-8-9913924-6-4 (paperback)

ISBN 979-8-9913924-7-1 (digital)

Cover art by: Sabrina Watts

Edited by: Kathryn Underwood

Proofread by: Laurie Starmer

 Formatted with Vellum

Prologue

JANUARY 1ˢᵀ, 1990

12:01 a.m.

Molly

I watch the clock flip from midnight to one minute past, then stare at the empty space next to me. It's officially the new year, a new decade, and my husband is nowhere to be found.

Not that I am complaining, since this will be a lot easier if he stays out all night. I throw the covers back and reach for my glasses before fumbling for my shoes under the bed. I walk softly to the bathroom without turning on the lights. If he comes home now my plan will—no, it won't be ruined, it will be delayed. I have a backup plan, and a backup to my backup. I blow out a breath and twist my long, curly hair up, then hold it in place with a claw clip. I unbutton my silk pajama top and slide the matching bottoms off, then put on my faded, ripped 501's. I pull my Fleetwood Mac concert T-shirt out from the bottom drawer and slip my feet into my old sneakers.

When I emerge from the bathroom dressed in my favorite clothes, I take my first step out of the life that I hate. I don't bother glancing around, I just make a beeline for the door, but since the lights are off, I slam my foot into the stupid baseboard.

"Son of a bitch." I grab my shoe and hop around a few times, then freeze when I think I hear a noise. I hold my breath and wait, then the sound happens again and I relax. It's just the neighborhood kids setting off firecrackers. I leave the bedroom and head down the hall to the stairs that lead into the kitchen. There is less of a chance I will run into anyone going this way. Isaac would never use this stairway, and Grant is at his friend's cabin for another two weeks. My eyes sting at the thought of my son.

I reach the kitchen and yank open the drawer that holds Jasmine's sharpest knives. After pulling it all the way out, I reach and push on the back of the drawer so it folds down, revealing a hidden compartment where I keep my keys. I tuck them in my palm and let myself scan the only room in this damn house that I will miss. I can see Jasmine's door and the light underneath seeping into the dark kitchen. I already said goodbye, even if she didn't realize it was forever.

I walk to the back door she uses to come and go from the house and twist the knob. Knowing I will never set foot in here again is like a shot of joy injected straight into my veins.

I step out of the house and into my new life.

Tom

I WIPE down the bar and take a deep breath, letting the smell of the pine oil settle my soul. I live all year for this moment.

June 1 is my favorite day of the year and August 31 is the worst. For now, I embrace June and all it has to offer. This is my sixth year taking my vacation on the West Coast and I have grown to love it more than my life back home. That's normal, right? I mean, most people hate their jobs and look forward to vacation. I am not alone in these feelings and thoughts. I look at the list Lyle left detailing all the things that need to be done, and I smile. It took a long time to convince my friend to let me do these things while I was here. The first year he hired piss-poor contractors who did half the job and charged him full price, thinking since he was out of the country he'd never know. That ended with one phone call from me.

Now, I'm not only the bartender for three months, but also the handyman, something that thrills me beyond belief. The first item on the list has me laughing out loud.

1. Take down Christmas lights

I glance around the small room and see his attempt at making the place festive. I am sure Jill had nothing to do with this. If she had, it would have looked good. I met Jill and Lyle when I was in grad school.

They had just started dating and were gracious enough to let me be their lifelong third wheel. Well, to be fair, they probably didn't understand the commitment at the time. My mouth curves upward when I think about our friendship over the years and how lucky I am that I sat at their table in the library all those years ago.

I grab a chair and use it to climb on the bar to reach the strand of lights that are drooping a little above my head. One quick tug and I have them down. I look around and see he has another strand tacked to the back wall, so I remove that. The last one is wrapped around the brass bar that people rest their feet on while they drink at the high-top bar. I notice more than one bulb broken or missing on this strand and wonder what Lyle was thinking when he put these here.

I glance at my tan Dockers and think about going upstairs before kneeling on the ground to get this last bit, but I have about fifty pair of pants exactly like this. It really doesn't matter if they get a stain. I kneel and start to unwind the lights, being careful not to cut myself on the broken pieces. The last little length of wire is wrapped around the bar and the bracket. It seems over time, part of the cord has gotten wedged into the space between. I crane my neck trying to see where it's stuck, then give up and plop down on my ass on the dirty floor.

From this angle I can see the problem, but I can't quite reach, so I scoot forward on my butt to get a better grasp. I am not sure if the ripping sound or the sharp pain catches my attention first, but the feeling of liquid spreading out from my ass has me cussing like a sailor who just found his best friend fucking his wife.

I roll my lips together to fight off any more obscenities and try to get up. My pants seem to be caught on whatever the hell stabbed me, so I grab my thigh and tug, and I hear a crack of old wood splinter beneath me. I roll to the side and reach back to feel and I find a very large sliver of wood sticking out of my left butt cheek.

Fantastic.

When I pull my hand back, I see bright red blood on my fingers.

Shit.

I manage to get up to a standing position and look down to see a rather big piece of the floorboard missing from where I recently was sitting. Great. There's a little puddle of blood and I feel more blood running down my leg. Damn it. I need to go to the doctor. I don't want to yank this damn thing out without help in case I've punctured an artery or something. I wonder if I'm being overly dramatic but allow myself some grace since it really fucking hurts.

I limp over and grab my keys then head to the front door cursing Lyle the whole way. As soon as I pull open the door, my eyes squint at the bright sunny day. Adjusting my gaze downward to let my eyes get used to the light, I see the feet of tourists and townsfolk hurrying past on the sidewalk. The bar I call home for the summer, The Floppy Fish, doesn't open for another five hours, so I have time. Thankfully there is a Doc in the Box type place only two doors down. I have never had to use them, but I am so grateful I know where to go. I lift my eyes and start to limp slowly along, still cussing under my breath. I am sure there is a plank of wood sticking out the back of my pants and with each step I can feel a gush of blood. I might die out here by the flower shop.

I smile and wave like nothing is wrong and keep my hand on the building for support as I scoot along at a snail's pace. When I finally reach the door to the medical clinic, I sigh with relief. I walk in, then inch toward the reception desk where a woman with grey hair is typing away. It's the only sound in the whole place and I hope that means there won't be a long wait.

"Hello, I need to see the doctor please," I say. My voice sounds strained, so I hope that it warrants an immediate response.

"Alright, you can fill this form out and we will get you back soon. You are welcome to sit over there." She points to the lobby and the hard plastic chairs that line the wall as she tries to hand me a clipboard.

"Well, actually, sitting is rather impossible for me at the moment. I seem to have a rather large splinter back there." I use my head to indicate the splinter is behind me.

"What are you talking about?" the older woman says, then stands to see. So I turn around to show her, wondering myself what it looks like.

I hear a sound that can only be described as air escaping a tire, then a thud. I twist back around and don't see the woman anymore. Crap.

I stand on my toes and look over the tall counter. I see black shoes that are covering long grey socks sticking out from a pleated grey skirt. I look around for someone else but don't see anyone, so I yell, "Help! I need help out here!"

A man with a large beer belly rushes out. Well, "rushes" is a stretch, more like waddles out. He's pulling on a white lab coat and from his vantage point he can see his secretary on the floor as soon as he rounds the corner.

"Jesus, Mary, and Joesph. Henny? Are you okay? What happened?" That last question seems to be aimed at me, so I start to explain, but he turns and yells over his shoulder.

"Molly, get in here! Henny fell. Bring me an ice pack and the smelling salts," he barks over his shoulder. I wait while a woman rushes in carrying what he asked for, and while I am not unsympathetic to poor Henny, my ass is starting to really hurt and my sock is now soaked with my own blood.

"I am sorry, I'm afraid she fainted when she saw this." I spin around and point to my ass.

"Oh! My! Yes, well, I imagine that would do it. Follow me. Molly, you help Henny, then meet me in Room 10." He waddles off and I follow him, glancing back only once to see a woman in pink nurse's scrubs snap a white vial and hold it under the old woman's nose.

The doctor has disappeared down a hallway with multiple open doors. I am grateful he said a room number to his nurse so I know where to go. I step into the room and see he already has a blue towel on a tray and is positioning a light above the patient table.

"Why don't we start with the basics? What is your name?" the doctor asks as he pats the table like he wants me to sit.

I raise an eyebrow at him and say, "Tom, and I'd rather stand, if you don't mind."

"Oh, of course, right. Turn for me and let me get a look at what we are dealing with." The doc does a little spin motion with his finger and I obey like a good ballerina. I place my hands on the table and wait while I hear him grunt and shift behind me. I have never felt more vulnerable in my life. He stands and grabs the light that is on some kind of hinged arm, and pulls it down close to my ass, then he sits again and scoots closer. His shoes are bumping mine and I make the mistake of clenching my ass cheeks. Pain and blood shoot down my leg and I hear the doctor sigh.

"I can't get a good look at it from this angle. Hang on." I hear the wheeled stool being pushed away and cabinets opening and closing.

"Molly! Where are the bandage scissors? Oh wait, never mind, I found them!" he yells to the empty hall. I am starting to worry that I killed poor old Henny since the nurse hasn't shown up yet.

"This part won't hurt, hold still please," the doctor says as he places a meaty hand on my shoulder. I feel something wedge between my pants and my hip then I hear a ripping sound. My pants fall away like the peel of a ripe banana. He kicks my Dockers out of the way and I feel cheap. He didn't even warn me, for fuck's sake. Then it hits me, how the hell will I get back to the bar? I hear him clear his throat then he puts a very cold hand on my butt cheek and lifts it a little.

"Nope, still can't see. I am afraid I will need you to lie down on your back. Let's see if we can get Molly in here to help you get on the table." The doctor pats my leg and I hang my head as he waddles out into the hallway.

"Oh, there you are! Molly, would you please get Tim up on the table. I can't get a good look at that foreign body. How's Henny?" he asks and I lift my head, curious about her well-being too.

"She's fine, Dr. Potter. Embarrassed, but she is fine," a sweet woman says. "Why don't you go see to her and I will get the patient set up."

The doctor walks away mumbling something and the nurse steps around so I can see her. In all the commotion at the front desk and the spear of floorboard in my ass I failed to notice how absolutely stunning Dr. Potter's nurse is. Holy hell. She isn't like any woman I have ever seen in real life. I wonder for a moment if I am hallucinating. She's tall, with curves for days. I wonder how I missed that the first time I saw her. She has short hair, I mean like short-short. Like it might be shorter than mine. She has wide brown eyes and a mouth that is so full and lush it can't be real. She's wearing simple gold hoop earrings that make me want to slip my tongue through them and tug.

Jesus, what is wrong with me. I clear my throat and say, "I think I have lost a lot of blood, I don't feel well."

"Right, let's get you up on the table. Put this hip here like this, then bend at the waist and roll to the table. As soon as you start I'll guide your feet. Don't worry—I got you," she says. She could have told me to do a handstand while holding a balloon between my butt cheeks and I would have agreed.

I nod, then do as I am told and am surprised at how easy it is. I sigh with relief. Now that I'm not standing, the pain has decreased a lot.

"Okay, now stay on your side for a second so I can get the stirrups ready," she says. She trails a hand down my leg and I get chills. I also feel like I might throw up. It wasn't a sexual touch, more like what people do when they walk behind a horse. I hear her moving things around and the table jerks a little as she snaps something in place by my feet.

She comes back around so I can see her, and she bends at the waist to peer into my eyes. "Now, I am going to have you scoot down on the table so that when you roll your bottom won't be on it, but I'll hold your legs while we get them in the stirrups."

"You keep saying that word like I know what you are talking about. The only stirrup I know is hanging off a Western saddle," I say with a grunt as she tugs on my right leg, encouraging me downward. Oh, she's strong.

"There you go, now roll, lift this leg a little, perfect. Feel that with your foot? Yep, your heel goes right there," she says, like I finally learned to ride a bike and she is super proud of me. I muster up some courage to say something, hopefully witty and charming, right as the doctor returns.

"Oh, good thinking, Molly. That makes things much easier. Now grab that light and position it, yes, just like that!" he says as he leans in. I can feel his hot breath on my thigh as he nudges my legs apart a little with his thick meaty hands. Holy crap, this is awkward. I blink up at the ceiling and try to block out what is happening to me.

Molly

WELL, this is the most interesting thing that has happened since I rolled into town six months ago. I know it's wrong for me to be excited by this poor man's predicament, but this made my whole week.

I feel on top of my head for my glasses then to my scrub top, then I do the "where the fuck are my glasses" pat down. Oh, right there in the front pocket where I put them. That used to drive Isaac insane. Nice that he doesn't have to be bothered by that anymore.

I slide my glasses on and lean against the counter waiting for Dr. Potter to let me know what he needs. I've already opened the sterile tray and helped him into his gloves and now he is poking around the most impressive splinter I have ever seen.

"You are a very lucky man, Teddy. One inch more and this would have speared your left testicle. Molly, hand me the hemostat please." He holds out his hand and I push the tray closer.

"It's just there, doctor. I am not sterile." I have to remind him all the time of things like this. He went to med school when gloves were for surgery, not in office procedures. Hell, when I started here he didn't even have biohazard trash!

"Ah yes, thank you. Now Trevor, I want you to hold still," Dr.

9

Potter says, as he picks up the man's testicles to move them out of the way. The guy jumps like ten feet off the table.

I walk over to his right leg and put my hand on his knee. "Hey, it's okay—he needs to get that out, try and hold still, okay?" I am using not only my nurse voice, but my mom voice. I hit him with the double whammy and it works, as his body relaxes and he closes his eyes.

"Please just hurry," the man says and I fight off a smile at how strained he sounds. I swear I am not a mean person, but I have been so bored. This is apparently the entertainment I needed.

"One quick tug and—" Dr. Potter pulls the wood splinter free and sets it on the tray next to the other instruments. "There you are, Theo, why don't you let Molly get you cleaned up and then we will see you up front. When was your last tetanus shot?" he asks.

"Um, I am not sure," the man says.

"Well, the answer from now on will be today's date! Molly, give him a tetanus shot and tell me, Trent, are you allergic to anything?" the doctor asks.

"Just penicillin," the man says.

"Well, good thing I asked! Alright, I was going to have Molly give you a shot of antibiotic but all I have is penicillin. Molly, why don't you order the clinic some Rocephin when you do your big month-end thingy. People like Ted need a safer option!" Dr. Potter heaves a big sigh then says, "Right, I'll just write a script for you then."

He takes his gloves off, leaves them on the tray, and walks out of the room. I pull on a pair of gloves and take up his spot on the stool. Man, that was a big-ass splinter. I chuckle quietly at my own pun. I lift my glasses to the top of my head so I can see and peer at the wound. It left quite a hole, and I touch the area gently. He flinches, so I apologize.

"Does he need to stitch it or anything? It feels like it's still bleeding," the man says.

"No, he won't want to close up the wound in case there are any little bits left in there. What's your name?" I ask, because it was clear the doctor didn't know.

"Tom," he says with a groan.

"Okay, Tom. I am going to get you cleaned up and apply a dressing, then we can get your vitals, that tetanus shot. Then I promise to get you out of here."

I start to work on the wound trying to ignore the fact that I am basically nestled between this man's thighs. I see that he has some blood on his testicle and I think about leaving it for him to clean off, but he's going to need to keep this dressing on for twenty-four hours then keep the area clean and dry after that. He might not be giving his boys a good scrub anytime soon.

"I am going to use a little wet gauze to clean you up, this is just sterile water, but it will feel cold. I want to warn you that I'll be touching you, okay?" I say, hoping he understands what I mean.

"No problem. Nothing could be more humiliating than having the doctor manhandle me without even knowing my name," he says.

I can't help but laugh at that. "Yeah, he is a little quirky, but he knows his stuff. For a small-town doctor he is pretty good." I wipe everywhere, saving the testicle for last. When I have nothing else to clean, I try and sound as professional as possible when I say, "Okay, only this last bit here."

I use quick soft movements and squirt a little of the sterile water over the area to make it go quicker. I hear him suck in a breath and see a not-so-subtle jump of his dick.

"Sorry, I know it's cold," I mumble, then quickly dry the area. I use a dab of ointment then hold a padded piece of gauze in place over the wound and tape it down.

"All done. I am going to help you get out of these." I pat the stirrups, and he blows out a breath but doesn't speak. I walk up so I can look down into his eyes then ask, "Are you okay, Tom?"

"Yeah, just embarrassed," he says, draping his arm over his eyes. I bite my lip to fight off a giggle. Damn, he is really cute. Older than me, I'm sure. He's got the start of a beard, and blond hair with a bit of grey around the temples.

"Nothing to be embarrassed about. Here, let me help you up." I reach for his hand and assist him to a seated position. Then for some reason it really sinks in that he isn't wearing anything but a shirt, socks and tennis shoes. I glance at the floor where his pants and underwear are in a heap.

"Here, I'm sorry." I hand them to him and try to turn to give him some privacy but he just laughs.

"These are going in the trash. He cut them off me. I'm going to cause quite a scene walking back home," Tom says. He has a nice voice, deep and rich and kind.

"Oh geez, I should have come back here to help him. I have a pair of disposable shorts I can give you." I pull open the drawer under the table and give him the paper shorts we use when I have to x-ray someone.

"Thanks," he says and bends to slip them on quickly. "Now that I am no longer flashing you, I can ask you a question?"

"Sure, what can I do for you?" I slip my glasses off my head and into my pocket.

"Oh good, you're all dressed! Fancy shorts you have there! You can thank Molly for that, she made me order those. Apparently people want to cover up while getting x-rayed!" Dr. Potter slaps Tom on the arm and laughs, then launches into his aftercare instructions. "You'll want to keep the area clean and dry for twenty-four hours. Don't change that dressing till then, and get this prescription filled. Also let me know right away if you have any blood in your ejaculate, or if you have pain with ejaculation. You didn't hit your testicle, but you came damn close and I want to know if there are any problems. If you have trouble getting an erection or if the erection is painful you can also let me know, or tell Molly. We can get you a referral to a specialist." He beams at Tom and I wish I could record this whole moment. It is incredible.

I have to admit, I knew Dr. Potter would say some weird shit to this guy. He just can't help himself. I don't know how his wife Henny puts up with him, but she must have some secret because they have been married almost forty years.

Tom shifts uncomfortably on his feet and refuses to look anywhere but the ground. The blue paper shorts fit him like they fit everyone, tight around the waist then billowing out like a skirt. Tom has nice thick thighs, but they are no match for the wide legs on these bad boys. I fight back a smile and turn to the tray instead, gathering the supplies so I can clean and sterilize them.

"Thank you, Doctor. I will let you know if I have problems," Tom says.

I carry the instruments out of the room and down the hall to our little lab. I set them on the counter so I can put them in the autoclave later. I feel antsy to get back into Room 10 and I pause to lean on the counter. What the hell, am I really rushing back in there? For what? So he can ask me on a date? So I can tell him I thought he was cute and I'd like to be that close to his balls under totally different circumstances? I rub my hand down my face to wipe away any of those kinds of thoughts. I take the tetanus vaccine bottle from the fridge and draw out the appropriate dose then recap the syringe and tuck it in my top pocket. I take a deep breath and walk back in to take his vitals, give him his vaccine, and then escort him to the front to get checked out. My plan is to do all those things without hitting on him, because that is creepy and not something I am good at.

I turn the corner into Room 10 and look around.

He's gone.

I wonder if it was me, Dr. Potter, or knowing he was getting a shot?

The rest of the day is filled with regular patients with regular problems. A sprained knee caused by too much bending to pick up sea glass, a cold that the patient was sure was a sign of a brain tumor, a bladder infection because she "doesn't like to get up to pee" so she holds it until she practically wets herself. I rolled my eyes at her so hard, but thankfully my back was to her. These people are ridiculous. That's probably why our first patient of the day stuck with me so much. Nothing was as interesting as him. Or as cute if I'm being honest with myself.

"We are going to close up at four today, Molly. I'm taking Henny up the coast for a nice dinner. She had quite the scare with that Terrance fellow and his splinter. Maybe a nice glass of red wine and a steak will make her feel better," Dr. Potter says. He is struggling to take off his lab coat and I could help, but it's kind of fun watching him spin circles as he tugs on it. He has these short arms and a rather large body so he's not unlike a T-rex. In fact, when I first started working here, I called him Rex in my head so many times I once said it in front of a patient. Thankfully, he didn't seem to notice.

"That's a good idea Doc. I am sure she will enjoy that. I will close up and forward the calls to the service," I tell him.

"Thanks, Molly. I don't know how we survived without you." He smiles at me, finally free of his coat, and walks to hang it on the hook.

"No problem. Have a wonderful night." I walk him to the back door, then lock up. I head to the front of the clinic and pull the blinds down and turn the sign that says we are closed until Monday at 8 a.m., then lock the door.

I have to do some charting and filing but it's okay. Not like I have anywhere to be on a Friday night. I fight the urge to pull the charts off the doctor's desk to see if Tom filled any paperwork out. I wonder what his last name is, or how old he is, or where he lives. Of course, none of that is my business, so I don't go looking.

I work until almost six and feel pretty good when I leave. All the rooms are stocked and ready to go for Monday. The charts have been filed and all the prescriptions have been called in. Now I have two whole days to find things to occupy my mind so I don't start wondering how my son is doing. First thing tomorrow morning I'll drive up to Fort Bragg to check my P.O. Box. Grant usually writes to me on Tuesdays, and I know by Saturday it will be there. I write to him on Saturday afternoon, and lately I have been able to do that without crying. He's doing well, and that is all that matters.

I walk down the street waving at the people I know and smiling at those I don't. Everyone that lives here is friendly and most of the tourists are great. Occasionally we get an asshole—I mean, what town doesn't?

Six months ago when I got in my car and drove up Highway 1 along California's coast I wasn't sure what I would find. I didn't really expect to stay, to be honest. I thought I'd keep going until I reached Canada, but there was something about Mendocino that captured my heart.

I am lost in thought as I make my way past the tourists. It's not too far up the street to my little cottage. I glance up as I pass the flower shop and see people heading into The Floppy Fish. I wonder if I should get a beer before going home. When the door to the bar opens, I hear soft jazz instead of the normal country music. I also notice the little sign that Lyle puts out front with the specials isn't there. Huh. I wonder what's going on.

My stomach rumbles reminding me I had a very light lunch, so I pass on the beer and reach my house a few minutes later. I live just off the main street of this small town, something else I never thought I would do. Choices were made for me at the age when most girls start to dream about their future, so I didn't think about what I would want, or where I would live if I could choose. I'm glad I eventually got the chance to learn this about myself.

I love being in the heart of the town. I walk everywhere. In fact, my car spends most of its days parked in the little garage behind my cottage. I pulled it in there after I bought the place, and I only take it out when I go check my mail in the town north of here.

I unlock my front door and set my keys down in the pretty blue dish I have on the wooden table in the entryway. I have light wood everywhere with white and blue accents. No dark colors, no dark pretentious wood. Definitely no heavy curtains covering views most people would die for. I have gauzy fabric that barely blocks my view out, and to be honest, probably gives my neighbors more information than they need. I take off my shoes and put them under the bench by the door, then turn and lock the dead bolt. It's a habit I can't break. I know I'm safe here, I know he doesn't know where I am. If he did, that little lock probably wouldn't stop him.

I pause and look down the hall wondering if I should shower first or eat first. It's the daily dilemma. I pull off my scrub top and head for the shower, knowing I will feel a hundred times better after washing off the day. I love how fast I can clean up now that my hair is so short. Not like I am going to leave it like this, but for now it's liberating. I have always had hair down to my waist, thick, long, gorgeous, curly hair that people would stop me on the street to comment on. It was how people recognized me, so it was the first thing to go.

I turn on the shower and wait for it to warm up then step in and sigh. Showering first is always the right answer. I pour a drop of shampoo in my hand and massage my scalp and my pixie cut hair, enjoying not needing conditioner. Maybe I will let it grow to my shoulders. That would be nice, and easy still. I do miss my curls, and the way they would bounce around my face like they had a personality of their own.

Now that I am all clean with legs and pits shaven, I pull my fluffy blue robe off the back door and walk out to the kitchen to make some dinner. Not having to cook for a family has been liberating too. I love that I can have a bowl of cereal if I want. Of course I rarely do that. I am far too in love with foods like enchiladas and pasta to live off corn flakes.

Once the enchiladas are in the oven I go into my bedroom and get into my pajamas. Another nice thing about living alone: my pajamas aren't the silk pants and button-up top that my husband expected to see me in. I wear a pair of ratty shorts and a thin cotton T-shirt, just like I did as a teenager before I met him. I never wear a bra when I am home and I love the way my big, heavy breasts feel when they are set free. They are only for me now, so I get to decide how they look and what does or doesn't cover them. To be honest, the first month I lived here, I walked around without a shirt on most of the time. I bet my neighbors across the street thought a nudist had moved in.

The timer goes off on the oven, so I grab a plate and lift the cheesy goodness out of the pan, then pour myself a glass of red wine. I sit at my small table and pull my latest novel toward me. When I stopped reading this morning, Kent Price was about to woo a gorgeous woman on a balcony. I love the way this guy writes, and when I found out there was a whole series I practically squealed. Patrick Smith does such a good job of drawing me into the fictional world he creates. I feel like somewhere out there Kent Price is still looking for his journal.

The evening passes like most of my nights since moving here. I eventually pull out my list and stare at the ten things I wrote down in my therapist's office a year ago. I am proud of all the things I have crossed off, but I don't know how to do some of these. I don't think I can. Sherry told me that lists help carve a path—they aren't commandments, and they can be changed, but she didn't know my drive to finish things.

1. ~~Leave him~~

That was a good one to cross off.

2. ~~Set up a way to correspond with Grant that feels safe.~~

I actually did that before the first item on the list. When I told Grant I was leaving and asked him to come with me, I wasn't surprised he said no. I knew he wouldn't leave his friends and his lifestyle. He had no reason to hate his father. That man gave him everything, I was just his mom. I set up a post office box for him and told him it was our little secret. I trust him.

3. Find Martha

Nope, haven't had the courage to do that one yet. Did it bother me that I wasn't able to complete these in order? Yes. It still makes me sweat to see number ten crossed out with the ones before it still waiting. Although number ten was a fun one to cross off.

10. ~~Have a one night stand.~~

Yeah, that wasn't something I ever thought I'd be able to do, but I actually enjoyed it. Even if he finished without satisfying me, and didn't seem to notice, it was exhilarating and helped me understand that I can do whatever I want. I can't really say it was his fault I didn't have an orgasm. I was so stunned it was happening I don't think I was actually in my body. It was like I was watching from a chair in the corner, like *wow, look at him go. He's really putting the work in.* I wonder if it had been a long time for him or if he was just one of those guys who thought of only themselves? I know going forward that I would not want that in a partner. I need to learn to enjoy sex and all it offers. I am in charge of me for the first time since I was sixteen and saw those two pink lines on the pregnancy test my best friend helped me buy.

4. Write something creative.

I guess I could tackle that one. Maybe I'll go to The Floppy Fish some night and watch the tourists. It might inspire me. I've thought about writing about Dr. Potter or his wife, but that seems like a cop-out since they are really the only people I know in town. I don't know what it is about this Northern California beach community, but it is so different from where I grew up. Where San Diego attracted money and beauty and power, Mendocino seems to attract hippies, families and artists. I should be able to find someone interesting enough to write about. I know my therapist wanted me to see that everyone has flaws, that on the surface someone can appear to have it all together, but the layers beneath are what she wants me to focus on. Her theory is that I'm too hard on myself, and while she is probably right, I'm not sure how to change.

I BARELY MADE it through the night. Every step was torture and I am pretty sure I bled through the bandage that cute nurse put on me.

I was so embarrassed about her washing my nuts that I ducked out of the room while she was gone and threw my credit card at the poor secretary I almost killed. She ran the card in record time and I was limping my way back to The Floppy Fish before I knew it.

I went straight upstairs and took a nap, waking up in time to drop off my prescription at the pharmacy before I had to open the bar. I prayed for a quiet night and since I am a lucky bastard, it was.

I turn off all the lights after locking up and then I limp my way upstairs. My apartment is just one room with a bed, a couch and a small table that sits near a kitchenette. The bathroom is pretty big and I stare longingly at the shower while I take a piss. God, it would feel amazing to wash off the day, but Dr. Potter and Molly told me to keep the dressing clean and dry for the first 24 hours.

I get undressed and reach under to feel the dressing, expecting to find it soaking. It's not. It's dry, so I imagined all the bleeding as I worked. I don't know how I feel about that. I have never been one of those lumberjack tough guys but I am not a wimp either.

I grab a paperback off the stack I brought and walk gingerly to my bed. Fuck, it feels so good to lie down. With a few pillows tucked behind me I get started on the first book in a series by a young author named Patrick Smith. My colleague recommended this book to me, so it went on my summer reading list. During the school year when I am teaching I can't read for pleasure like I want. I am preparing lessons or grading papers or writing grant proposals. Then there are the fundraisers and galas that require a tux and a date.

I sigh and flip the book open, folding the cover back to curl around the spine. I never do this with other books. It's a bad habit and destroys the novel, but I am a rebel during the summer months and this is one of the ways it manifests.

When the sunlight hits my face, I realize I must have fallen asleep reading again. I glance over to the small table serving as my nightstand and I don't see the book, which means that uncomfortable lump under my right shoulder blade is probably *Kent Price, A Man on A Mission.*

I tug it free and put it on the table, then roll to my stomach. My ass is feeling a lot better this morning, so I reach back and push on the bandaged area. It's a little sore, but not bad. Thank God. I don't think I could face seeing that nurse again. Fuck, she was pretty. I don't think I have ever seen a woman with eyes like that. Her lips too, Jesus, those things could stop traffic. I roll to my back and stretch my arms above my head, then I think more about Molly. When she held my knee and used that stern voice or when she leaned over to check on me with those kind, beautiful eyes. The gentle curve of her ear and those sexy gold hoops, understated and dainty, they begged for teeth to nibble on and around them.

My cock jumps at that thought so I reach down and give it a squeeze. I wonder if I should test out the boys and see if they're okay? I mean it's research really. A need-to-know kind of situation.

I slide my boxers off and grab my hardened length. Fuck, how long has it been since I have had actual sex? My hand and I spend way too much time together. Yvonne? Was that her name? My date for the last fundraiser. She was very attractive and had a nice figure, but her speaking voice was rather off-putting. Call me shallow, but I prefer to have a deeper voice than my date. Once in the middle of sex when she moaned I actually thought a bear had broken into our hotel room.

Fuck, why am I thinking about that right now? I clear my head and try to summon a good experience, college days, nope. Grad school? No.

Then the image of Molly bending over to help Henny pops into my head. Her pink scrub top had pulled up a little exposing her lower back as it sloped down to that full, round ass. There were no pockets on the back of her pants, so the curves stood out. I imagine what that ass would look like uncovered. She doesn't strike me as the type that exercises too much, creating one of those firm hard butts. No, she was soft and supple. I picture grabbing her hips from behind and guiding her onto me slowly at first. I'd tease her dragging my cock up and down through her slick heat, then thrust in and pound away until I felt her clench around me.

My hand is moving faster now as the scene unfolds in my head. In my imagination she throws her head back and cries out "Tom!" as I slam into her again and again. As she tightens and her orgasm takes her under, she looks back at me, mouth open, eyes wide and I come hard, shooting my load into her deeply and relentlessly.

Reality fades in and my come hits my stomach and chest, as my balls continue to tighten. Holy crap. Well then. Experiment complete. No pain and, as I glance down at the mess I made, I'm happy to see no blood.

I grab my shorts off the floor and wipe myself clean, then get up to use the toilet. When I am finished, I stick my head under the sink and scrub my hair as best as I can. I'll shower tomorrow and since I don't shave in the summer it looks like I am ready to start my day. I really need to try and find a girlfriend or at least a friend with benefits. Maybe even go on a date or something this summer. I feel a little shame at how hard I came fantasizing about that nurse. Since I have never seen her around here before, there is no reason to assume I will run into her. Mendocino isn't that small of a town. I am sure there are a lot of people that don't come into The Floppy Fish, or get their groceries every day at The Harvest Market. Those two places make up the extent of my summers, unless I need lumber or supplies Lyle didn't think of for his list of repairs.

I make my usual summer breakfast, an omelette with every vegetable I can find. Summer squash, spinach, mushrooms, red onion, and green peppers. I scramble three eggs with a bit of water, then tip it into the hot buttered pan. I scrape away the edges, letting the uncooked liquid eggs fill in the open space. When I have a mostly cooked surface I dump in the veggies and shredded cheese, expertly folding the egg to make a pocket. My mouth is watering just looking at it.

I don't have time for this during the school year. I am up and out the door with coffee and maybe a bagel or toast. I eat something from the cafeteria for lunch then come home too tired to cook a nice dinner. Every year when I return from my summer here I swear to myself that I will cook like I do here. Every year I don't. Maybe if I did I'd be happier? I flip the omelette and let it cook for a little longer, then slide it onto a plate as my toast pops up. Love it when I get the timing right.

After breakfast I clean up the small kitchen and pull out the list of things I need to do. I add "repair splintered floorboard" below all Lyle's requests. I look at number two and sigh. I hate doing things out of order, but I really don't know if I am up to climbing a ladder today. I opt for the third and fourth items.

The boxes are right where Lyle said they would be. I grab the one on top and take it to one of the high-top tables near the front of the bar. I can see out the window from here so I'll get to people-watch as I fold.

Every year Lyle creates a flyer of all the summer activities available in the area. There is a map on the back, and the center contains the events and the dates of each. I've told him he should get the local shops to pitch in and advertise on this, but he says no. He doesn't want it to be a sales thing—he just wants to share information. Since his is the only place that carries it, he gets a ton of foot traffic and customers. I guess that makes him pretty damn smart.

I have to watch what I am doing the first couple times to make sure I get the seams right, but then it becomes easier to glance up. It's about eleven and the sun is bright and cheery overhead. I look down to put my folded flyer in the box and almost miss Molly crossing the street and walking right toward the bar. We aren't open. The door is locked. Should I get up and unlock it? I should. I don't want her to pull on the handle then never try to come in again. I hop off the stool just as she veers past The Floppy Fish and keeps going down the sidewalk. I press my face to the glass to try and catch a glimpse of her, but she is gone.

Should I go after her? Fuck no, of course not. What would I say? Hey, just wanted to let you know when I jacked off to thoughts of you this morning everything was okay! Then give her a thumbs-up and a smile? I push myself off the window and go back to folding the flyers grumbling to myself about my sad life.

When I am done with these I need to go to the hardware store and get some heavy-duty hinges. Lyle wants me to cut into the bar on the right side to make another way out. It's a reasonable request and should be fairly easy to do, and since we are closed on Sundays I can start on it first thing in the morning if I have all my supplies.

Molly

I SPEND my Saturday running errands and enjoying the beautiful weather. One of my Saturday errands is to drive up to Fort Bragg to check my post office box.

Grant is so good about writing to me, and I find that these letters from him give me a sense of myself that I wasn't expecting. He is seventeen now, almost eighteen. Sometimes it feels like only a few years have gone by and other days it feels like a few lifetimes have passed.

He writes about his days at the beach, playing volleyball with his friends, surfing and bonfires. He has no idea I was younger than him, doing those same things when I met his father. I mean, he can do math, so he knows I was only sixteen when I had him, but he never asked questions, so I never told him the story. Of course my therapist made me put that on my list. It's hovering at almost the last spot because I thought I was doing them in order and I wanted to put it off.

#8 Tell Grant about how I became his mother.

I pull into the parking lot of the post office and look around for any sign of my husband. It's dumb—he probably doesn't even care I'm gone, but I am sure his parents do. Mr. and Mrs. Densworth do not like surprises or lies. Grant said they ask him often if he's heard from me, then I'm sure they lament my poor parenting choices when he says no.

Grabbing my keys from the center console, I jump out and open the door in time to help Mrs. Johnson make it inside unscathed. I honestly don't know how she gets in when I'm not here. Maybe she has a team of people who know she can't manage her walker and the stupid heavy door with the broken spring.

"Good morning, Miss Molly. How are you this fine Saturday?" she asks.

"Wonderful. How are you?" I duck down a little and speak loudly into her left ear.

"Fair to middling, all my joints are working and my heart is still thumping!" She gives me a bright, beautiful smile, one I return easily.

After I grab my mail, I wait so I can hold the door open for her, then I walk with her to the bus stop to make sure she is safe. I have never asked her how old she is, but I am guessing she is about 150. I know that isn't possible, but there is no way she's younger than ninety-five. Her wrinkles have depth like that of a topographical map of Hawaii. I don't know if I want to live that long to be honest, although she seems pretty damn content.

Normally I wait to open my mail at home, but for some reason today I feel antsy to read the letter from Grant. The envelope is thicker than normal so I slide my finger under the flap and pull out his letter.

Dear Mom,

I am so excited. I wish I could see your face when you read this, but I got into Willmore University! Grandfather said he went to school there and thought I had a good chance, so I applied and got my acceptance letter a few days ago. We are going to Coronado on Saturday to the steakhouse you love, to celebrate. It's going to be weird not to have you there Mom, but I know you will be celebrating for me. Maybe after my birthday, I can come see you? I will be moving out to Connecticut in August, so this might be our last chance for a while. I hope you can make it work. I am trying to understand why you left, I know you must have had a good reason, but times like this it really hurts. I've included some pictures this time. Grandfather caught the moment I read I was accepted, I thought you would like that. I also put in a few other pictures, me on the rowing team and me at prom. No, we are not a couple. She is a good friend who is going to UC Davis to study animal sciences. She thinks she wants to be a veterinarian but she's not sure. You'd like her, Mom.

Dad has been on a trip for work so I haven't had the chance to tell him about my acceptance to Willmore. I wish you were here. I can't wait to hear what you think about all this, Mom.

Love you,
Grant

Well that's a punch to the gut. I let my forehead fall to the steering wheel, not caring if there are people watching. One thing about my big, long hair was I could hide under it to cry. Now with my hair not even covering my ears the sobs escaping me are obvious.

Connecticut? That's on the other side of the country. I knew he was going to apply to Ivy League schools, but he also talked about smaller ones on this coast. The guilt for wishing he had been accepted to Washington State instead, sits in my throat, making it hard to swallow. I wipe my eyes and force myself to sit up, shoulders back and smile. My son is going to Willmore. That is something to celebrate, not cry over. I tuck the pictures in my purse and fold the letter back into its envelope, setting it with my other mail.

My mind slips back to when Lisa and I stared down at that stick with its two bright pink lines that shouted "pregnant." It might as well have said, "You are in so much trouble," given how my stomach twisted in on itself. I can still feel that pang when I remember the day I found out I was going to be a mom. It's one of the many things Isaac stole from me and one I would never get back. I would never look at a pregnancy test with hopeful joy. Instead, I worried about what kind of a life I could give a child. I worried about how I would finish school, get a job, or have a place to live. That was all before I knew the truth about the father.

Isaac was a baby-faced, dark-haired surfer who caught my eye in the fall, the night of my sixteenth birthday. He was at the beach with his friends like I was, and we hit it off so quickly I was under him before I gave it much thought. I fell hard, and at the time I thought he did too. We spent a lot of time together after school and on weekends. I didn't really think about the risks, and he did wear a condom sometimes. When my period didn't come in November, I took a test with Lisa just before Thanksgiving.

My mom worked at the local diner, and she was on the late shift that night. The flash of the car lights as she turned into the carport seemed to sear the pain deep into my heart. I had to tell her. I had to disappoint her. I will never forget the look on her face when she came in. She set her worn leather purse on the TV tray by the door where we kept the mail, then caught sight of me, on the couch clutching the stupid test, bawling my eyes out. I think she knew without me saying a word. She wasn't as supportive as I wanted her to be, but she was as supportive as I expected her to be. We were barely making it with only two of us. How could we manage a baby? My baby.

When Isaac came by the next day, I told him. I knew I didn't have a lot of choices and I wanted his help, I thought maybe he would know what to do. Maybe that naïve part of me thought he'd tell me how happy he was because he had fallen in love with me. What. A. Joke.

My mom came out of her room and demanded he take care of me and the baby. Mom went on about how he was going to have to get a job and pay child support and help with the medical bills. She peppered him with questions about how he planned to pay for a child, and how his parents would feel knowing he knocked up a sixteen-year-old. When I think about that particular comment, I remember his face turning very pale. That should have been my first clue.

I remember feeling so ashamed that she was talking to him like it was all his fault. When he stood and shoved his hands in his pockets saying, "Don't worry. I'll handle this," before leaving, I thought I'd never see him again. Maybe that would have been better.

I stop before I can fall down that rabbit hole again. My therapist said I can turn the channel. I don't have to watch the reruns. So I shift my car into reverse and head back to my home where I can write a congratulations letter to my son and look at the pictures he sent.

As I drive back up the freeway I try and form the feelings I have into words. How do you tell your kid that they mean the world to you after you left them? How do you convey their importance when you are hiding from the people who surround them?

I toy with saying, *Grant, once you are on the other side of the country and away from the horrible people you call your family, I will come see you as often as I can!* I won't say that of course. I promised myself, and to a lesser extent, Isaac, that I would never speak ill of his family around our son. Grant deserves to love them, and for all their faults I will say, they love him fiercely.

By the time I make it back home I am more of a mess than I want to be. It's only four but I grab an enchilada from the fridge and put it in the microwave to warm up. I shove my list and a few notebooks in my favorite bag knowing that I need to do something besides sit here all night. I had the idea of going to write at The Floppy Fish, so after dinner, that's what I will do. I can write Grant back when my head is in a better place. He doesn't need my frustrations and anger. He needs my pride and joy. Those things are there; they are just buried under all the negative thoughts at the moment.

An hour later, freshly showered and with a full belly I lock up and head to The Floppy Fish to try and erase my crappy mood.

Tom

SATURDAY NIGHTS ARE USUALLY the busiest and it seems tonight will be no exception. I already switched out the kegs, and my waitresses were kind enough to help get all the cases of alcohol unpacked and restocked before we opened at four.

Now at five, I have a bachelorette party on the patio out back and four locals bellied up to the bar. All the high-top tables are full as well.

"Can I get you another one, Dave?" I ask the man who has already told me his life story over one beer. I hate to think about what he will spill with a second one.

"Nah, just the bill. I need to get home and soak this wart or Dr. Potter said he will take the scalpel to it," Dave says, slapping a ten on the bar. I shudder and turn to the register to make change and when I spin back around to hand it to him, a beautiful face greets me instead. I look over her shoulder and see Dave waving at me as he pushes out the door.

"Oh! Hey! It's you! Hello there. Molly, right?" I stammer like a fool. She cocks her head at me like she is trying to place me.

"Have we met?" she asks, then her eyes flash with recognition and she dips her head. I wish the lighting was better in here, because I'm sure she is blushing.

"Hi. Yes, well, not formally." I extend my hand to her and say, "I'm Tom."

"Hi, Tom, you must be new in town," Molly says with a small smile.

"I was going to say the same thing about you," I respond, leaning in like I have nothing better to do than chat up a pretty girl at my bar.

"Hey Tom, I need two vodka tonics, a white wine, a bud light and one shot of tequila," Misty says as she wedges herself in between the locals. I should take care of #6 on the list and put those bars up to give her an area. We'd lose a seat at the bar, but I hate watching her squeeze in like that when it's busy and I know Lyle feels the same way.

"Sure thing, Misty. Coming right up." I start pouring and set everything on her tray as Patty comes to the other end of the bar with her order. Doesn't look like Molly and I will be chatting too much this evening. I do manage to get her a glass of red wine that she requests, and I sneak glances at her whenever I can.

She has a notebook and a few pieces of paper in front of her, and she is writing, then crossing things out. She also has been chewing on the plump bottom lip of hers which is very distracting. Not like it's any better when she nibbles on her pen while looking off into the distance. I only overflowed one beer mug while watching her, which isn't too bad.

The bachelorette party finally leaves the patio, allowing for some of the patrons that are crammed in here to filter outside. I roll my head trying to relieve some of the tension I feel. It's not the crowd, it's her. I glance around and since everyone seems happy for the moment I lean over and ask, "So Molly, can I get you another glass of wine?"

I swear she blushes again, but that also might be wishful thinking on my part or it's just really fucking hot in here. I mentally add "improve lighting" to my list.

"Sure, Tom. I'd love another. Thanks." She slides her empty glass toward me and our fingers brush as I take it from her. It's not much but that little touch is enough to make me remember my fantasy about her. I turn from her quickly before I make an ass out of myself and pour her a glass of our finer wine. She asked for the house wine, but that crap is gross. I'll pay for her to have the good stuff. Giving her way more than the four-ounce pour too, I spin around and attempt my best smile.

"I'm glad you came in tonight, Molly. To be honest I was hoping I

—" I start but Misty steps up with another huge order, effectively stopping my attempt to ask Molly out.

"Are you new in town or just visiting?" Misty asks.

"I've been here for about six months, but I haven't been in for a drink in a while," Molly answers.

"That explains it. I know I would remember you if you had come in. I love your hair. Who cut it for you? I want to go that short but I've been chicken," Misty says. I am strangely interested in this exchange because I also love Molly's hair. She has such a beautiful face, it would be a shame if you couldn't see it from every angle.

"I had a really good hairdresser where I used to live. She did the big cut and now I go to the barber shop over on Forest for a trim," Molly says.

"Oh man! I am so jealous. I want that kind of carefree life," Misty says with a chuckle then looks down to see her full tray. "Shit, sorry, Tom. I didn't see that you were back. Thanks!" She takes the tray and heads back into the crowd.

"What are you working on, Molly?" I ask, because that is all I've wanted to know for the past hour.

"A short story. I thought if I was here, I would get some good ideas for characters or something. So far all I have gotten is a little tipsy," she says with a giggle.

"Are you a writer?" I ask.

"Apparently not," she says, and I laugh at that unexpected reply.

"I mean I can write words, and I can string them into sentences, even form a paragraph, but tell a story? Not really." She sighs and rests her chin in her hand. With her other hand she lifts her wineglass and stares at it before taking a drink. "You are a little heavy-handed with the pour, aren't you?"

I shrug and grin, "Maybe, when it's for a beautiful woman."

"Oh, wine and charm! I like this side of you, Tom." Molly takes another drink and licks her lips as she sets the glass down. "Don't think I didn't notice you poured me a glass of the finest merlot. There is no way this is the crappy house wine that Lyle buys."

"You caught me," I say with a wink. "It's on me. I'd really like to ask

—" I start then jump about ten feet in the air when Patty slams her tray on the bar.

"Tom, can you please go toss Mr. Cowboy? He's on the patio and he grabbed my tit and felt up two women who are trying to talk and have a nice girls' night out," she says.

Patty has her arms crossed over her chest in a protective manner, making me see red. I storm out from behind the bar and push past a few people to get to the back patio. I see the guy right away since it's hard to miss a six-foot-four cowboy who is trying to motorboat a very angry woman.

"Alright, Tex. That's enough!" I grab him by the back of his pants and twist, jerking him back to me.

"What the fuck, man? Oh hey, Tom, what are you doing out here?" he slurs at me. Jesus. A wave of relief washes over me, knowing this won't turn into a fight.

"Kicking you out. Time to go home, Dylan. You've had enough and these women are not interested." I still have a hold of him just in case he decides to stop being my best buddy.

"Okay, Tom. I'll go, let me get my keys out." He staggers into me, and I reach into his front pocket and retrieve the keys before he can. I pocket them and start marching him to the door. "Patty called you a cab, Dylan. You aren't driving home." I pray that's true since I don't want him inside the bar causing more problems.

"Thank fuck. I love that Patty. Will you tell her that? Tell her I love her," Dylan says, tipping his hat at everyone we pass like he's on a parade float. He's a decent guy, when he's sober. I know I'm lucky that he isn't a mean drunk. He just gets handsy. Patty will probably get flowers and an apology tomorrow from him.

I walk him out front and park him in the back of the waiting taxi. I lean in and say, "Thank you, Earl. If he doesn't pay, come back and I'll take care of it."

Earl nods and I slap the roof to say goodbye, then head back inside. I hope I can finally ask Molly if she would like to have dinner with me. I tried what feels like at least five times tonight and was stopped every single time.

I step back into the bar that has finally settled to mostly a mellow local crowd. My shoulders sag immediately when I see the empty barstool where Molly was. Her bag is gone and I see a twenty tucked under her wineglass. Damn it. How long was I gone?

I sigh heavily then walk back to get behind the bar and run into Molly as she comes out of the bathroom. I grab her elbow to steady her and apologize. "I'm so sorry, I didn't see you there. Are you okay?" I wonder if she can tell how relieved I am that she's still here.

"I'm fine! Sorry, I wasn't watching where I was going either. Some cute bartender poured me a lot of wine, so I am a little wobbly," she says with a wink.

Cute? Damn, I like that. "I kind of assumed you would stay longer if you had a full glass, are you leaving already?" I ask.

"It's after nine, Tom. I should probably make my way home." She adjusts her bag on her shoulder. Fuck, I wish I could make sure she gets home safe. I glance around the still bustling bar and know there is no way. We don't close till midnight, and I can't ask her to hang out and watch me work, for fuck's sake.

"You aren't driving, are you, Molly?" I ask. I still have my hand on her elbow, but she hasn't pulled away so I keep it there.

"No I live up the street. I walked here." She gives me a shy smile.

"I wish I could walk you home," I say before I can think too much about it.

"Do you now? That is very sweet, but I think I can manage," she says. She puts her hand on my chest and I take a sharp breath in at the contact. I step closer to her and see her eyes widen a bit.

"Can I get your number, Molly? I would really like to take you out for dinner," I say. I can't believe Misty or Patty didn't pop up out of the floorboards or something when I said that. They've had the worst timing all night.

"Sure. I'd like that, Tom." She reaches into my pocket and pulls out my pen, then trails her long delicate fingers down my arm to my hand. She pulls my hand up and squints while she writes out her phone number on my palm. My heart is thumping out of my chest and I fight the urge to snag her wrist in my hand when she caps the pen and slides it back into my shirt pocket.

I stare into those endless brown eyes and give a little nod before I say, "I'll call tomorrow so we can find a day you are free."

This time I know I am not imagining the blush that crosses her neck and face. She stares down at her shoes, then at the wall behind me, then at my shoulder before letting her eyes settle on mine. "I look forward to hearing from you. Don't lose that number," she says with a wink. I grin at her, enjoying that I watched her go from insecure and unsure, to confident and sassy in the span of a few seconds. It was like watching a butterfly break free of its chrysalis.

"Tom, I have an order for you!" Patty yells from over my shoulder so I give Molly a smile and a wave and get back behind the bar. The first thing I do is grab a napkin and write her number on that so I won't live in fear of water for the next three hours.

Patty's order is only four beers from the tap, so I fill that and start wiping down the bar top and then grab the empty glasses to take to the back. I bend to put them in the bin under the cabinet and see a folded piece of paper on the floor. I pick it up and unfold it to see a list. I must have dropped Lyle's list out of my pocket. I fold it back up quickly and shove it in my back pocket just as the cab driver that took Dylan home wanders in.

"Hey, Earl, let me know what I owe you," I say, but he shakes his head.

"Nah, I'm off duty, came in for a drink and to catch up. I haven't seen you since last year. How was teaching?" Earl settles in the seat that Molly had vacated.

"It was good, the same as usual. Do you want a beer or is tonight a whiskey neat kind of night?" I ask, reaching for a glass.

"Beer, I had whiskey one time! Never again," he says, shaking his head. "I should have known it wasn't going to be my thing, I hate the taste of most hard liquor. They make it sound so good in books and movies, you know?" He chuckles.

"Yeah." I lean in and whisper, "I'm actually a red wine fan. I hate whiskey. If I have to have a mixed drink I usually order something with vodka, then sip it all night."

Earl laughs and slaps the bar top. "I wouldn't have guessed that about you."

"Dylan get home okay?" I ask while the tap fills a beer mug for Earl.

"Sure, he's probably passed out just inside his door but I don't offer a turndown service." Earl says and I laugh, but he's holding up his hands to stop me. "You think it's funny, but he asks me to tuck him in every damn time. I help him to his front door, get it unlocked, then run back to my cab. I have no interest in getting more involved than that."

"Jesus, I don't blame you," I say with a laugh. I wander down the bar checking on the other people and making small talk with everyone. Eventually I am back with Earl and his endearing questions. He is a great guy and one of the many people I miss when I am in Connecticut.

"So, favorite student and why?" he asks as he watches me wipe down the beer mugs and rehang them. Jerald came in at ten to start washing glasses for us so he can get Misty home on time for once. He's learned that she won't leave a lot of extra work for me so if he wants her home, he helps out.

I scratch my head and think back on the different classes I had and all the students. Only two stand out and I know immediately he will agree with my assessment.

"Robert and Gwen. Both grad students, separate classes so they didn't know each other but they were by far the best. Robert because he kept me on my toes with his research and questions. He had a way of phrasing things that I found intriguing, and before you ask, I am trying to think of an example." I shake my head with a laugh, knowing that was his next question. "And Gwen because she was brave in her requests. She was doing her thesis on the ancient people who inhabited Scotland, specifically how they traded with others. She wrote a grant—which was funded, mind you—allowing her to study abroad for an entire year with accommodations rivaling a queen."

Earl laughs at that even if he probably doesn't know how ridiculously lucky Gwen was to have that experience. The postcards I received before I came out here from Gwen made me laugh out loud. She basically had enough funding to hire a ship builder to replicate the ancient vessels and plans on spending the summer traveling the trade route.

"They sound like quite the pair. How did the fundraiser event last September go?" Earl asks. He drains his beer and slides the mug across the bar for a refill. He lives about a mile from here and I know he walks, so I never question his alcohol intake.

"Oh, that was an interesting evening indeed. Remind me to tell you about my experience with deep throat," I say, wiggling my eyebrows.

His eyes go wide and he throws back his head in laughter. "I demand to hear that story right the fuck now!"

I hold up a finger to him to indicate I need a minute, then tend to my other patrons. Sadly, it's midnight before I make it back to Earl. He's sliding off the bar stool and pulling out his wallet when I reach him.

"Another night I will hear this tale, no?" he says in a fake accent. I am not sure if he's trying to sound like an Italian mob boss or a Frenchman, but I chuckle at his attempt either way.

"Yes, I promise," I say, holding my hand over my heart and the other in the air.

After I see the last of the people out, I check the back patio area happy to find no empties or beer mugs. Jerald's help always makes closing go quickly. When I make it back to the front, Patty, Misty, and Jerald are at the door ready to go. "Thanks for your help tonight. Jerald, I am going to put you on the payroll. You can't keep doing that for free. I mean it." I point my finger at him and he laughs.

"Whatever man, I want to get Misty home. I like helping her." He squeezes her hand and leans in for a kiss. I see Patty roll her eyes and nudge them toward the door.

"I want to go home too, see you later Tom," she calls over her shoulder as she steps into the cool night air, followed by Misty and her boyfriend. I walk over to lock up, then turn off the sign in the window before heading upstairs to my apartment.

Once I am inside, I pull my pen out of my shirt pocket and the napkin that has Molly's number on it. Then I dig my keys out of my jeans then do the pat down, making sure I haven't forgotten something. I feel the crinkle of paper when I pat my ass, so I pull the folded sheet from the pocket and toss it on the table. My eyes catch on the purple ink.

That's not my list. What is that? I pick it back up and unfold it, seeing a list of ten things. Some crossed out already. It's in a woman's handwriting and I hold it up to my nose and take a sniff. Perfume like

Molly wears floats around me, and I close my eyes. I should fold this back up and give it to her when I see her, but I don't have that kind of control.

1. ~~Leave him~~

2. ~~Set up a way to correspond with Grant that feels safe.~~

I should stop. This is obviously very private, but my eyes betray my good honor and I see #10 ~~Have a one-night stand~~. Damn I wish that one wasn't crossed off. Not that I would want to be that to her, but I still feel weirdly jealous of whoever was.

I fold the paper over and take a deep breath. Do I keep reading?

Yes. I am a horrible person, but yes.

3. Find Martha

That one isn't crossed out, I wonder who Martha is. I smile when I see #4. Write a short story. That is what she was working on tonight. This is like a bucket list or something. I scan over the ten things she felt were important enough to write down and cross off as she completed them.

9. ~~Buy a home~~

That is crossed off too. She hasn't accomplished very many of these and is obviously not a weirdo like me and doing them in order. I don't know why that makes me think she is exciting and wild, but it does. My eyes squint at the seventh item on her list. Fuck, I should definitely not be reading this.

7. Buy a vibrator and use it

It's not crossed off. Interesting. She had a one-night stand before she bought a vibrator? Has she never owned one? I assumed all women had one, but if you ask me why I think that, I wouldn't be able to give you an answer. I just assumed. I mean if men had an actual equivalent I am sure I'd have one. A blow-up woman with an o-shaped mouth? Gross. No. Not interested.

I fold her list back up and pull the napkin from my pocket. My hand still has her number written on it, but I liked the assurance that I wouldn't lose it. I strip out of my clothes and take a shower before collapsing into bed, happy and intrigued for the first time in my whole damn life.

I SCRIBBLE out what I wrote. It's like the tenth time I have tried to start a congratulations letter to my son. Why can't I find the words? Maybe I used all my words in that horrible attempt at a short story last night. I should just burn that. It didn't seem half bad in my semi-tipsy state but when I reread it this morning, all I felt was shame.

I take a deep breath and stare up at my ceiling, letting my feelings wash over me like I was taught. What rises to the surface? Pride. Awe. Wonder and joy for sure. I would have never dreamed of a moment like this, maybe I should say that? No. That opens the door to all the things I have never told him.

He thinks his father and I met, fell in love, got married young and had him. He doesn't know the truth and there is so much I don't want him to know. Not yet at least. I want him to have his memories unvarnished by my mistakes. I want him to have the family he thinks he has. I don't want him to know who they were to me—yet.

My dearest Grant,
I am so proud of you! If you could have seen my

face as I read the letter it would have been exactly like you imagined. I cried like a baby as I read the words and even more when I saw the picture. Thank you for sending that. You have worked so hard to get where you are. I know you scored very high on your SAT's and I am sure the essay you wrote clinched your admission. I hope you are planning on majoring in something that will highlight your gift for writing.

I would love to see you before you leave for college. Once you are 18 you can come here, or we can meet somewhere in the middle. I don't want to explain or talk about this again, please know that once you are a legal adult things will change. I will be sending a card for your birthday that will explain more. I love you so much and I am sorry I couldn't be there to celebrate with you.

Thank you for carrying the burden of keeping my whereabouts a secret. I hope soon more of this will make sense. I am sure your father will be as excited as me to hear your news.

You deserve all you have earned.

I love you,

Mom

P.S. You and your date looked lovely. She sounds like a nice person and I am glad you have found a friend in her. Maybe you can keep in touch through college.

I reread the letter and sigh. It's not everything I want to say but it's what he deserves to hear. My baggage doesn't need to be unpacked at his expense. That is something I worked on with my therapist. I want to continue to give him every opportunity available to him because of the ties his father and his grandparents have. I sacrificed so much to get him the life he deserves, but he doesn't need to know that.

I fold up my letter and put it in an envelope, then grab my bag to pull out my list. I flip through the notebook several times and even shake it out. Damn it. I shove my hand in the bag and feel around, like it has a secret list-stealing compartment I don't know about.

Fuck. It's gone. I tip my head back and moan in frustration. I must've dropped it in the bar last night. It's probably in the bottom of a trash can somewhere. I hang my head and put my face in my hands. Do not cry. It's just a list. I can rewrite it. I know what's on it. It's paper and words. Words that took me a year to compile. Words that helped me find my way.

My phone ringing stops the spiral I am about to embark upon. I stand and walk to my kitchen and pull the phone from the cradle on the wall. "Hello?"

"Hi, Molly? It's Tom. I hope it's not too early to call." A deep sexy voice comes through the other end of the phone, and I feel my stomach flip. I put my hand over my heart and breathe before answering.

"Hi, Tom, no it's fine. Nice to hear from you."

"I want to let you know I may have something of yours. Did you lose a list?" He says and I sink into the nearest chair. Oh thank God.

"Is it written in purple ink and contains things I hope you didn't read?" I say, a nervous chuckle bubbling out.

"It is and, I owe you an apology," he says in a sheepish voice.

"Damn. Well, I guess we'll have a lot to talk about at dinner. Unless you are only calling to tell me you found my list and you were hoping I forgot you wanted to take me out?" I ask, trying to sound light and airy and not mortified and miserable.

"I called to ask you out, Molly, but I wanted to be up-front. I am sorry that I let my curiosity get the best of me. We don't have to talk about it. You are allowed to have your privacy," he says in such a warm tone it brings tears to my eyes.

"Well, thank you for that. I would love to go out with you, Tom. I um, I work Monday through Friday for Dr. Potter. Eight to five so if weekdays work for you—" I ramble.

"How about brunch today? Have you had a big breakfast already?" he asks quickly, cutting me off.

"No, I've only had a cup of coffee," I say. My smile takes over my face easing the anxiety I was feeling.

"Great. I can pick you up or we can meet somewhere?" he asks.

I look around my house, my sanctuary, and say, "I'll meet you."

Tom mentions a restaurant he likes and asks if I know it. I nod even though he can't see me. It's my favorite place too. "Yeah, I know it. Ten?" I ask.

"Yeah, I'll bring your list and we can pretend like I didn't see it. We can also pretend like I am not a jealous fucker over number ten," Tom says, and I bark out a very unladylike laugh.

"I should be embarrassed, but I am not. I'm proud I was able to cross that off my list," I say. I'm so glad he can't see me, I'm probably the color of a beet. I do feel proud of that, but it took a lot to get to that point. I am not going to pretend I didn't call my therapist the next day in a complete meltdown. I also went to a doctor and got every test I could even though we used a condom. But now, five months later, yeah, I'm proud of myself for that one-night stand.

"I look forward to seeing you Molly," he says, his voice deep and warm. It's so soothing I could listen to him for hours. I wonder if he has ever worked in radio? He sounds like one of those DJs I'd listen to in my room as a kid. Playing the Top 40 hits and melting my preteen heart with smooth vocal rumblings.

"I'll see you soon, bye, Tom," I say and hang up before letting myself squeal like I wanted to when he asked me out to brunch.

Today.

Like he can't wait until next weekend. I do a little shimmy dance and hurry to my bedroom to find something to wear.

Glancing at the clock I see I have enough time to walk to the café on the cliffs, aptly called Cliffside Café. I put on mascara and a light pink lip gloss and a new dress. I haven't had any occasion to dress up since moving here, and it feels good to have on something so pretty. When I step out onto my little porch, I look around out of habit. I wonder if that will ever go away. I know Isaac isn't even in California right now, but I still feel nervous. I opted for my white saltwater sandals since I have to walk. I am sure this dress would look great with heels but I haven't worn a pair since I left San Diego and I don't know that I ever will again.

Stepping into the street, I smile as a gust of wind pushes me forward, like the heavens are encouraging me to this fresh start. The light cotton fabric of my skirt swishes around my legs as I make my way through the neighborhood. I push my sunglasses up to the top of my head when the sun tucks behind the clouds. My silver hoop earrings are a touch on the big side, but I fell in love with them when I tried them on. Now that my hair is short, I can wear things like this and they actually show. My wicker boho bag with the leather strap hangs from my arm and I wish I had a picture of me walking down this street for a date. I wish I could show the me of a year ago that this was possible. A piece of my heart mends with each step forward. I feel so free and light as I turn onto Cliffside Way.

My newly healing heart stutters in my chest when I see Tom standing by the little white picket fence that surrounds the place. He's wearing light tan Dockers and a button-up dark blue shirt with yellow polka dots. I glance down at my yellow dress and chuckle softly to myself. We match. How fucking cute is that?

"Hi!" I say as bright and confident as I can, even if inside I am a trembling mess.

He dips his head and I see the grin spread across his gorgeous face as he shakes his head. "I see you are crossing number five off your list today."

I blush at his remark but quietly tell myself to keep it together. "I am, and number six," I say. When he cocks his head like he doesn't know what I mean I explain, "That one was to go on a first date."

"I am glad I get to help kill two birds with one stone," Tom says. He pushes off from the fence and walks toward me with a swagger I didn't notice before. He grasps my elbow and leans in to kiss my cheek gently. Before pulling away he quietly says, "You look lovely in yellow, Molly."

His gaze is dancing over my face and my breath catches as I blush and look down at my feet.

I say, "Thank you," then fight the urge to explain I have always loved yellow, but Isaac hated it and told me to stop wearing it. It's been almost eighteen years since I've worn my favorite color. Wearing it today on a date, is like my silent middle finger to him and his controlling family. I remember walking out to make breakfast when Grant was about three. I had bought myself a new shirt that was bright yellow. It had a bee on the front that was dancing and said something cheesy like "bee happy." Isaac scowled at me and asked why I was dressed like a child, then told me yellow made me look green. He left before eating and I swore to never wear yellow again.

"Ready?" Tom asks, nodding to the restaurant and breaking me from my thoughts.

"Yes, thank you for inviting me," I say nervously as he lets me lead us into the quaint little cafe.

"Don't thank me yet, you might find me horribly boring and wish you had said no." Tom holds up two fingers as the waitress approaches. I watch as she grabs the menus then she leads us to a table by the big window. "Is this okay? There will be a spot on the patio in about five minutes if you'd rather wait?"

Tom looks to me for my opinion and that little gesture has my head spinning. "This is fine," I whisper.

"This will be fine, thank you," Tom says keeping his eyes on me the whole time, his brows furrowed. He pulls out my chair and then sits across from me the concern on his face never leaving.

"You weren't given choices," he says, but then shakes his head as if clearing the thoughts. "I'm sorry, that was too forward of me." He reaches into his shirt pocket and pulls out my list and hands it to me.

"Thank you. I was looking for this when you called. I have it memorized, so it wouldn't have been the end of the world if it went missing," I say. I tuck it away in my purse, happy that I will be able to cross two more items off at the end of the day.

"I am a man of my word, so we don't have to talk about it, Molly. Tell me something that wasn't on that list. When did you move to Mendocino?" he asks.

"About six months ago. I needed a change, as I am sure you gathered." My body relaxes as bit as I realize maybe it's a good thing he's read my list. He was probably able to gather enough information about me to not ask uncomfortable questions. He seems like a gentleman who will respect my boundaries, but I am sure I'll find out. "How about you, Tom? When did you move here?"

"About six years ago, but to be honest I only live here in the summer. I don't think I count as a true Mendocinian."

"Mendocinian?" I ask.

"Yes, one who lives in Mendocino," he says with a smile. There is something so refined about him. He reminds me of the people I would meet at fundraising events with Isaac and his parents, but Tom has a kindness about him those men lacked.

"I see," I say with a chuckle.

The waitress comes over and we both give her our order. I notice Tom didn't have to look at his menu since he knew exactly what he wanted. I mean if you come here, there is only one choice for brunch, the lobster quiche. It's the best thing I have ever eaten and I don't miss Tom's smile when I order one as well.

"You fit right in here," he says with a wink.

"I lived in San Diego before moving here, and of all the seafood places I had the joy to visit, nothing compares to this quiche," I say.

"I have never been that far south. To be honest, I have only ever seen this little sliver of California. I don't have a lot of time while I am out here." Tom pauses as the waitress comes with our coffee, then continues when she is gone. "My friends own The Floppy Fish and they travel every summer, so I offered to come out and run the place in their absence. It's my favorite time of the year."

"That's very nice of you. You must be a teacher to get summers off like that," I say, and he nods. "So how are you healing up, if you don't mind me asking?" I am desperate to talk about him and not me and my list of self-discovery.

The cutest red flush crosses his cheeks and he takes his napkin from his plate and unfolds it like he might find the answer to my question inside. "If you don't want to talk about it, I understand," I say quickly.

He shakes his head and laughs a low deep rumble of a laugh. "No, it's okay. I guess I was kind of hoping that you had forgotten how much you know about me." He sighs and leans back before saying, "I guess that's why I read your list. I mean it seemed only fair since you've had my balls in your hand."

The small sip of water I had taken decides to go in two different directions as I laugh out loud at his remark. Some went up my nose and sadly some hit Tom in the face. Seeing him wipe his face with his napkin made the laughing and choking worse. Thankfully he joined in and I was delighted to see his silent, shoulder-shaking tears streaming down his handsome face.

He reaches for my hand and squeezes it when we regain our composure. "Sorry, Molly. That was a little blunt. Although, I haven't laughed that hard in years, so I'm going to say it was worth it. To answer your question, the hole, which was way too close to my testicle, is healing nicely," he says with a smile.

I rub my thumb over his hand and give him a little squeeze before pulling my hand away. I am not ready for that kind of intimacy with him. "Good. I am glad you haven't had any problems. I am not going to ask any more questions because I am sure if there were problems you would have contacted Dr. Potter." I wiggle my eyebrows at him and he starts laughing again.

"I can, in fact, report that there was no pain or blood and everything seems to be in working order," he says with a wink. God, he is so handsome. He has dark blond hair with a hint of grey mixed in and light blue eyes. He has a full bottom lip that I want to chew on and a deep divot in his top lip. He must've skipped shaving this morning because he has a light stubble.

"Well, that's good to hear. I am sure Dr. Potter will be happy to know that as well. For information only, of course—" I say and he nods and says, "Of course," then waves his hand for me to continue. I clear my throat and lean in before saying, "Can I assume this was a solo experience or did you have help testing the equipment?"

"Are you asking me if I am seeing anyone, Molly?" he says with a smirk.

"Yes. To be honest, I am." I sigh and lean forward a bit. I might as well lay this on the table, he must know already anyway, and I promised myself to do things differently. Ask lots of questions, answer honestly. "I haven't really dated before, so I don't know the protocol for things like that. Forgive me for being so forward," I say, using his words. I squeeze my hands together under the table to steady myself.

He smiles and says, "It was a solo experience, strictly for peace of mind, of course." He winks at me then continues, "To be honest, Dr. Potter's comments scared me more than the splinter did!"

"I have to tell you, that was the most impressive splinter I have ever seen. You handled it really well. Better than Henny, that's for sure. I couldn't stop laughing when I was bent over trying to help her," I say. Then I add, "But I was quite impressed when I saw what made her faint."

"Do you think I could add that to my resume? Has ability to make women faint with just a glance at his ass?" Tom says. He leans forward resting his chin in his hand. My stomach does that little flip again as his smile spreads across his handsome face.

"I don't think you need to advertise your assets Tom," I say with a wink. Not sure why I suddenly feel more confident, but it must be because he is very easy to talk to. The waitress brings our food out and tops off our coffee, apologizing for the wait.

"It's no problem. I was enjoying my date so much I didn't notice," Tom says, and the waitress smiles at us before leaving.

"You are quite the charmer, aren't you?" I say.

"I have been known to charm, in the past. Not recently. Mostly I teach and sling drinks."

We dig into our food and fall into a comfortable silence.

Tom

I CAN'T GET over how easy she is to talk to. I haven't had this much fun on a date, well, to be honest, ever.

Once we finished eating, I pay the bill and ask Molly if she wants to go for a walk. I have things to do this afternoon, but I'm not ready to say good-bye yet.

"I would love to. I assume you've been to Portuguese Beach?" she asks.

"I have, but I always enjoy it. Would you like to go?" She is smoothing her hand over her dress and I sense she is a little more nervous now that we are done eating. I don't want her to feel uncomfortable.

"Or we can walk along through town. It doesn't have to be the beach," she says, glancing around. She looks over her shoulder before pulling her sunglasses down to her face. They are the latest style, cat-eye with a black frame and silver writing on the side. I can't make it out, but it looks like a designer label. That kind of surprises me. I bet they cost more than her dress and shoes combined.

"Let's go to the beach. If it's low tide we can look for shells." I hold out my hand and she slips hers into it easily.

"What subject do you teach, Tom?" she asks as we wind down the street that leads to the ocean.

"I teach at a university, mostly archeology but I had a few sociology classes last semester that I hope to keep. I filled in for a colleague who doesn't appear to be coming back," I explain. I don't get into how I still haven't gotten tenure after all these years and my job is at the whim of the administration. Still, teaching at Willmore is a dream and I don't want to complain or sound ungrateful. My father certainly would raise an eyebrow at any hint of my being anything but completely enamored with whatever crumb they throw my way.

"That sounds interesting. Do you have a favorite subject aside from what you teach? Like is there a class that interests you so much you wish it was yours to teach?" Molly asks.

"What a great question. I guess that would be the sociology class. When I was teaching archeology there was a lot of pressure to write grants for upcoming digs, and with my time split last year that lightened up a bit. I made the mistake of writing a few grant proposals that were accepted early in my teaching career and now they expect magic from me," I say. We have reached the end of the paved road, so I motion to the bench and wait for her to sit before joining her. I slip off my loafers and wait while she removes her sandals, then we continue down to the beach. I notice she juggled her shoes quickly to her other side so that we could continue to hold hands, and my heart feels ridiculously warm at that little gesture.

The wind is picking up and I glance over at Molly who has slid her sunglasses up on top of her head. The waves are crashing and couples like us walk along the shore. There is a woman with a bag full of shells that waves at Molly.

"Hi, Mrs. Christopher. Find any good ones?" Molly asks as we pass her.

"You know it! It's late in the day now, but I can't resist. Enjoy your walk!" The old lady scurries off after yelling, "A sand dollar!"

Molly chuckles and says quietly, "I am not supposed to reveal this, but she is one of our patients. She is a real hoot and comes in often with shell-related injuries." She glances back over her shoulder to make sure the woman is out of earshot. Then she stops and grabs my arm, turning me toward her. "Hey! You left before I could give you that tetanus shot! I also didn't get your vitals. My chart is incomplete thanks to you. I had to write 'patient went AMA' on the bottom." She squints at me like she's mad, but her grin gives her away.

I drop her hand and let my finger trail up her arm as I stare into those big, beautiful brown eyes of hers. I feel the goose bumps form under my touch, so I drop my shoes and do the same with the other hand until I am resting both hands on her shoulders. I watch as her tongue peeks out, licking her bottom lip. Her chest rises as she takes a sharp breath in. I lean in a little and say, "I am so sorry that I ran out on you, Molly. What can I do to make it up to you?"

A sweet humming noise comes from her as she cocks her head to the side contemplating. I step a little closer and see her eyes widen as she takes in a quick breath.

"May I kiss you, Molly?" I ask, stepping in a little more. I am betting no one ever asked her that based on the look she is giving me. She blinks slowly, then nods yes with a subtle dip of her chin. I slide my hands up her shoulders to the back of her head, then I move one, letting it fall a little lower onto her slender neck. I want to make her feel cherished, special. I want her to know how attractive I find her, so I let my other hand trail down to cup her cheek.

A little whimper escapes her as I lean in and gently press my lips to hers. She is soft and warm and smells like lavender and the sea. I move both hands so I'm gently holding her face as I kiss her. I slowly take my time to explore her luscious mouth. She parts her lips, but I don't change my pace or deepen the kiss. I pull back slightly and rest my forehead to hers. My breaths are short and ragged. I am afraid to continue out here in the open where I would get arrested for what I'm thinking of doing.

"Wow," she says in a breath out.

"Yeah, you took the words right out of my mouth." I step back so that I don't maul her the way I want to. In the distance we can hear Mrs. Christopher yelling about another kind of shell she found, and it breaks the tension a bit.

I bend to pick up my shoes, then grab her hand again and lead her down the beach, trying to calm my racing heart. When was the last time a kiss affected me like that? Did she feel that too? I promised myself to not rush her, to not ask too many questions about her life because from what I gathered from that list, she is in the middle of a divorce. I mean at the very least, that is what she is dealing with.

I am assuming Grant is her son and even though I have a million questions, the way she looked at me just now, and at the restaurant when I asked if she was happy with the table, I am betting she wasn't in a great marriage. I don't know if she was abused. I hope to God she wasn't, but there is a timid almost fearful nature about her sometimes. It's layered under her confidence and laughter, but it's there.

"What made you want to be a nurse, Molly?" I ask, assuming this is a safe subject. There was nothing on her list about school, so I am taking a guess.

"Oh, I'm not a nurse. I am a medical assistant and I have a limited certificate for x-ray. I didn't go to college for that, it was a trade school," Molly says as I feel her squirm a little.

"Don't do that. Trade schools are important, and what you do is as well. What made you interested in working in the medical field?" I ask, giving her hand a little squeeze.

"That's hard to say. I guess I liked the idea of helping people. I actually started in the EMT program, but I, well that didn't work out." She pauses so I squeeze her hand again and look over at her and nod encouraging her to continue.

She blows out a little breath and says, "There was another program that started a few days later and it was a better match. I got certified as a medical assistant first then got my limited x-ray certificate right after."

"How long have you done this? I only ask because you are very good, Molly. You helped set me at ease that day, even if I did run as soon as I could," I say, and she laughs.

"Thanks for that. I've been working for about five years," she says and I can feel her relaxing again. "I really like it, and so far, Dr. Potter is the best physician I have worked for." She stops and turns toward me with a twinkle in her eye. "I know you might find that hard to believe, but he is a really good doctor."

"He couldn't remember my name, Molly. I didn't find that confidence inducing." I laugh as I say this, and she dips her head and smiles before looking up at me again. I could get lost in her eyes, so big and round and innocent.

"Yes, but that is part of his quirky side. Seriously, as a diagnostician he is one of the best in the state. Mendocino is lucky to have him." I can tell she believes this even if it isn't true.

"Okay, I will take your word for it, Molly," I say with a little chuckle.

"How long have you been teaching?" she asks.

"A while." I shrug. I don't want to talk about me, I want to learn more about her and the things that aren't on her list. I want to know about her list, of course, but I am a man of my word.

"Do you like it?" she asks, and I nod.

"Do you want to talk about something else?" she asks with a laugh.

"Yes. Please," I say. I nudge her toward the ocean so we can get our feet wet a bit. A man with a golden retriever jogs past and waves at us. The sun is out from behind the clouds now and our little quiet walk is quickly turning into a group activity.

"So where does Lyle go over the summer?"

"Oh! Another great question, Molly," I say, and am rewarded with her beautiful laugh. I continue, "This year it was Jill's turn to pick, so they are in Ireland working on a farm."

"Working? I thought they took off for a vacation!" Molly seems as surprised as most people who don't know Lyle and Jill.

"They don't have an off switch. That is a vacation to them, working somewhere else." I shake my head, then explain further, "We all met during college, undergrad years. He, Jill, and I became friends quickly because they were as serious about school as I was. Lyle was taking a double major and had big plans to join the Peace Corps and travel the world. Jill was studying marine biology and had aspirations of joining Greenpeace. A week before they were set to graduate Jill's mom got sick. Jill graduated but gave up on her dream so she could care for her mom. Lyle spent about one week away from her and came right back here." I assume Molly knows who Jill's mom was since she has been here for six months. Everyone knows her story, because she was the heart of this town.

"Oh right. Frances! I learned about her from Dr. Potter. I am sad I didn't get a chance to meet her. Isn't the park by School Street named after her?" she asks.

"Yeah. They did that before she passed. I heard it was a touching ceremony. Frances loved kids so much and she was an incredible teacher," I say with a sigh.

"That's what I heard. She had such a rare form of cancer it was missed until Dr. Potter saw her. He's the one that figured it out, did you know that?" Molly asks with an eyebrow raised in challenge.

"Seriously? No, I hadn't heard that. Okay, I concede to you. He must be a good doctor."

"Tom, I hope this doesn't make you feel like I am not having fun, but I really need to get back. I have some things to do before my work week starts tomorrow," Molly says. It doesn't feel like a brushoff, but I'm still disappointed.

"I understand. I actually need to get to the hardware store and start on a few projects at The Floppy Fish. It's part of our arrangement. Lyle lets everything go to crap all year so I'll have more to do than just tend bar," I say, not meaning to be funny, but Molly grabs my arm and laughs.

"You are so hilarious, Tom, I have had so much fun today," she says.

"Me too, I hope we can do it again sometime, unless second date is not an option. I didn't see it on your list," I say feeling all kinds of nervous.

"Neither was 'have the best kiss of my life,' so I think the list can be amended," she says with a wink.

Damn, that felt good to hear.

Molly

TOM OFFERED to walk me home but I told him I had to make a stop at the store first. I didn't. I don't know why I feel this way; it's not him. I had a wonderful time today. He's funny and smart and God, can he kiss. I have never gone weak in the knees from a kiss before and didn't even believe that was a real thing. Isaac was an okay kisser, I guess, but he was always in a hurry to get to the next part.

My one-night stand and I kissed once at the bar and I felt zero chemistry, but I had already decided I was going to cross that off my list, so I went for it hoping it would get better.

It did not.

When Tom kissed me, the earth seemed to move under my feet. The way his big hands cradled my face so gently, reverently almost, was more sensual than anything I have ever experienced. I don't know if he really felt what I did, or if he was caught up in the whole first-kiss thing.

I walk to the market and grab a basket to get a few things so if Tom sees me walking home he won't think I lied. I pick up a new bottle of red wine and some cheese and crackers. Then I head over to the bakery and pick out a few of my favorite cookies. I know it's Sunday and I need to work tomorrow, but I want to extend this lazy, romantic feeling I have. I plan on curling up with my book and spending the rest of the day snacking and reading.

After I pay for my goodies, I start back toward my house and spot one of our most difficult patients heading right toward me. He hasn't spotted me yet, but if he does, I'll be trapped listening to him prattle on about all his perceived medical problems. He once spent ten minutes explaining to me that he was having secret heart attacks while I was trying to pick out a book at the library. That is how I ended up with the third book in a series I hadn't started yet. Worst part is, I was halfway through the damn thing before I realized it wasn't a standalone.

I turn and scurry down an alleyway and pop out onto a street I don't usually walk down. There are some cute little shops, so I decide to hide in the first one I come to, in hopes he hasn't followed me. A little bell above the door jingles as I push in.

"I'll be right out!" a woman yells from the back.

"Take your time, I am just looking around," I call to her and sigh when I see the selection of delicate bras and nighties on display. I run my fingers over the soft yellow silk tap set that is on the rack by the door. When I glance up, I see one I like better and quickly walk to it like someone else might get there before me. It's the most beautiful thing I have ever seen. I pull out the large and hold it up wondering if it would fit.

"You need the medium, there is no way that size will fit you," a sweet voice says from my left.

"Are you sure? I am pretty chesty." I nod to my front in case she somehow missed my big boobs.

"I know, but this is cut loose. If it's too big it doesn't look good. Here, let me show you." She takes the hanger from me and slips the top off. "See? It has a little bit of polyester so there is some give. You want it to pull across your chest a bit to highlight those amazing breasts of yours. Why don't you take this and the medium in there and try them on," she says, grabbing both sizes and handing them to me. I don't have a chance to protest before she is pulling a few more items and leading me to the back of the store where there are three stalls for trying things on. Each has a deep blue velvet curtain that is held back with a gold braided rope. It's lovely and opulent and reminds me of the stores in the downtown area of San Diego.

I never wanted stuff like this when I was married to Isaac. The less desirable I was to him, the better. He bought me something from Frederick's of Hollywood once, but it had more of a stripper vibe to it. I couldn't get my body to fit into the damn thing, then I think he called me fat or something. I don't remember all the details, but it wasn't my favorite experience.

I step in and release the curtain then face the mirror. My cheeks are a little pink and I am not sure if it's from walking on the beach or if my complexion is betraying my feelings about being in here. I take a deep breath and blow it out, placing one hand on my heart and one on my stomach like my therapist taught me. I repeat the words she said to me, "You deserve to find joy. No one gets to define what that means for you."

I slip out of the yellow dress and try on everything the saleswoman gave me. She was right, the medium fits perfectly. I stare at my reflection and tears form in my eyes without warning. I look beautiful. The light pink tank top is simple but flattering with its scooped neckline and the shorts are cut high with overlapping edges at the hip. The fabric has a shimmer to it so when I turn and the light catches it, the color changes slightly. I am not even going to look at the price. This is mine no matter what the cost.

I get dressed and step back out into the store where the saleslady is waiting. "What did you think?" she asks with a big smile.

"I love them all, but I think I'll get this pink one. You were right. The medium was perfect," I say.

"I didn't mean to snoop but you must be planning a special evening," she says, motioning to my shopping bag I had set outside the dressing room.

I laugh a little and shake my head. "A romantic day to myself, that's all."

"Ah, those are the best days. Have you seen our selection of toys?" she asks with a cocked eyebrow and a grin.

I lean in and whisper, "You mean like vibrators?"

She laughs and says, "Yes. Here let me show you."

Ten minutes later I walk out with a sexy outfit and an even sexier toy. Looks like I get to cross three things off my list today. Walking up this road, I find a crossover to Main Street, then it's only a block to my street. I hope to avoid running into anyone so I can get home, get comfortable, and enjoy the rest of my day.

As I unlock my front door, I glance down the street before stepping in. I look over my shoulder up the street the other way then sigh. I hate that I do that. I want to stop, but it happens before I even think about it. Once inside, I set my keys in the little blue dish and take my bag to the kitchen. I put everything away and grab the bag from the boutique when I see the light on my answering machine flashing. I rush over and push the button.

"Hi Molly, it's Tom. I wanted to say thank you again for having brunch with me this morning. I had a really nice time. I hope to hear from you soon, but if you are too busy today maybe stop in for a drink during your week. You know where to find me. Bye."

I rewind the tape and play it a few more times, enjoying the deep sexy voice he has. God, he missed his calling. He should have been a radio DJ. Actually I bet his classes are filled with young, beautiful girls who lean forward, with their chins in their palms, listening to him speak. I know I would. I know I'll think about that voice and that kiss with my new toy.

I pour myself a glass of wine and feel my nerves start to wind up. Jesus, it feels like I am about to have sex for the first time or something. I decide to put on my beautiful new tap set, then I put on some music to help me calm down. The sales lady was very helpful explaining all the settings and what it could do and how to wash it afterwards. I pull the box out of the bag and stare at it. It's a subtle box with small writing and if I didn't know what was inside, I wouldn't have guessed it was a sex toy.

My hands are all sweaty. Maybe I should drink a glass of wine first. There is no reason to rush this, right? I leave the box on the table and walk over to the couch and settle in with my book and my glass of wine. I only get a few pages in and I'm looking over at the table where I left my new friend.

"Fuck it, or rather, fuck me I guess," I say and then giggle nervously.

God, I am so glad no one is here to witness this. It's like the most awkward first date ever. I bend at the waist and peer at the box and say, "Hey there, you come here often?"

The box remains silent.

"I've got an itch that I can't scratch on my own, how's about you come with me and see if you can help?" I thrust my hip out and slam into the chair. "Ouch! Shit, that hurt." I rub at the sore spot and shake my arms then roll my neck back and forth like I am getting ready for a fight.

"Okay, mister. You're coming with me, or rather I am coming with you soon I hope," I wink at the box then roll my eyes. "Fuck, Molly, stop. This is embarrassing and not helpful."

I take the box off the table and open it. I pull out the bright pink toy. The salesclerk said her friend up in Seattle has a large shop, and she can't keep these on the shelf. They apparently hit all the right spots. I stare at the vibrator that has a realistic shape to it. It's thick and veiny and as I look at it, I feel my upper lip start to sweat. I suddenly realize the woman who sold me this knows I am going to masturbate. Why did that not occur to me when I was buying it? What if I run into her in the grocery store? Or what if she comes to the clinic!?

"Hey, I remember you! I sold you the vibrator! How'd those little extra bits work out for you?" she'll ask and I will burst into flames on the spot. People will walk by and stare at the charred mark on the floor and wonder what happened.

Fuck, why is it so hot in here?

I set it on the table and back away, like it might chase me down and perform nonconsensual vibrations. More wine. I need more wine.

Two full glasses later I saunter over to the table and pick up Fred. I've decided he needs a name and I refuse to name him Tom, because that's a little weird. Plus, Fred the Fancy Friend has a nice ring to it.

I may be drunk.

I walk down the hall to my room and slip out of my pretty new outfit then pull the covers back on my bed. It's only like four in the afternoon so it's not dark in here, but with the curtain drawn it's not super bright either. I lie down on my back and bend my knees, resting my hand on my belly. Okay, I guess I should think sexy thoughts or maybe I turn it on and get to work? I should have asked more questions. I am not turned on, I'm nervous and I want to get this over with, so I push one of the three buttons on the bottom of Fred and it starts to vibrate. I hold it down, pressing it between my legs and just about fly off the bed.

Holy shit! That was intense. Okay, maybe I can ease into that a little better. I have never felt anything like that, so it was shocking. I trail the vibrator up my thigh and skip over the sensitive area then go down the other thigh.

"Oh you like that? You like it when I tease you?" I say, then laugh because this is seriously the most ridiculous thing I have ever done.

I get brave and let the vibrator rest on my clit and moan with pleasure. It's like someone lit a fire between my legs and I pull it away to catch my breath. Jesus, I may never leave the house. I put it back and I am hit by the most earth-shattering orgasm I have ever experienced. It came on so fast I didn't have time to think. I sat up and looked at the toy in my hand. "Well, you are very talented. Let's see what else you can do."

I slip it inside, which now that I have had an orgasm, is a lot easier. That was a happy accident. I remember her saying there were different settings, so once it's in as far as I am comfortable with, I fumble with the buttons on the bottom and feel the extra bits kick on.

Oh.

My.

God.

I move to push the button again, because holy crap that was a lot, but I must have hit a different one because the whole vibrator starts to move, in what can only be described as a thrusting motion. It sounds like maybe the motor is working extra hard too as it punches me in the cervix. Over and over and over. Well, that isn't enjoyable at all. I grab at it to turn it off and manage to kick it into overdrive somehow. I think the extra bits just flicked my clit into the next room and my cervix has a black eye now.

I pull it free and toss it on the bed next to me, then I collapse on my back. I am a panting, sweaty mess. One sneak attack orgasm followed by an assault.

I might not be cut out for sex toys.

Tom

I STOPPED off at The Floppy Fish to grab a few things and decided to call and leave Molly a message. I had such a great time with her this morning, but I am kind of glad she had stuff to do. I really need to get started on my own list and not obsess about hers.

The hardware store is thankfully quiet, so I'm able to get all the things I need quickly. I had Frank order the brass bars I'll use to make a waitress stall. He says it will take about a week for them to arrive, but he had the right size hinges for the flip-up section of the bar. I also got some wood putty and a sander so I can fix that bit of floor that almost castrated me.

When I get back to the bar I run upstairs to see if I have any messages then try to pretend like it's cool that I don't. I change into my work clothes and grab the knee pads and saw from the shed out back. When I get back into the bar again, the phone is ringing, so I hurry to pick up the line. This is a different phone number than the private line upstairs, so it's probably not Molly, but my stupid heart gets excited anyway.

"Hello?" I say, sounding more breathless than I wanted.

"You okay there, Tom?" Lyle asks with a chuckle.

"Oh hi, yeah. I just got back from the hardware store. How are you?

What time is it over there?" I ask. I know he told me at one point, but I forgot.

"We are eight hours ahead of you, so it's almost nine. Jill is in the shower before we turn in, so I thought I'd call and check in with you," Lyle says.

"Things are great here. I had to kick Dylan out the other night, but he was cool about it. I had a little incident with a splinter but I went over to Dr. Potter's place and he took care of me," I say for some dumb reason.

"Oh, did you now?" Lyle says. He has been in Ireland for a week and he already sounds like he has an accent. "And did you meet our sweet Molly?"

"You know Molly?" I ask. I don't know why I am surprised by this. Of course he would know her; she works two doors down and lives in the same town as him.

"Everyone knows her. She's gorgeous and probably one of the nicest people you'll ever meet. Be nice to her," he says, like I might not be.

"I am, I will be, I took her on a date," I blurt out before really giving it any thought.

The line goes silent then I hear a muffled sound and suddenly Jill is on the line. "A date? Tom, you went on a date?" she shrieks, like I had been a celibate monk or something.

"I date!" I say incredulously.

"When? Before taking Molly out, when was the last time you went on a date, oh and galas don't count," she says. I can picture her tapping her foot and I pinch the bridge of my nose reflexively.

"It's been a while, but only if I can't count the gala," I mumble.

"She's a really nice person Tom, but she's very private. I get the feeling that someone hurt her pretty bad. When she first moved to town I noticed her constantly looking over her shoulder, and she keeps to herself. I got to know her because of my desperate need for allergy shots." Jill laughs.

I don't say much, but I assure her that I have no intention of hurting Molly. I know more about her—thanks to her list—than Jill probably does. I think Molly was hurt too, and fuck, I don't want to add to that. I am only here until August, so it's not like I plan on starting a long-term relationship. I was hoping to spend some time with her, get to know her better. She is enchanting and beautiful and those lips are like a beacon in a storm.

"Tom? Are you still there?" Lyle has the phone back now and I rub my hand down my face hard to clear the sudden unease I'm feeling.

"Yeah, listen, I'd love to talk. but I am about to start on the bar top door you wanted. I ordered the waitress stall and I'll put that in next week. You've gotten pretty busy, so I bet that will help," I say. I don't want to talk about Molly anymore. I shouldn't have brought it up.

"That's fine, thanks for doing all that, Tom. I really appreciate it, and I feel bad every year asking you to take care of these things," Lyle says.

"I don't mind, and I'd be very bored if I didn't have stuff to do. Now get some sleep and maybe try to send me a postcard or something. I bet the farm is beautiful," I say.

"It is. Amazing family too. We might not come home!" Lyle jokes. One of these days that will be true. Now that Jill's mom is gone they really don't need to stay in Mendocino. Last year when they went to Germany to work with troubled teens I thought they were going to stay or bring home a few of the kids. Jill got very attached and still writes to a few of them.

"Well, enjoy your time off," I say, then say my good-byes. My stomach feels like I ate rocks and my shoulders are tense. That wonderful warm feeling I had at brunch and during our walk on the beach has been replaced with a feeling of guilt. Not just guilt, that feeling is laced with a touch of regret. I don't regret spending time with Molly, or that kiss. I regret that I didn't think this through. I saw an attractive woman and jumped with both feet. That isn't like me at all and I honestly am struggling to understand why I did it. I mean I have been lonely, but fuck, it's been years since I have had a woman in my life. Being alone isn't new. Why did I feel the need to ask Molly out even when I was naked and lying on the exam table? Who does that? I groan at the memory of her washing my balls. I was literally going to ask her on a date right after that? I didn't consider her feelings at all. I shake my head, resolving to give her space and not pursue her any further. I am sure she doesn't want a casual thing with a summer-only guy.

I get my tools out and set everything out where I need it. I measure the bar top and snap a chalk line where I want to cut, then walk around behind the bar to start on the base. It's not much, a couple of two-by-fours and some wood panels. The main supports for the bar are a few feet over, so this won't affect anything. I pray to God that I don't run into any electrical wires. I am sure Lyle didn't think about any of that. He has a vision and it's my job to see it through. I bend down and yank the first panel board free, then cough and sputter at the years of dust I unearthed. I grab the next panel and pull, holding my breath this time.

I have quite a pile of construction debris that I need to deal with before I get too much further. I love this kind of work, since it's different than what I do during the school year, but it still engages my mind. Using my physical strength instead of my brain helps loosen some of the tension I've been feeling, but when I break through the false wall of the bar I come face to face with the wood plank that tried to skewer my balls, which of course makes me think of Molly.

Molly with her short dark hair, big wide brown eyes and lips that felt like velvet against mine. My dick jumps at the memory of her mouth and I set the saw down so I can collect myself. Fuck. It was one date. One kiss. I moan miserably and scrub my hand down my face again. Not more than a few minutes ago, I decided to leave her alone and now I'm fighting the urge to run upstairs and call her again. How am I going to get through this summer?

I don't think I *can* leave her alone.

Molly

THE WEEK FLEW by and every night after work I thought about calling Tom, but I know the Floppy Fish opens at 4, and I am not off until 5. He works until midnight and I am sound asleep by then. I guess I should have called and at least left a message, but I kind of started wondering if I should let this go. Do I really want to date someone?

When I wrote "go on a first date" on my list in my therapist's office, I didn't think past that. I wrote it as a reminder of what I missed out on, what I never got to have as a teen or even a young adult in my twenties. When all the people at my high school were going to class, attending football games, going to prom, I was getting tutored in a house that didn't belong to me.

I glance over at the phone on my counter and wonder if I should call and tell him that I had a good time, but I am not interested in a second date. That seems like what a good person would do, not string along a nice man who kisses like sin and promises. I groan and drop my head to my table, squeezing my eyes shut in frustration.

Every night since our date, memories have been flooding in. Memories of my life before Isaac, our relationship before I knew I was pregnant, then all the things that happened after that. In some ways it seems like it happened to someone else, because I got so good at detaching myself from what was going on. In therapy, the first thing I had to learn was how to handle my emotions once I opened the floodgates. I was numb for so long that when that first spark of the idea to leave ignited, I almost went up in flames.

Without thinking, I stand up and cross to the front door, grab my keys, and walk out with one thing in mind. I go the few blocks up my street and turn to Main Street where The Floppy Fish is before I realize I didn't check over my shoulder. I didn't look around even once. I freeze in my tracks and my stomach tightens as I slowly look around. It's just after sunset and the wind has picked up, but that's my only company on the street. People are probably at dinner or already settled in for the night. I wipe my hands on my jeans and push on toward the bar, wanting to be inside. I walk up to the front door of the bar and tug on the handle to pull it open.

It takes a minute as I scan the room to find him, but then I see Tom rising up from behind the bar like Poseidon rising from the depths of the sea. His eyes lock onto me and the corners of my mouth turn upward.

"Hi, Molly, how are you?" he says. He straightens the rest of the way up and grabs a rag from the bar to wipe his hands. "Have you been here long?"

"Just walked in." I glance around and notice the bar is empty. "Are you open?" I ask with a nod to the empty room. Then I hear cheers and shouts from the open door that leads out back.

"Yeah, everyone is outside. I was tapping a new keg and didn't hear the door," he says.

"Right, well I wanted to stop by, you know, and say hi, like you suggested when you called, Sunday," I say. It feels like it was so long ago and I worry he forgot that he had extended the invitation.

"I am glad you did. I worried since I hadn't heard from you that maybe I had done something wrong," Tom says. He's wearing a black V-neck T-shirt instead of a button-down and I can see his throat working as he swallows. It's almost like he is nervous, and his unease gives me the confidence to step forward and climb onto a barstool.

I shake my head and smile at him again. "No, Tom, you did nothing wrong. I got busy during the week. We have very different schedules," I say. Then because I want to reassure him more, I lean forward and say more quietly, "I also had to find my purple pen to add something to my list."

"Oh really?" Tom's eyebrows shoot up and he leans in across the bar to hear what I have to say.

"Yeah, I added *ask a handsome bartender on a second date*, do you happen to know anyone that fits that description?" I say, with what I hope is a flirty tone.

Tom's face lights up with a smile and he tips his head back and laughs. "I might be able to point you to someone."

"Oh good. Well, while you do that, could you also get me a glass of red?" I put my chin in my hands and wait.

Tom leans over and says quietly, like he's sharing a secret, "I bet the next guy to slide a glass of red wine across the bar would be willing to take you on a date, Molly. Don't be afraid to ask." Chills dance down my arms and spine as I feel his warmth and smell his intoxicating cologne. I smile and cross my legs while Tom pulls a bottle of wine off the top shelf. It shouldn't be sexy to watch a man uncork a wine bottle, but watching his wrist and forearm flexing and working the corkscrew has me breaking out in a little sweat. He turns from me and slides a wineglass off the rack then sets it on the back counter of the bar. I can't see his face as he pours the wine, but I watch his wrist twist a little as he finishes and I take a breath in waiting for him to turn around. I expect him to, but instead he pulls a second glass down and pours another one.

When he turns around to face me, he has the sexiest smile on his face. My stomach flutters and I take a desperate breath in, hoping to calm my nerves. I watch his eyes flare and the corner of his mouth tilts up. He sets both glasses down and slowly slides one to me. His gaze never leaves my face as I reach for the wine and bring the glass to my lips. I take a small sip, praying for a steady voice.

"Hi," I manage to say.

"Hello." He smiles again and raises his glass to me in a silent toast before taking a drink. "Delicious. This bartender really knows his red wine." He cocks an eyebrow at me and I giggle like a teenager. I am trying to be seductive but am afraid I'm failing miserably.

"I was wondering if you are available on Sunday? I'd love to spend some time with you," I say. I don't mean it to come out so quiet, but he is smiling and leaning in like my words are a rope tugging him closer.

"Why, Molly, I would be honored to spend Sunday with you. I would be even more honored if you'd share a bottle of wine with me tonight. Can you stay a bit?" he asks and when I nod his smile grows. "Wonderful. I have a private party out back, with a bar set up there so it should be pretty quiet in here. Not like last time you came in." Tom raises his glass and takes another drink without letting his soft gaze move from my face.

"I was wondering why it was so quiet," I say. My shoulders relax a little and I don't know if it's from the wine or his easy smile.

I am about to ask him a question when the door opens and a group of people come in. Tom stands up straight and asks, "Carrera wedding?" and they nod. "They're all out back." He gestures with his head towards the patio door.

We both wait as they make their way out back, and I laugh when the door opens, and the shouts and hoots pour in. They must be very well liked to get that kind of welcome. It sounded like when Norm would walk into Cheers.

"So what would you like to do on Sunday, Molly?" Tom asks, leaning forward on the bar. I clear my throat and lick my lips nervously. I hadn't realized I would have to come up with the plan if I asked him out. I didn't think I was going to do this at all, so there wasn't much planning. Tom waits patiently, taking another drink of his wine. I stare at him, suddenly hit by the contrast between him and Isaac. I can't think of a time where Isaac asked me what I wanted to do or even waited for me to pick between two things. He told me what we were doing. I squint at Tom, tempted to see how long he will wait for me to decide.

"I'm not sure yet. Is that okay?" I say with a small smile.

He leans in again and smiles back at me. I see the little wrinkles by his eyes when he does that. He must have spent most of his life laughing and smiling. "Molly, maybe I shouldn't admit this, but I don't care what we do, as long as I get to spend time with you."

I feel myself relax and take a big drink of my wine letting the warm sweet feeling of his words spread through me like the merlot. I bet I could suggest a walk in the Botanical Gardens, or looking through local shops and he would be happy. This is such a different feeling. I'm getting drunk off power so I announce, "Let's go to the bookstore!"

"The little one on the corner? Happy Endings?" he asks with clear excitement in his voice.

"Yes! I want to see if they have the second book in a series I am reading. That's another thing I should have added to my list. I'd like to be able to say I read a whole series by the end of the year."

"I just finished the first book in a series too. I think that is a wonderful idea, Molly. Tell me, what are you reading?" Tom asks. He pours a little more wine in my glass, and I nod a thank you.

"I read *Kent Price, Man on a Mission* by Patrick Smith. I can't wait to find out what happens next. Have you heard of that author?" I ask.

"There is no way you're going to believe me if I tell you. Can you wait here a moment?" Tom asks with a chuckle. I nod, and he turns and hurries out from behind the bar to the stairs in the corner. He comes back down quickly and sets a paperback in front of me. He's right. I would have thought he was making it up.

"I couldn't put it down. If I don't find out what happens with Fernando and that woman on the yacht soon, I might lose my mind," Tom says.

"Right? And what about the notebook? I wonder who stole it?" I hold up my hands and say, "Wait, don't tell me what you think, I want to be surprised and I bet you have it figured out." I laugh and Tom shakes his head.

"I don't have a clue," he says with a chuckle.

I smile again as another warm feeling spreads across my chest and swirls down to my stomach. I try to remain casual since climbing over the bar and wrapping my arms around him might come across as stalker-level crazy. So instead I say, "I think he's such a good writer. I haven't read for fun in a long time, and I am glad I stumbled across this book."

I see the crinkles near his eyes again and his face softens as he says, "I don't get to read for pleasure during the school year, so I build a stack of books for the summer. This one did not disappoint. I think book two is *Kent Price, Mission at Risk*. It should be good."

The evening gets away from me as Tom continues to refill my wineglass, and his. I've laughed so much my sides ache and my face is tired from all the smiling. What a wonderful night. Earlier, in my house when I thought about telling him "No, thank you" to another date I had a flash of what my days and nights would be like in September when he was gone. Did I want to be able to look back on a summer filled with fun or regret? Nothing about seeing Tom would cause me to feel regret, but passing on this chance? I decided that wasn't something I wanted. My list was about growing and exploring and testing the limits of my comfort.

"Thanks again for letting us rent the back patio on such short notice." A short, round man is aggressively shaking Tom's hand and it snaps me out of my thoughts.

"Of course, I am so glad you were able to get everyone here. I hope the wedding is as magical as you and your fiancée," Tom says bowing his head a little to the man. His smile is wide and genuine, and butterflies take flight in my stomach as I watch him. I glance over as the partygoers file out, and I blink at the strange assortment of people. It's not my place, but if you had told me these people were all about to attend a wedding together, I wouldn't have believed it.

A tall, willowy lady slinks out and drapes her arm over the short round man. She is at least a foot taller than him and while he's soft, she is nothing but sharp angles. She reaches out with her free hand and pats Tom on the head like he is a child who did a good job at the science fair. "You have a lovely place here, Thomas. I think we should come perform sometime, yeah? People love us and you will enjoy the show!" Her eyes twinkle as she waits for his reply.

"That sounds wonderful, Victoria, whenever you and Victor are available just give me a call. If it's after the summer tell Lyle—he's the owner—that I recommend you highly," Tom says, sounding sincere and kind.

"Will do!" the short man, who is apparently named Victor, says as he slaps Tom on the back. The two leave and I turn to look at Tom, who is rubbing his hand down his face.

"Jesus. That was an odd couple if I ever have seen one," he says in a breath.

"Oh, thank God it wasn't just me!" I say. I adjust myself on the stool and wobble a little. I catch myself before Tom notices.

"Are they performers? What did she mean by that?" I ask because that seems nicer than asking why those people were so strange and if they reminded him of the evil couple from the Rocky and Bullwinkle show.

Tom steps back behind the bar and takes my empty glass of wine, finally putting it in the rack to be washed instead of filling it up again. He turns to me again and rests his forearms on the bar top leaning into my space. "That was Victor Victoria, you know, like the movie?" he says with a chuckle.

"Wait, the movie with Julie Andrews? She played both parts! Oh my God, that is really funny. Do they sing all the songs from the movie?" I ask.

"One would think, but no. They have their own songs apparently, and," he leans in closer and whispers, "she juggles while he sings a jaunty little tune about how opposites attract."

"Oh God, I would pay to see that." I laugh out loud.

"Don't, it's not as amazing as it sounds," Tom says. Two girls that I think I met last time I was here, and a man, come in from outside.

"We are all cleaned up out there, Tom. I left the keg but Jerald said he'd help move it in tomorrow. The glasses have all been brought in too. They are in the kitchen," one of the women says.

"Thanks, Misty. I appreciate your help. I'll make sure you all get extra pay for doing that. I know it meant you missed out on your usual tips," Tom tells her.

Misty laughs. "Um, I think we did better tonight than we have all summer. Those people were very interesting. They threw money around like they printed it themselves. Patty said she has enough to pay off her Corolla!"

The girl who must be Patty laughs at that. "Yeah, well I only owe about 250 dollars so don't get all excited!"

"Shit! That's great!" Tom says.

"Need help closing up?" Patty asks. I notice her glancing at me and then at Tom like maybe she's wondering if she needs to save him from me.

"Nah, thanks though. I'm going to wipe down the bar, then walk Molly home. I'll clean the rest up tomorrow," he says. I try not to react to the fact that he said he's walking me home. Instead I smile and wave.

"Okay, well, if you're sure. Good night, Tom." Patty walks out first, followed by Jerald and Misty.

I speak up as soon as the door closes. "You don't need to walk me home, Tom, I'm fine."

"Don't be ridiculous. It's after midnight and I gave you roughly a whole bottle of wine. It would be very ungentlemanly of me to—" he stops and scratches his chin then continues, "Unchivalrous? Ungallant?" I notice for the first time that Tom is a little wobbly too.

"How much wine did you have this evening? If you walk me home, will I have to walk *you* home? That seems like a lot of work." I stand up from the bar stool and grab the bar top so I don't sink to the floor, then giggle like a drunk person. Fuck, I am a drunk person.

"I had just enough wine to know that I can in fact walk you home, if we can get past the fact that there are two front doors. I guess if we pick the right one, that means we can leave!" Tom declares.

I hiccup, then start to slide a little to the left. He is there quickly, grabbing me by the elbow to set me back up. He stares into my eyes and says, "You look like the pilot on that show."

"*Airplane*?" I ask, and we both fall into each other laughing. Tom snorts, then wheezes and slaps himself hard on the chest, trying to recover. I take a deep breath and grab onto the bar before I say, "What pilot? If you say Tom Cruise, I will punch you in the dick and balls."

Tom covers his crotch with his big hands and his eyes go wide. "Please don't do that. They are afraid of Dr. Potter." This makes me laugh again.

"No the pilot from that new show *Northern Exposure*, Maggie. You are beautiful like her," Tom says, holding one hand over his chest and keeping the other in a protective cup shape down lower.

"Oh! Huh, yeah, I guess we have the same haircut," I say, then add, "I like that show. It's so funny."

"Well yeah, your hair but your eyes are like hers too. Big, wide, and so fucking pretty," Tom says. This time I don't laugh at all because the air has left my lungs. The way he's looking at me right now is a drug that I am going to become addicted to very quickly. Suddenly, I don't feel so drunk. He steps closer, his gaze locked on mine. I watch as he runs his tongue along his bottom lip and when I look back to his eyes, they're zeroed in on my mouth. He reaches me and places his large warm hands on my hips and pulls me into him. I can feel the heat coming off him, or maybe that is me. My breath is coming faster as his fingers curl in, squeezing me. I watch as his eyes close and he groans and his hands move a little more to grab my full hips. My breath catches and his eyes open as he pulls me into himself, his mouth crashing down on mine.

It's not like that kiss on the beach, slow and sweet. It's firm and wet and tongues and teeth clashing as he pulls me impossibly closer. His hands are everywhere, but I am doing the same, running my hands up his back and over his shoulders and fisting his shirt then wrapping my arms around him. I am pulling him closer because I can't stand to be even a millimeter away from him. We are moving, he's steering me as he backs up a few steps then he stops and pulls away, chest heaving like he ran a mile.

"Fuck, Molly. I'm sorry. I didn't mean to—"

"It's okay, did you hear me complaining?" I ask still breathless myself. He shakes his head, so I step closer. "I don't want to go home yet." I tug at him and he crashes into me again, this time moving his lips slower more sensually over mine.

After a few minutes he pulls back so our lips are still almost touching, and he asks, "Would you like to come upstairs?"

I kiss him like that will be enough of an answer and he seems to understand. We stumble to the stairs, kissing and pulling at each other's clothes, then stop because neither of us can make it up the stairs like that. He grabs my hand as we climb up to his place and I want to melt into this moment. Hold it forever in my heart because this is what I missed out on. This excitement, passion and can-barely-stand-it-another-second lust.

I want this.

I want him.

Tom

AS SOON AS I push the door open to my little summer getaway, I spin and kiss her. Those two minutes it took to get up the stairs are two minutes my body wasn't touching hers. Two minutes that I wasn't nibbling on those full sweet lips, tasting that delicious mouth of hers. Merlot on Molly is my new favorite flavor.

She is tugging at my shirt, so I help her pull it off as I walk backwards to my bed. This room has two choices and while I don't expect to have sex with her tonight, I know we will be more comfortable here than on the couch. I sit on the edge of the bed and Molly straddles me without hesitation. I slide my hand slowly under her white cotton T-shirt, giving her the option, and I feel her tense a little. I pull back and look into her eyes. "Molly, we don't have to do anything you're not comfortable with. We can just kiss, I don't want to rush you."

She nods and a small smile crosses her lips. "Thank you, I'm okay. I haven't, it's been a while since anyone has seen me, and I—I guess I got a little nervous."

"You are beautiful, Molly, you should know that. I find you so fucking attractive that I can't believe this is happening. Also would this be a good time to bring up the fact that you have seen not just my balls, but my dick too?" My eyes show the smile I'm trying to hide.

She laughs and pulls her shirt off in one quick motion, tossing it on the floor. "I didn't know this was going to happen, or I would have worn a better bra," she says. I lean back on the bed, propping myself up on my elbows. It leaves her exposed as she straddles my hips, and I see she wants to fold down onto me, but I stop her.

"Wait, please. Let me look at you. Jesus, Molly. You are perfect." I sit back up and trace my thumbs across the hardened nipples that are peeking out of her satin bra. I take her breasts in my hands and groan at their weight. "Can I take this off?" I ask as I tug gently on her bra, and she bites her lower lip and nods.

I slide my hands to her back to unhook her bra and slowly lower one strap off her shoulder, then the other. I want to unwrap her like the gift she is. I ease the white satin cups down exposing the most beautiful nipples I have ever seen. I lower my head and kiss along the top of her full, plump breast then run my tongue into the valley of her cleavage. Cleavage that still exists without a bra pushing her tits together. Fuck. I am about to lose my mind with desire for this woman when she pushes me to my back.

She pulls the bra the rest of the way off, tossing it on the floor near her discarded shirt, then she stares down at me. She takes a ragged breath in before leaning forward pressing her chest to mine. Our lips meet again and I am lost in her kisses instantly. I let my hands roam across her bare back and down to her ass, that luscious, round ass. That ass that took over my thoughts as I gripped my cock the day after I met her. I slide my hands up under her skirt to pull her up because I need to feel her heat on me. She knows where I want her and she settles over the button fly of my 501's. It's painful how hard I am but if these pants come off, I am not going to be able to stop myself.

She starts to rock and grind against me and I groan and reach for her beautifully full breasts. I knead and squeeze gently, loving how she feels in my hands. Her breasts are heavy and round and I never want to let them go. I think about all the ways I could enjoy them, all the ways I could make her feel good.

"Oh, Jesus, Tom, that feels so good," Molly says in a strained voice. She starts to move faster over me, so I flip us over quickly, taking control. I don't want this to end, and maybe we need to slow down a bit. I don't want this to be fast, and I was seconds away from coming in my jeans like a teenager. I dip my head and kiss her like she is my air and hell, does it feel that way. Her lips, wet and warm, move over mine in slow, languid strokes, as I settle my hips between her legs. I love that she's wearing only a skirt, since I am only in my jeans. I get a rush, a thrill like I am back in high school and am about to be caught making out with the hottest girl. Purely fantasy back then, but now in this moment, in my tiny studio getaway, it's real. This woman beneath me is like a work of art, with her soft curves and inviting eyes. I rise up so I am straddling her and I think of the painting Venus of Urbino as I stare down at Molly.

I move my hands slowly up from her belly to the swell of her breasts. I don't know how I like them best, because flat on her back like this they still arch up as if they are begging to be touched. The way they fall a little to the side allowing me a path between to lavish kisses. The round curve at the bottom of each breast calls to me to cup it, hold her in my hands as I drive into her again and again.

"Why did you stop? Is something wrong, Tom?" Molly says in almost a whisper and it snaps me out of my thoughts. Was I really fantasizing about this woman in the middle of ravaging her?

I look down to see I am holding her breasts in my hands and just staring at her. That's fucking weird even for me. "Sorry, I got overwhelmed. Your body is so—" I stop because there are no words coming to me that would do it justice.

"Sorry, I didn't—" Molly starts to squirm to try and get away and it hits me that she thinks I was going to say something negative.

"Molly, stop, please." My voice comes out strained and she takes a breath and looks up into my eyes. I see it. The hurt, the fear lying there just beneath the surface waiting for someone to pick at it and set it free. I lower myself to my elbows, caging her whole body with mine, then I let my lips settle on hers. Slowly kissing her, worshiping her mouth until she moans with pleasure. My actions mean more than any words I could say, any words she's heard before, so I kiss her like that is all that matters. In this moment it is all that does.

When I feel her body relaxing and her trust building again, I move down her body, kissing my way to her stomach. I feel her breathing change and I can tell she is nervous. I don't know how to reassure her that I want this, I want her, so I show her. I lift off of her and stand at the edge of my bed, then flip her skirt up and drop to my knees in one motion. I tug at her cotton panties and she lifts her ass to help me along. I think about putting her underwear in my pocket because I think that is what Kent Price does in the book we are both reading but I worry she will think I'm weird, so I drop them on the floor next to her shirt.

I press her thighs apart and I feel her tense a bit. I let my thumbs trace up her legs to her center where I apply soft gentle pressure. She lets out a quiet moan that sounds like a yes, so I dip my head and trace my tongue along her. God, she is exquisite, hot and wet and quivering at my touch like I own her body. I exhale and my breath across her lips must feel good because she arches up. I slowly move my hand so my fingers are close to her entrance, hesitating for a moment to be sure she wants this. I look up at her, noticing for the first time that she is up on her elbows, looking down at me.

"Tom, please," she begs, spreading her legs a little wider, allowing me access to the place I have fantasized about since meeting her.

I dive in, kissing her everywhere with my lips and tongue until she is writhing beneath me. I scoop her leg up over my shoulder as I slide one hand under her ass. I use the other hand to trace soft circles up her thigh as I inch closer to where my mouth is. She whimpers, so I slide two fingers inside her, hoping to bring her closer to the edge. I thrust my fingers in slow and steady in rhythm with my tongue and when I feel her tighten around me, I curl them up and hit that spot. The sound that comes from her is like nothing I have heard before. It's a prayer mixed with lust and joy and I continue to work my mouth over her until she's begging me to stop.

I crawl up her body as she breathes in short quick bursts. I can feel her heart beating against mine as I lower myself to her and kiss away any residual doubts of my attraction to her. Our lips melt together as I hold her face in my hands. I think I feel a tear slide under my finger so I move my lips to capture it, kissing her there. In this moment all I want is to make her feel cherished.

"Oh my God, that was so intense. Tom, how did you do that?" she asks, but I don't know if she really wants an answer, so I drop to her side and wrap my arms around her pulling her close. Her breathing slows and I feel her whole body go slack in my arms. Even though I am as hard as stone and still in my jeans, I fall asleep with her lips pressed into my neck.

The thing about falling asleep half hanging off a bed after drinking too much wine, is that it sounds romantic and impulsive, but in reality, at age thirty-eight, it's painful. My eyes feel like someone poured sand into them, so I know I didn't take out my contacts. I groan and turn a little, not wanting to dislodge Molly from my body but desperately needing to remove these contacts. Luckily, she sleeps like the dead. I wiggle free and walk to my bathroom, where I take out my contacts and brush my teeth. I empty my very full bladder, then turn the light off before I make my way back to bed. I notice her white cotton panties on the floor and decide Kent Price was probably right. I need to keep these. I tuck them in my front pocket and climb up onto the bed next to Molly.

I tug at the blankets so I can have something to cover us with, then pull her up with me to the pillows. She sleeps through the whole thing and for a moment I worry, but her breaths are steady and strong. I gather the blanket around us and as soon as my head rests on the pillow again I am out cold.

Molly

THERE IS something very firm and hairy under my cheek and it takes me a moment to remember where I am. A smile spreads across my face as I replay last night in my mind. I have never blacked out from an orgasm before, but that is the only way to describe what happened. I had no intention of staying the night. I thought we'd fool around and then I'd have him walk me home. Something that didn't seem so scary after a whole bottle of wine.

Instead I am waking up with my face pressed into his rock-hard chest. Not going to lie—I love it. I can hear and feel his breathing. Slow and steady with an occasional snore tossed in, reminding me he is human and not a god from the land of orgasms. I stretch under the covers and let my hand reach lower, surprised to find he is still in his jeans. I move my hand to my hip and feel my skirt, but I know I don't have a shirt or bra on, because I can feel his warm chest against mine. I fight the urge to rub myself all over him, to wallow in his chest hair and breathe in his delicious scent.

Jesus, Molly, you are not a cat.

I roll away and lift my arms above my head, pausing a moment to relish the way my body feels. I have not had a good night's sleep like that in years. Or maybe ever. If that came from having one mind-blowing orgasm, I am going to need to give my friend Fred another try.

"If you expect to leave my bed today, you are going to have to stop looking so goddamn beautiful," a gravelly voice says.

I turn and tuck my hands under my face. He has one arm under his pillow and he's lying on his side facing me. "Good morning, Molly."

"Good morning, Tom," I say. My smile betrays any thoughts of playing it cool.

"How did you sleep?" he asks. He's looking at my face even though my breasts are out and mere inches from him. I am either impressed or insulted. I must look like I'm trying to solve the world's problems because he reaches up and smooths my forehead with his thumb.

I grin and say, "Really, really good. I'm sorry. I hope I didn't overstay my welcome. I don't think I even remember falling asleep."

"Red wine and a talented lover will do that to you," he says with a wink. "You were out pretty quick, you didn't seem to notice that I moved you up here to the pillow portion of the bed. Our activities took place a little further south."

I cover my face to hide my embarrassment. "You picked me up and I slept through it? Good Lord, I am so sorry."

"Please don't apologize. I had to get up to take out my contacts and I really didn't want to have you curl up on the foot of the bed. I treat my guests better than that," he says. I know he's joking but it does make me wonder if he has had a lot of "guests" who stay the night. He could, since he's handsome. Plus, on any given night, there is a bar full of women downstairs who would probably kill to be with him.

"There's that look again," he says, smoothing my brow once more. "Are you always so contemplative in the morning?"

"Not normally. I don't usually wake up in bed with men I hardly know, so that's probably it." I hope that sounded as airy and bright as I intended. I wanted to ask him how many women he has brought up here and if last night meant anything to him, but I keep my mouth shut. Is this what dating is like? Not knowing how the other person feels, but wallowing in your own doubts and regrets? This sucks.

"I wouldn't say we hardly know each other, Molly." He rolls away and grabs a pair of glasses off the nightstand. They are simple metal frames and they make him look impossibly handsome. He props himself up on his elbow and smiles down at me. As he does the covers fall away revealing his toned chest. He pushes the blankets down a little further as he adjusts himself in bed. In an attempt to cover my obvious lust for this man I look down away from his face and spot my underwear hanging out of the pocket of his jeans.

"Are you trying to take tips from Kent Price, or have you always stolen women's underwear?" I ask. The laugh that comes from him as he flops on his back is so endearing I want to dive on top of him and kiss him until he can't see straight.

"Busted. I was hoping you would think it was sexy, like the woman on the balcony, what was her name? Does he ever tell us?" Tom asks.

"If he did I can't remember. So speaking of names, Tom, Thomas, Tommy? What is your last name?" I ask as I playfully poke him in the chest.

"I thought you would have seen that in my medical chart, Molly." He raises an eyebrow at me.

"Well, had you filled out the standard patient intake form I would have all kinds of information about you, but you ducked out before we were finished. I believe your chart is labeled Man with Splinter." I poke him again and he grabs my wrist. He looks like he wants to kiss me, at least that's what I hope. Or if I'm being honest, that is what I want.

"My name is Thomas James Hemingway, no relation," he says, with a nod of his head.

"Well, Thomas James Hemingway No Relation, it's nice to meet you," I say. He loosens his grip on my wrist, so I reach up and pat him on the cheek.

"And you are?" he asks with a smile.

"I am Molly Kristen Sparrow. It's nice to finally meet you, and may I ask how old you are, Tom?" I prop up on my elbow then realize that I am not wearing a top and the whole big boob side flop isn't very attractive, so I lie back down.

Tom gets up and walks around the bed to where my shirt and bra lie on the floor. He hands them to me then waits as I tuck myself back into my bra and slip my shirt on. He seemed to have picked up on my discomfort at being topless and that makes me feel odd, but not in a bad way, more unsettled, like he can see inside my thoughts.

"I'm thirty-eight. My birthday is in November and I'm one of five kids. The oldest, to be exact." He sits on the bed after pulling his T-shirt back on. "Your turn, age and birthday, please." He smiles again and I can't help but join him, a huge grin spreading across my face. Why is this so fun?

"I'm thirty-three, and my birthday is in October. I am an only child, and I should probably get going. I have taken up enough of your Saturday morning." I stand and look around for my shoes and purse. When I spot them I rush over and slip my feet in and duck under the long strap of my purse. "Well, thanks, Tom. Did you want to still get together on Sunday? It's okay if you can't or are busy or something, I would understand." The words are tumbling out of my mouth now, like someone knocked over a tower of blocks.

Tom stands and crosses to me, then grabs me by the shoulders. He is probably trying to get me to stop blabbering. Is this when people get slapped? Snap out of it Molly, with a little shoulder shake, then whack! I can see the appeal.

"Molly, there is nothing I would rather do on my Sunday. What time are you available?" His voice is low and kind and he leans in as he stares at my mouth.

"Um, can we say ten?" I ask wiping my hands on my skirt.

"That works for me. That's less than twenty-four hours from now, so I will allow it." This time he does lean in and place his lips gently on mine. I feel my knees get wobbly as he moves his mouth over my lips in gentle strokes. When he steps back my mouth tries to follow him and he laughs.

I attempt to play it off by quickly saying, "Okay, sure. Ten is great. I'll come here, or we can meet at a restaurant or . . ."

This time his brow furrows, but he shakes it off and says, "You can meet me here. I'll be downstairs."

"Okay then. Well, thanks, Tom. I had a really great time." I turn to go, but then I remember he has my underwear. "Are you really keeping those?" I say, pointing at his pocket.

Tom looks at me a little sheepishly and nods, then says, "I'd really like to, Molly."

"Okay, Mr. Price, man of mystery, I'll see you tomorrow," I quip, then hurry down the stairs to the bar then over to the door. I grab the handle and pull only to find it locked. Shit. I glance over my shoulder to see Tom walking up behind me with a set of keys.

"Here, let me get that for you." His voice is calm and soothing and it makes me feel like a coward for trying to run out of here instead of playing twenty questions. Which I remind myself, I started. I spin and force a smile before saying, "I'm sorry. I have a hard time sharing about my past, but I will. I need some time. I know you have probably figured out some, since you saw my list." I pause and take a breath but before I can explain more, Tom stops me with a gentle kiss.

"Molly, you don't owe me any explanation. I don't want to make you feel uncomfortable, but that being said, I would love to hear about you. Whatever you want to share." He trails his hands down my arms until he reaches my hands, then he holds mine in his and gives me a squeeze.

"Thank you. I didn't really think, I wasn't planning on . . ." I stop and shake my head to clear the jumble of words that are trying to get out all at once. Tom reaches past me and slips the key in the lock and then steps aside.

"I'll see you tomorrow at ten." He smiles warmly at me so I lean in and give him a quick kiss then I leave before I can do or say anything else weird.

Once I get home I take a shower and eat a quick breakfast before starting my normal Saturday chores. The drive to Fort Bragg is slow due to road construction that seems to be a year-round thing here. I am excited to see what my son has to say this week, and I am counting down the days until I can see him. It's only two weeks until he is eighteen. I have the letter telling him where I live already written out and ready to send, when it's time.

He will get a portion of his trust fund on his birthday, with the rest being released when he is twenty-five. As much as I hate my in-laws, I could never have provided Grant with the life he has had and will continue to have. His opportunities, including being able to go to a prestigious university like Willmore, would not have been a possibility if my mom and I had raised him in our run-down trailer. Not because the love and affection wouldn't have been there—in that sense he would have had a better life. But the summer camps, world travel with tutors in tow, and all the best food and activities money could buy, gave him a leg up a single teen mom couldn't give him. I know that, but it still bothers me that it was never my choice.

I think back on that first meeting between his parents and me and my mom. Isaac wasn't there and I remember feeling scared and overwhelmed. When they took my mother to the other room to talk I felt not just left out, but furious that other people were making decisions about me, without me. Everything was happening so fast, I didn't know how to fight it.

"You're going to, um, stay with them for a few days. I'll pack some things. They think this is best and Molly, I need some time to wrap my head around all of this." My mom leaned in like she was going to kiss my cheek but instead whispered, "They have money, play your cards right."

That was the last thing my mother said to me. She climbed in her beat-up Datsun pickup and left the parking lot in a puff of black exhaust fumes. I blinked a few times to clear both the smoke and tears from my eyes. Mrs. Densworth came up behind me and waved her hand in front of her face as well, to clear the lingering cloud. "Well now, come with me. We have a lot to do in the next few days."

It wasn't until months later that I understood fully that my mom wasn't coming back. Mrs. Densworth never spoke of her again, and she took legal custody of me before Grant was born. That is why I want to talk to my mom one last time. I want to understand what happened, why she left me. When Grant was about one, I drove to the mobile home to show her what she had missed. I wanted her to see how wonderful my little boy was, but she was gone. The new renter said they had moved in almost two years ago. Somehow knowing that my mom wasn't just across town ignoring me made the pain shift. It wasn't gone, but it did lessen with knowing the disconnected phone line meant she had moved.

I sigh, and inch along with the rest of the traffic. I can see the driveway to the post office, but we have come to a stop again, so my mind continues to wander over the details of what's to come. Like how once Grant is a legal adult, I will have fulfilled my "obligation" to the family and will be free to file for divorce. If I hadn't left early I would have also had my own hefty trust fund, but I forfeited that. I knew what I was doing when I walked away. I knew my leaving broke the contract I signed the day I married Isaac. I never had any intention of taking that money. Leaving early was my way of giving them the middle finger I was never brave enough to do in person. I don't want anything to do with Isaac or his family and that trust fund would tie me to them forever. I only regret that I didn't get to see the shock on their faces when they woke up and learned I was gone.

In therapy I realized that the guilt I carried for taking things from them would continue if I relied on their money the rest of my life. They made sure I finished high school and even paid for my college education. I guess they paid for me to become a medical assistant too, although they didn't know about that. I had saved cash whenever I could, money left over from shopping trips or my allowance that Isaac so graciously (insert eye roll here) gave me every month for "whatever girly things I needed." I think he didn't trust me with a credit card or checks because he thought I would leave. When I got certified as an MA, I found a job that wouldn't keep me away after Grant's school hours. As long as I was home when he got home I had enough time to make dinner and tidy the house.

I worked for five years and not one person in my family knew I had a job. I opened my own bank account with my maiden name and started to build credit slowly. I was able to save every dime from my paychecks so that when Grant turned seventeen I started enacting a plan. He was seventeen and a half the day I left. My stomach turns a little sour at the memory of my last hug with him, and I have to remind myself I will see him very soon.

The traffic finally moves and I am able to pull into the parking lot and run into the building key in hand. My box is full this time with catalogs and bills, but I see Grant's letter on top as I pull the stack free from my tiny box. I tuck everything against my chest and head back out to the car, anxious to read what he has to say.

Dear Mom,

I was so happy to get your letter and to know that you are excited for me. I don't know if I will take any classes in writing, but I love your confidence in me. You have always been my biggest cheerleader and for that I am grateful. Dad wasn't as happy about my news as I had hoped, but I think his business trip didn't go as planned. Maybe by the time I am there, he will be more excited.

I pause and reread that part. What an asshole. Why on earth couldn't he just be happy for his son? What could have gone wrong that would take away from the fact that his only child got into Willmore, for fuck's sake? He's probably mad it isn't one of the other Ivy League schools, but we all know he didn't get into those even with the sizable donations from his family. Like my uncle once said, you can't put a shine on a turd no matter how much you polish it. I blow out a breath and keep reading.

I know you said you will be sending me information on my birthday about where to come see you and I want you to know I cleared my calendar. I told Dad and Grandmother that I am taking a road trip with some friends. This isn't entirely a lie, since Trevor and Max are heading up Hwy 1 to see more of California before they leave for Italy. I might hitch a ride out of town with them but I am pretty sure they are stopping in Santa Barbara. Grandfather told me he likes to golf there and for a terrifying moment I thought he was going to try and come along. Don't worry, he is heading to France to settle an issue with one of the hotels there.

I really miss you. I am excited to see where you live now, and what your life is like. I hope you can make me enchiladas because Jasmine does a crap job compared to yours. Don't tell her I said that, she is so sensitive.

I have a small party planned for my birthday and of course I wish you could be here, but I understand. I will see you soon Mom!

Love,

Grant

I fold his letter and tuck it in my purse. That is one I will read again at home, with wine, or maybe even whiskey. My anger is so close to the surface I make myself sit in the parking lot until I can calm down. I don't want to run over an undeserving pedestrian because my son's father is an asshole.

Tom

SATURDAY DRAGS on for about five years. Every person at the bar who wants to talk to me reminds me that I'd rather be talking to Molly. Every glass of wine I pour reminds me of how her lips looked wrapped around the glass, and how they felt and tasted against mine. I'm like an addict jonesing for another hit. Each time the door opens I whip around or crane my neck to see if it's her. It's not, and on a logical level I know it won't be, but my heart has other thoughts apparently.

When the last person settles their bar tab and walks out the door I am cleaning like a madman and dashing upstairs to take a shower and go to sleep. I feel like a little kid on Christmas Eve as I lay in bed and try to make myself feel tired. I roll over and bury my face in the pillow that Molly slept on because then I can almost imagine she is here. She isn't though, because she's somewhere a few blocks over asleep in her house. The house she doesn't want me to see. I noticed how tense she got both times I suggested meeting at her place. I am not sure what her ex-husband did to her, but it was significant and I am not going to be the one to push her out of her comfort zone.

Eventually I must fall asleep because when I open my eyes, there is light peeking through the curtains. Dim, diffuse light that is morning here on the northern coast. It's foggy today, the perfect type of day to visit a bookstore and grab some lunch. I have a spot I'd like to take her if she doesn't have plans after Happy Endings.

At ten sharp I see Molly walk up to the front of the bar and I don't even bother waiting for her to come in. I rush out and pull her into my arms.

"Good morning, Molly," I say into her neck as I pepper kisses all along the slender slope. I have my arms wrapped around her with one across her back and one lower at her waist. There is no hesitation as she melts into me and her sweet voice rings out with a little moan.

"Oh my. Well, that is how every woman should be greeted. Not by you, of course. I hope you aren't doing this to everyone," she says nervously. I think she was trying to be funny, but there is an undercurrent to her words. I pull back and level my gaze right into her eyes.

"No, currently it is only you that gets this greeting. Now, can I tell you that I missed you terribly? Or is that bordering on needy?" I say with a big smile.

"I think I like needy, so yes please, tell me how you could barely sleep because you were so excited to see me this morning," she says with a laugh.

She is smiling up at me and I wonder if I should rein in my overzealous attraction a bit. This is, after all, nothing more than a summer fling. I shouldn't be making an ass of myself.

"I think I'd rather pretend to be cool and aloof instead. Are you ready to go to the bookstore?" I slip my arm over her shoulder and lead her back out to the street.

"Yes, besides the second book I also want to see if they have any books about Connecticut or more specifically, Willmore," Molly says in a breezy, casual tone. I freeze in my tracks and pull her to a stop alongside me.

"Why?" I ask. We haven't talked about where I live the other nine months of the year, and I wonder where this is coming from.

"Well, my son got accepted and will be attending in the fall. I want to learn as much as I can about the area before he comes out to see me next month." Her eyes are bright with excitement but mine are filled with confusion.

"Is your son a child prodigy or something?" I ask.

"He turns eighteen in two weeks, so just a regular prodigy." She laughs and I quickly do the math. She was a teen mom. Little pieces are starting to click into place, but I don't want her to think I am judging her, because I am not, so I smile and nod.

"Oh well, Willmore University is a very good school indeed. They have excellent scholarships and opportunities for kids from all back-grounds." I pause and hold my hand on her arm as a car passes us. When it's clear I lead her across the street so we can be on the correct side of the road for the bookstore.

"How do you mean?" she asks. She's got the wrinkle in her brow again but this time I don't try and smooth it down.

"Well, I mean if you don't have the ability to pay—" I stop because I realize I have no idea about her life or what she can or cannot afford. My presumptions are offensive, that is clear by the look on her face.

"Oh, right. Thanks. I think Grant has it all figured out," Molly says, but she looks away right after, then steps away from me. She walks at a little faster rate toward the bookstore. I jog to catch up and try to fix whatever the fuck I just said.

"Of course. I . . . listen, I don't know why I said that, I have experi-ence with Willmore." I want to explain that is where I work, but we have reached the store and she gives me a tight smile and pulls the door open.

"Don't worry about it, Tom. It's fine." She turns and walks into the bookstore but once inside she gives me a soft look and says, "I'll be up there in the nonfiction section. Why don't you see if you can find the book we want." She doesn't sound angry any longer, but it's clear she wants a moment, so I nod and walk toward the bookcases that hold all the fictional works.

Damn. That was real smooth, Tom. I want to punch myself in the face but that seems a bit drastic for a Sunday morning in the stacks. I sigh and run my finger along the spines of books. The S section is always big so it takes me a minute to find Patrick Smith's books. There are three copies of the first book in the series, and only one of the second. There are plenty of copies of the rest of the series, but I don't want to be tempted to sneak a peek, so I pull the single copy of book two. I walk up to the register to see if they have an extra copy in the back.

Molly is coming out of the nonfiction area with her nose in a huge color hardback. She is smiling and when she looks up and finds me at the register her smile continues. My shoulders relax a little as I assume this means she isn't mad at me for my blunder earlier.

"Did you find it?" she asks. She glances to the book on the counter by the register.

"Yes, but there is only one of *Kent Price, Mission at Risk*. I asked them to check in the back for more. They have a few of the others but—"

"Oh, I would peek and see what happens, no, don't get those," she says. I laugh before she continues, "I guess we could share book two." She cocks an eyebrow at me and asks, "Are you a fast reader, Tom?"

I am, but I don't know if that is what she wants to hear. I get a vision of us curled up together reading the same book while sharing a bottle of merlot.

"That depends," I say with a smirk.

"On the book?" she asks. I shake my head. She raises an eyebrow at me and opens her mouth to speak, as the clerk comes out from the back.

"I'm sorry, we don't have any other copies of that book and it appears they are on back order. We won't get any in until August. I'm so sorry," the tall, thin woman says to me.

"That's fine." I grab the book that Molly is holding and set it on the counter with the Kent Price book. "We will take these."

I expect Molly to fight me on the purchase but she doesn't, and once our books are in the bag we head out into the morning fog. Molly slips her hand into mine and asks, "Where to now?"

"If you are hungry I'd like to take you to my second favorite breakfast spot. They don't have a lobster quiche but, I think you'll like the ambience." I wait for a beat for Molly to respond and she nods and flashes me that big smile again.

"I'd love that. I had a small breakfast when I got up at five, but I could use more food," she says. She tucks her arm into mine and I inwardly sigh at how right it feels to have her on my arm.

"Why on earth were you up so early on a Sunday?" I ask. We weave among the cars parked along the road so we can cross to the ocean side of the street.

"I had a hot date this morning and I couldn't sleep because I was so excited," she says. Her voice is low and sultry and suddenly this foggy Sunday morning feels too warm.

I clear my throat and slide my hand down her arm so that I can hold her hand before I say, "Well whoever he is, I hope he knows how very lucky he is."

This earns me a laugh. I guide her down the street past a little park then up the hill. I finally pull her to stop in front of a little white picket fence.

"It's here, they're expecting us." I push open the gate and motion for her to walk through. The look on her face is a mix of confusion and something else I can't place. Thankfully the front door opens and my good friend Angus steps out onto the porch. His restaurant looks more like a home from the front. He holds his arms open wide and smiles.

"Thomas! It is about time you brought me something so lovely. Where have you been hiding this beautiful creature? Come in, come in. I have your meal almost ready! You brought books? I hope you plan to share, I am in need of a good story."

"You can't hold your tongue long enough to hear a good story, my friend! These are for us, not for sharing, so keep your hands off!" I say sternly even though he knows I am only joking. Angus and I met my first summer here and he and I became fast friends. He is a retired professor of anthropology, so we have a lot to talk about. He traveled the world teaching in the most incredible places, never worrying about stability or tenure. For him, it was always about the adventure and the people he would meet. In the end his career was something out of a novel, instead of mine that so far reads more like a footnote in a textbook.

He waits for us to step into his small, homelike café, then grabs Molly's hands and peers into her face. "How is someone as lovely as you walking this earth? Tell me, what is your name?"

"Molly Sparrow," she says. A sweet blush rises on her cheeks and I almost feel bad for not warning her about Angus. I knew he would be smitten with her.

"English first name with a Gaelic last name! Tell me, where was your family from?" He is still holding both of her hands in his and I know he will not step aside and let us sit until he hears her family history. Thankfully Molly laughs at his question and pats his hands. She has to bend a little to look him in the eye, then she says in a conspiratorial tone, "Well, if my father ever comes back from the store I will ask him. He left to get a pack of smokes in 1958 and he must have gotten lost, because we haven't seen him since." Molly winks at him.

"Shame. He missed out on raising such a lovely woman, your mother did a fine job without that bum, I am sure. Come on in, I have the table set out back. The Silvermans are already here as well as that couple from Fort Bragg. I think you met them last time Thomas. Richard Jones and his wife Glenda." He stops then whispers, "I gave you the best table, don't worry."

He scurries off ahead of us and Molly grabs my hand, slowing me down. "What is this place?" she whispers.

"This is The Cellar, named after a famous restaurant in Edinburgh. To be honest, I got lucky getting us in here. The Fitzpatricks canceled." I give a little one-shoulder shrug trying to appear nonchalant. I really want to impress her, make her feel special. Being with Molly is a weird mix of comfort and anxiety. My stomach is in a constant state of unrest and my heart beats wildly without warning. Describing that to Dr. Potter would probably earn me a cardiac workup, so I will keep those symptoms to myself.

I guide her to our table, nodding and smiling at everyone already seated. When we reach the table, I pull out her chair and help her get settled before taking my place across from her. Thankfully we don't have much time before Angus and his wait staff start bringing out the food.

Molly

AFTER EATING MORE in one meal than I usually do in a day, Tom, or Thomas, as Angus called him, walked me back to The Floppy Fish where we said our goodbyes. He apparently has a few projects to take care of today, so he didn't have as much time as last week.

I feel bad that he was uncomfortable with my reaction to his comment about how Grant could afford Willmore. He didn't bring the subject up again and neither did I, but I could tell he was trying extra hard to smooth things over. To be honest I don't know why it ruffled my feathers so much. It never occurred to me that he thought of me as middle-class or maybe even poor. I haven't given much thought to my social status since leaving San Diego, but I guess I am no longer considered wealthy. I have one designer thing left over from my marriage and the only reason I hung on to it was because it is my prescription sunglasses. Yes, they cost a fortune, but it's not like I could donate them or anything like I did with some of my other things. I left most of my clothes in my closet, taking only what I had bought with my own money.

Tom handed me the book about Connecticut I found. It has a few chapters on the Willmore campus and surrounding areas, and the second book in the series we started. I am going to read the first three chapters then drop it off at the bar on Wednesday night for him to read. We have plans for next Sunday to discuss. While I am excited about that, I felt like things were off today. I don't know if it was the comment or the fact that we went to Angus's for brunch and it was hard to really talk.

Every time we would get into a flow, that short little bearded man would pop up like a Scottish jack-in-the-box. Once I literally screamed because he appeared as if by magic over Tom's shoulder with a story about a dig he went on off the coast of Africa. While it was fascinating, Tom had just started to tell me about where he teaches. Instead he spent five minutes with his hand on his chest trying to control his breathing. I almost took his pulse to make sure it was regular and he wasn't throwing any PVC's.

I toss the books on my coffee table and pick up Grant's letter. I guess it's a good thing this didn't turn into an all-day date, since I want to reply to my son. I have calmed down since yesterday, when I read that his father wasn't excited for him about getting into Willmore, so that's good. I have spent over seventeen years pretending that Isaac didn't drive me up the wall, I can do it for another few weeks.

Dear Grant,

I am sorry to hear you didn't get the response you were hoping for from your father. I am sure Grandmother and Grandfather were very proud of you and I hope you know I am as well.

It is going to be so hard for me to be absent from your eighteenth birthday party, Son. I love you so much. I can't wait for you to see where I

I stop writing and look around my home. Do I want him here? I mean if it was only him, yes. The thought that he may let slip where I live and

Isaac could come here to my space, my sanctuary, has me second-guessing all of this. Crap.

A few deep breaths and I consider my options. If I have him meet me somewhere in Fort Bragg where I get my mail, he will know I don't live there. I don't want Grant to feel like I don't trust him. If I want to start a life on my own, build a relationship with my son away from my ex and his parents, then I need to do this.

> *I can't wait for you to see where I live. I have so much to tell you. The next letter you receive will have my address. As I said before, please keep that close to your heart and don't share it. I hope someday you can understand that all I have done has been for you. I love you so much. Happy almost birthday, my dear boy.*
>
> *Love,*
>
> *Mom*

I set the pen down and wipe my face with my hands. I can do this. It's almost over. I have my attorney ready to serve Isaac on Grant's eighteenth birthday, and once that is done any contact, other than through our attorneys, will result in a restraining order. That little notice will be sent to Isaac's parents too, and God, I wish I could see the look on Vivian's face when she reads that. They will be so shocked to learn I don't give a flying fuck about their money or their status. I wanted to pay them back for my college education but my attorney said I shouldn't. He said that for what they put me through, I at least deserved my bachelor's degree. Even if it is in something I will never use.

I got more enjoyment and use from my community college certificate program than I did from four years at UC San Diego. Like I was ever going to work for them, for fuck's sake. I remember Vivian calling me to her study to tell me I was enrolled, and that my major would help me fit in with the family business. When I asked why that major, why I couldn't pick my own, she had said, "Because it will make you useful, you see? You can play a part in the advertising and press releases. We will put you on a team of others who work hard to make sure our brand stays at the top. We have done so much for you, it's time to repay that." Her smirk is still seared into my brain and I can almost smell her suffocating perfume as I remember that day.

"Grant is only two, I thought I would start college when he starts kindergarten. That way I won't have to be away from him," I said, frustrated that my voice was cracking as I spoke. I hated that I had to ask permission to spend time with my son, but if it wasn't for Isaac's family I'd be working full time somewhere and Grant would be in some subsidized daycare for eight hours or more.

"Dear, we have talked about this. You are eighteen now and in the summer you and Isaac will be married. In the fall you will start college. Isaac is going to be in Europe for a year learning the business, so why not get yourself an education? Women should be able to stand on their own two feet. I'd like to see you do that with only a high school diploma! No, you'll be a college-educated woman and you'll make a name for yourself. Strong women make this world go around and educated women lead the charge. We are done talking about this." She waved me away like I was a gnat. I knew it was pointless to argue, so I nodded and bowed my head.

"Thank you. Yes, that does sound like a good idea."

I walked straight into the living room and picked Grant up off the rug where the Nanny was playing with him. I scooped him into my arms and hurried down the hall before she could stop me. He snuggled into my body as I stepped out into the garden with him. He always seemed to know when I needed his snuggles.

I remember being so confused by her insistence on my education. What did it matter? They were richer than anyone needed to be and I couldn't imagine my contribution to their business would add even a nickel to the wealth of the family. It was like she wanted to make sure I could stand on my own in case Isaac came to his senses and left me.

My therapist thinks Grant knows on some level how dysfunctional our family is, but I disagree. He has a ton of friends, has gone to the best schools and summer camps. He has played multiple sports and musical instruments over the years. He's the most well-rounded kid I have ever known. How can he be aware of the terrible life I lead alongside his charmed existence?

I fold the letter and place it in an envelope that I've already addressed and stamped. It's my last one. I filled all these out when I moved here, calculating a letter a week until he turned eighteen. It helped to see there was an end, a goal to reach.

I set the letter by my keys and return to the couch where I curl up with Patrick Smith's book, *Kent Price, Mission at Risk*. It is as fast-paced as the first one and I reach chapter four before I know it.

I close the book and sigh, wondering why I agreed to only three chapters at a time. I lean my head back and close my eyes thinking about what I read and how I want to talk to Tom about it now, not a week from now.

* * *

A phone ringing in the distance pulls me from what must be sleep since I don't actually own a llama or live on a mountainside like Kent Price. I peek out from under one eyelid and expect to see my phone jumping around like a cartoon, since it sounds that loud. My answering machine kicks on so I wait.

"Hi, you've reached Molly Sparrow, the bird you cannot change. Leave me a message, since I'm traveling at the moment."

A beep sounds and I hear Tom's laugh, then, "I just got that. I love that song, Molly. Did you know "Free Bird" by Lynyrd Skynyrd is one of the most requested songs that live bands get? Did you also know it is the most hated? Well, I don't know if that is true, but a drummer friend of mine told me that. He said the song is too damn long and people only ask for it at the end of the night. Not sure why I am telling you this—"

The machine cuts him off and I chuckle to myself and wait. Sure enough the phone rings again. After the machine picks up and the message plays again Tom says, "I totally deserved that. Your machine cut me off. I called to check on you and to tell you I had a lot of fun this morning. Can't wait until Wednesday, Molly."

A warm feeling spreads across my chest. Tom is such a great guy. I don't know how it's going to feel when he leaves at the end of the summer, but I am betting it won't feel good. I decided that having a summer fling is an important part of my journey to discovering what I want out of life, but I hope September me remembers that.

I stretch out and yawn before walking to my little kitchen to grab my cordless phone. I hit redial since Tom is the last person I called, and I wait for him to answer.

"Hello?" He sounds like maybe he ran to get the phone and for some reason that makes me giggle.

"Hi, Tom. I got your messages, I think all the food I ate this morning and a very good book sent me off to dreamland. Sorry I didn't answer."

"Reading all about Willmore?" he asks.

"No, well, I did look at it a little bit, but I read the three chapters. Can I bring it to you before Wednesday? I don't think I can wait to talk about what Kent Price has gotten himself into."

"Damn, you read fast! Yes, please. I'm not going to lie, Molly, handing that lone copy over to you was the hardest thing I have ever done. If you want to come down to The Floppy Fish, I'll unlock the door."

"Why don't you come here?" I say before I can second-guess it. "Unless you are busy or something?" I add as my stomach twists into knots.

He's quiet for a moment but then says, "I'd love to. Can I bring anything?"

"No" I glance at the clock and see it's past five. "I can make something for us to eat if you're hungry, or we can just—"

Tom cuts me off. "I am starving. I didn't eat lunch and I've burned off all of Angus's delicious brunch with the work I did around here."

I give Tom my address, then rush down the hall to freshen up. My eye makeup is smeared a bit so I wipe under my eyes with a washcloth and stare at my reflection. I am due for my haircut soon, but I think I might let it grow out. I want to feel like my decisions are for me, and cutting off my hair was more of a middle finger to Isaac.

I run my hands under the water at my bathroom sink, then try and tame the weird patch of hair that is proof I did fall asleep on the couch. There is a knock on the door and I laugh to myself knowing he must have jogged here to make that kind of time.

I place one hand over my heart to settle the damn thing, because it seems to think Tom coming over is equal to running a marathon. When I feel like my heart isn't about to jump out of my chest and attach itself to Tom, I open the door and burst out laughing.

Tom

"WHAT THE HELL happened to you, Tom?" she finally manages, after a fit of laughter.

"I was hoping you wouldn't notice," I say with a grimace. She stares at my face, which is speckled with very bright green paint. I think it's glowing. It feels like I could bring a ship to shore right now.

She snickers. "I'm sorry. I can close the door and we can try this again. My acting is shit though, so I can't guarantee the second time will be any better."

I sigh and chuckle a little before I try to explain. She holds up her hand and stops me. "Come in, I don't want my neighbors to think I am dating Kermit the Frog."

I like her saying we're dating more than I probably should. I hand her a bottle of the merlot I always overpour for her, and she thanks me.

"I couldn't show up empty-handed, and to be honest I thought if I gave you enough wine, you'd look past my imperfections," I say sheepishly.

"I would argue that the Day-Glo green is making you more attractive." She takes the wine and walks toward her charming little kitchen. I try to act like a gentleman and not stare at her ass as she walks away. I fail miserably.

"It's black light paint. Lyle wanted me to paint arrows on the floors pointing to the patio and the bathrooms. Most of it went well, I had only two arrows left to go when the sprayer malfunctioned. My face took the worst of it."

When she sets the wine on the counter she turns to face me. Her eyebrow arches, "Did you get paint in your eyes, Tom?"

"No. I had on goggles," I say and watch as both her eyebrows reach her hairline. I clarify, "Swim goggles. They were all I had, and they worked so you can stop laughing." I'm waiting by the door because I really want to ask her if I should take off my shoes before coming in. Her house is spotless and fits what I know about her. It's bright, airy, and so feminine. Not in an obnoxious Barbie Dream House kind of way, but mature beauty. Elegance with refined touches of grace, without being ostentatious.

"Why are you standing there, Tom? Is the paint still wet or something?" she asks.

"No, should I take off my shoes? I don't want to get your floors all dirty."

Her face softens and her smile fades but she doesn't look angry. Her eyes crinkle at the edges as she says, "Thank you. Yes, please. I put my shoes there by the bench." She points to a white bench with a blue toile fabric cushion. When I sit, I see the print is lighthouses and whales. It's subtle, and if you didn't look closely, you probably wouldn't even notice. There is something about living by the ocean that makes people want to line their whole world with nautical-themed decor, and I am unreasonably happy that Molly hasn't fallen into that trap.

I slip my shoes off, tuck them under the bench, then walk toward her marveling at how beautiful she is. How on earth did someone let this woman go? How did her husband not cherish what he had? I am about to tell her something along these lines when her phone rings. I watch as her eyes go wide and something like fear crosses her face.

"Sorry, I don't get a lot of calls. It might be Dr. Potter," she says, grabbing the cordless.

"Hello? Oh, hi. No, I understand, can you give me a minute?" she asks, and pauses to cover the phone with her hand before saying, "I need to take this, Tom. I'm sorry. Make yourself at home." She scurries down a small hallway to an open door where she disappears. I hear the click of a door latch, but her voice is still audible through the wall, and I know she wants privacy, so I try to busy myself. I wander around her kitchen and living room area touching things like an unsure burglar. She has a stack of mail on the counter that looks to be mostly bills and magazines. There is one letter ready to go out that is addressed to Grant, her son.

"But I thought the judge was on our side!" I hear Molly yell from the other room. Shit. I walk to the farthest corner of her small house, which is in her kitchen. I open the fridge and look at her food, but I don't want her to think I am snooping so I close the door and straighten up.

"No, Jeff, I don't want him to have this address! What else can we do?" Molly's voice is frantic and it breaks my heart a little. She sounds so afraid, and I am here awkwardly staring at her belongings. Do I go in and try to comfort her? Should I leave? I spin around and lean against the fridge running my hands through my hair. Fuck, I wish I knew what to do.

Something bumps my shoulder on its way to the floor. I look down and see a box that I must have knocked off the top of the fridge. I pick it up and read the side where light pink writing scrolls elegantly from edge to edge: *The Fancy Friend.*

Huh. It must be some kind of cooking thing. I pull open the flap and reach inside, hitting some kind of button as I do. When I pull out the item it is pulsating and well, thrusting. Jesus Christ. It's not a cooking thing, it's her vibrator. Who leaves a vibrator in the kitchen on top of the fridge? I scramble to turn it off, pushing the three buttons in every possible order but it seems to only anger the damn thing.

"I guess I have to get used to the fact that I will never be free from him or his family. No, I understand. Thank you," I hear her say from the other room. She really needs thicker doors. What is the point of a door if it can't block out sound? I look down at the angry pink thrusting, vibrating dildo and panic. She's coming out here after arguably getting the worst news of her life, and she is going to find me holding her vibrator.

Shit.

I shove the thing down the back of my pants and hurry to sit on her couch. I arrange myself a few times praying the cushions will muffle the thrusting I can feel. It seems to be crawling south with each movement. It's like an angry inchworm after a rainstorm searching for a tuft of grass to hide in. I really don't see a way out of this mess, especially since Molly has emerged from the bedroom and is coming right toward me.

"Sorry about that. I got some bad news from my lawyer." She flops on the couch next to me, which normally I am happy about. Her being near me is one of my new favorite things, but the flop has caused the vibrator to jump even closer to my ass crack.

"Do you mind if I order us a pizza? I really don't feel like cooking and I definitely feel like eating a bunch of cheese." She laughs, and I am struck by how calm she sounds after that call.

I clear my throat and say, "Sure, Molly, that would be fine, or I can go if you need to be alone." God, I really hope not. I want to spend time with her but I also don't want to stand up and walk out with her vibrator violating my ass. Oh, it sort of tickles. Do I like it? Maybe. That is something I'm not ready to explore, especially not at this moment.

"No, I want you to stay. I want to explain, if you're up to listening to a story," she says. She's still holding the phone in her hand and she's turned towards me now resting her knee on the couch. "Let me call Rico's. Do you like pepperoni or do you want something fancy?"

"Pepperoni is fine," I manage to say. I push back against the cushion a little bit hoping that she can't hear what I am hearing. The thrusting vibrator behind me is starting to get warm. I don't think trapping it like this is good for the motor. I am probably voiding her warranty at the very least, but I might also cause a fire.

Molly orders us a pizza then takes the phone to its base in the kitchen. She pulls two wineglasses out of the cabinet and opens the wine. Maybe when the pizza guy gets here I can excuse myself and go to the bathroom and flush this damn thing down the toilet. It's vibrating between my ass cheeks now and thrusting itself closer to a place I really don't want it to be. I'm sweating and with all the stupid paint speckles on my face it's getting uncomfortable. I am about to excuse myself to the bathroom and risk getting caught when Molly returns to the couch with my wine.

"Here, a nice big glass Tom, you look like you need a drink as much as me." She gives me one of her heart-melting smiles and I force myself to relax. The batteries can't last forever, right? Eventually this thing will stop violating me and I can go back to my life.

"Thanks. Is everything okay?" I ask her because I really want to know, but I also want a distraction.

She sighs and takes a big gulp of her wine before turning to face me again. She tucks her leg under her and rests one arm across the back of the couch. I wish I could mirror her pose, but I don't dare move away from the cushion that is currently muffling my shame.

"It is. It will be. Next week, my husband will be served divorce papers. I was trying to make it so my post office box would be listed as my new address, but the judge said no. Now he will know exactly where I live," she says. She is tracing her finger over the top of the wineglass, making tiny squeaking noises.

"Is he a dangerous man, Molly?" I hope the concern in my voice makes up for the fact that I am still facing forward like I am on a bus.

"Maybe? I wish I knew for sure. I have never gone against his wishes or his family's, so I don't really know. He always gets what he wants, so if he wants to hurt me, he will." Her voice is small and fragile. I turn, more worried about her than my own predicament.

"I'll protect you, Molly. I won't let him hurt you," I say over the now loud grinding, sputtering sound.

She cocks her head and looks at me, then around the room. "Do you hear that?"

"Hear what?" I say like every clichéd movie line I have ever not believed. Just like me, Molly looks suspicious.

"It sounds like a blender or something. It's grinding," she says, and her eyes narrow. I am sure she is on to me, but instead of leaning closer to me she stands and walks to her fridge. She presses her ear to the door and says, "This thing is on its last leg. It came with the house and I have put off getting—" her voice trails off as I watch her look down. I know the moment she sees the empty vibrator box because I see it at the same time. Holy hell.

She snatches it up and peers inside, I am sure hoping to see her little friend nestled where he belongs. She doesn't of course, so then her eyes snap to me where the sound of unrequited love is coming from my pants.

She rolls her lips in forming a thin line, then puts her hand on her heart before saying "Tom?" in a very high-pitched voice.

"Yes?" I try and act nonchalant but sweat and green paint are pouring down my face. Well, that's probably an exaggeration but I do have a bit of paint in my eye thanks to all the sweating and now that I'm away from the cushion, the vibrator has officially reached its mecca. I whimper and bite my lip as the tip starts to thrust against the very puckered flesh of my asshole.

"Tom, are you getting to know Fred?" she asks in almost a whisper. She sounds horrified. Can't blame her.

"Maybe. Is Fred pink?" I ask, in case maybe she has other malfunctioning vibrators.

She puts her face in her hands and her shoulders start to shake. It feels like hours pass before she looks up at me with tears streaming down her cheeks. She holds out her hand and says in a strained laughing voice, "Give it to me, Tom."

I reach back and dislodge Fred from my pants and hand it to her. Now that it's free from my waistband prison, the thrusting is more violent and the little leg things aren't just vibrating—they're whipping back and forth like windshield wipers in a storm. I have no idea how that would feel good for a woman. Unless women like it rough. That seems unlikely. This thing is pure violence. Pink violence.

"Oh my God, it's possessed. I can't turn it off," she says in gasps between her laughter. She whacks it on the counter a few times and I cup my groin in sympathy even if the pink dick is getting everything it deserves.

It makes what I hope is its final thrust, and I swear a puff of smoke comes out of the tip. Molly sets it on the counter and backs up like it might spring to life again. Really, if this were a Stephen King novel, it would.

"Is it done?" I ask, peering over her shoulder.

"Maybe. I don't know for sure." Molly bends forward like she's examining an art exhibit. Fred gives a little kick and we both jump back.

The knock on the door saves us from further assault as we both decide to retrieve the pizza. I beat her to it and hand the delivery boy a fifty from my wallet. He is beyond excited when I tell him to keep the change. My motivation is purely to get rid of the kid before Pinkzilla comes to life again.

"Do you want me to set the pizza here?" I motion to the small table she has near her kitchen.

"Yeah, that's perfect. I'll get our wine." We both move about her house pretending there isn't a vibrator fighting for its life on her counter. It has mostly stopped kicking now. There is an occasional shudder as it tries in vain to please the tile.

"So you crossed off another item from your list?" I ask innocently.

She snickers and nods. Since she doesn't elaborate, I press on and ask, "Was it enjoyable?" Then I lean in and whisper, "Do you like it rough, Molly?" Because if I am going to be with this gem of a woman, I want to please her.

Her eyes fly wide and she puts her hand over her mouth to hide the snort of laughter. "God, no, Tom. That thing assaulted me. I assumed I did it wrong, but I am beginning to think it's broken." As if on cue Fred kicks on again and vibrates himself right off the counter. Before it can crawl toward us, I jump up and grab it, then toss it in the trash.

"I have to say, I am really glad to hear that. I don't know if I have it in me to be that aggressive," I explain as I make my way back to the table. Molly is wiping her eyes in vain as she continues to laugh. Seeing her like this is a treat. She's not just relaxed, she's euphoric.

"I don't want aggressive, or I don't think so at least. I haven't had a lot of experiences to go by, but I am pretty confident about not wanting you to windshield wiper my lady parts. Or punch me in the cervix. That wasn't enjoyable at all." She takes a bite of her pizza before I can ask any questions about that.

After another big gulp of her wine she places both hands on her chest and takes a settling breath. "Okay, first of all I want to say thank you. I got some pretty frustrating news tonight but your run in with Fred erased all my anxiety. I am so glad you came over. I am not glad you were assaulted, but I *am* glad you are here."

"Glad I could be of help." I tip my wineglass toward her and she raises hers to match. We clink glasses and drink.

"I want to explain—" she starts but I hold up my hands to stop her.

"Only if you want to, Molly. You don't owe me anything," I say.

"I know, that's why I feel like sharing. You have been so patient with me." She looks down at her plate then lifts her head and looks around her small cottage. "You are my first houseguest. I haven't had anyone in my personal space since I moved here. Now, in light of the judge's decision, I am grateful that it was you that walked through my door and not him." She pauses and takes a deep breath in then blows it out. "That came out wrong maybe, I didn't feel comfortable sharing my sanctuary, and if Isaac, my soon-to-be ex-husband, was the first, I think that would have been very upsetting. Does that make sense?" she asks.

"Sure. You got to control it. You were in charge. It makes perfect sense. Tell me, when was the last time you felt like you were in charge of your own life?" I ask, hoping I'm not pushing too much.

"When I was sixteen. I met Isaac on my sixteenth birthday, had sex with him the same night and got pregnant with Grant, probably that night if not shortly after," she says. I notice that it sounds practiced, like she has told people that story before, or she prepared herself to tell me.

"That must have been really tough. Was he supportive? You married him, so he must have been a little at least?" I ask.

"No, it wasn't his choice to marry me. That was all Mommy. I think it was his punishment, to be honest. He screwed up her plans for the social event of the year. I am sure she thought after he graduated college, she'd pair him with a show horse and they would go on to produce pedigree offspring. Instead he knocked up a teenager who lived in a trailer in a mobile home park by the beach. I was the farthest thing from her plan."

"That's awful. Why did you agree to that if you knew?" I ask, trying to understand what she must have gone through, but failing miserably.

"I didn't have a choice. At least, at the time I didn't think I had a choice. I could have signed over my rights to my son and walked away. I'm sure they had a story all ready to explain how Isaac's true love had died in childbirth and now he was forced to raise his son on his own."

"What the hell? That sounds like a horror movie, not real life." I shake my head in disbelief, bile rising in my throat as my anger starts to take root.

"It was a horror movie and my life. Once his parents found out I was carrying his child, they moved me into their house. I am grateful for some things. They paid for a private tutor so I would graduate high school, then they paid for college. I'm sure their motivation was so their son wouldn't be to be married to a dummy."

"You went to college? I thought you only had that certificate training?" I ask.

"I graduated from UC San Diego with a degree in communications. They were hoping that I would work for their family business, promoting their brand. Of course once I had my degree they didn't place me on a team where actual work was being done. I had a small office I was supposed to go to each day and pretend to work. No one checked on me or gave me any assignments, so I started looking at other things that interested me," Molly says with a little shrug.

"What did your parents think of all of that?" I ask. I picture my sisters going through something like that at sixteen and feel a little sick about it.

"My mom gave her consent. Well, to be more exact, she sold me to them." Molly drains her wine and reaches for the bottle, but I take it and pour her another glass, then top mine off. I should have brought two bottles.

"Okay, now I do need more information on that. What happened?" I ask. I reach across the table and give her hand a squeeze.

"Well, I told you that I was sixteen when I got pregnant, I thought Isaac was seventeen. Turns out he was twenty," she says. She takes a big bite and I wait as patiently as I can. My chest feels tight and I am sure my face is turning red. I am so angry for her that I want to stand up, get in my car and drive to wherever the fuck her ex is and kick him right in the dick.

"So my mom met with his family and signed some papers then walked out with a check for five grand. That is the amount her grandchild and I were worth, I guess." She gives a little shrug, like what? Like it doesn't matter? Like that is a reasonable price for her freedom and autonomy?

"Molly." I pause to consider my words then say, "That is so fucked up. I'm so sorry." It's not what I want to say, but by the look on her face it was the right choice.

"Yes, Tom, you hit the nail on the head. I've had a few years of therapy and for the past six months I have come to terms with a lot of things that happened to me. I'll never let myself get into that kind of situation again. I will be the one who makes decisions about my life, no one else." She smiles at me and I try to return it, but I rub my chest instead and look down.

"Tom? Are you okay?" she asks. Her head is cocked and she is about to push up out of her chair.

"I'm fine, Molly. Maybe I shouldn't be, but I'm really bothered by all of that. I feel so bad for you." I have put my hand out on the table and she reaches for me and gives it a squeeze.

Molly

I KEEP my hand on Tom's not because I like touching him, but also because I am a little worried about him. I noticed him rub his chest a moment ago and his face is like a beet. His skin feels dry and warm though, so maybe he really is mad, like he said.

I wish I had a blood pressure cuff here. Maybe he will come by the clinic and let me check him out.

"So, is your son coming to visit?" Tom asks, breaking my thoughts about a covert blood pressure check.

"Yes. He's getting a letter next week with my address. That's what the phone call was about, I am sure you heard," I say.

"Yeah, sorry about that. I tried to not listen but your doors are like paper, and then your vibrator attacked me," he says and I chuckle.

"I owe you something for that, but I am not sure what. Therapy? Dinner?" I ask as I sip my wine.

"Dinner works." He winks at me then asks, "When do you expect Grant?"

"Probably around the first of July. He and some friends are heading up the coast on a road trip. They're stopping in Santa Barbara, and he'll go on from there," I say. My excitement at seeing my son is, I am sure, obvious.

"Well, I've tried to tell you this many times but keep getting interrupted. You are never going to guess where I teach," Tom says. He is looking more like his normal color again as he's leaning back in his chair with his wine in hand.

"Are you going to tell me of all the schools in this country you teach at Willmore?" I ask, sure that he's teasing me.

"I am. That is exactly what I tried to tell you today. I've taught there for ten years," Tom says then goes on, "My father taught there, and my mother for a few years before going into consulting."

"Are any of your siblings teachers, or just you?" I ask.

"No, my sisters are overachievers. One is a pediatrician, another is a nephrologist, and the baby girl of the family is a cutthroat lawyer." He laughs and takes a big gulp of his wine.

"You said you were one of five, so you have a brother too?" I ask and Tom nods but I see his expression fall a bit.

"Yes, my brother Nicholas isn't quite like the rest of us, unfortunately. He is a bit of the black sheep of the family, although I have never liked that term. He had a rough go of it when he was younger and to be honest he never pulled out of it."

"What happened? If you don't mind me asking," I say.

"No, it's fine, I don't mind talking about it. Nick was bucked off a horse when he was about twelve and sustained a head injury. He dealt with a lot of rehab, and pain. More pain than a little kid should go through to be honest, and by the time he got to high school he turned to weed to help him with his headaches. I think he liked the way it made him feel, so he's spent the next fifteen years chasing a better high." His gaze drops to the table and he shifts in his seat a little.

"Oh God, that's terrible. I am so sorry." I don't know what else to say, so I pour us each more wine and offer a smile.

"Yeah, I think if my parents had been around more, things might have been different. We had a great support system of friends and family in the area, but with Mom and Dad both working I think Nick kind of fell through the cracks." Tom runs his hand over his face and looks at me. "I don't want to blame them, God knows they do that enough themselves, but it was hard to watch, hard to know what he was getting up to and no one was stopping him. He's been in rehab a few times now but always falls right back into those patterns as soon as he is out. I think it's who he is now."

"So what's the order? You're the oldest?" I ask, hoping to lighten the conversation a little. I want to hear all about his family, what his life is like, but I can tell he's uncomfortable.

"Yes, I am the oldest, then Julie, the nephrologist. Next is Kimberly. She is the pediatrician, then Nicholas, then Laura, the attorney, finishes off the group," he says.

"Did you enjoy growing up in a big family?" I ask.

"Yes and no. I don't think there is a memory of mine that doesn't involve pushing or shoving of some kind. I am glad that we are all still friends, I guess. We talk a few times a month, either on the phone or via mail."

"Do they all live in Connecticut?" I ask.

"Everyone but Laura. She lives in New York. She visits as often as she can and sends my parents tickets to Broadway shows so she can stay in their good graces. They still hold it against her that she moved. Being a real estate attorney in Connecticut isn't quite the same as practicing in the Big Apple."

"That makes sense. Did you get enough to eat?" I ask before I close the lid to the pizza box. There are only three slices left so I guess we both absentmindedly devoured it while we talked.

"I am beyond full. Thank you." Tom stands and takes the box to the counter the starts opening cupboards.

"Tinfoil is in the drawer by the sink," I say feeling the corners of my mouth tilt up. I can't remember a time when Isaac helped clean up after dinner. We move to the couch and talk more, in a relaxed way that I imagine usually comes with years together. Tom makes me feel so comfortable and I get the feeling he thinks the same of me. Is this what it's like to date as an adult? I really have no idea. Dating in general is such a foreign concept to me. Isaac and I didn't really date. He never showed up at my house with flowers or took me to a movie. I think he bought me a hot dog the night I met him, but to be honest I don't remember. I spent a lot of time blocking out that night, wishing it hadn't happened, or that I had gone home when I was supposed to.

When Grant was a baby, I remember lying with him in the room I was given at the Densworths' house. I curled up on a bed bigger than my whole room at the trailer where I had lived and I'd stare into his eyes and wonder where I would have been if he hadn't come along. I'd touch his soft, chubby cheeks and trace my finger over his beautiful lips, then cry at not what I had lost, but what I had now. From the outside looking in I must have appeared lucky. I went from having nothing, going hungry some nights, worrying about how we were going to pay bills, or if my mom would want me to quit school and get a job now that I was sixteen. That was the whole point of going to the beach that night—I wanted one last chance to be wild and free, be a kid who had no responsibility or worries. I left the beach, albeit unaware, that I had gained one of life's biggest responsibilities.

"Do you want more wine? If you say yes, I will have to run back to the bar and grab a second bottle," Tom says. He's leaning on the counter in my kitchen with a dish towel slung over his shoulder. He looks so comfortable here in my home and I am surprised at how happy that makes me.

"No, I think two glasses on a Sunday night is more than enough." I pat the couch next to me so he will join me. I am rewarded with his heart-melting smile as he drops the towel on the counter and walks towards me. My heart does a little flip and my stomach does that swoopy flutter thing. Damn, I like that. I like how he makes me feel and that scares me a little. I know he's leaving in August, I know this is temporary, but as he reaches me, and bends to place his lips gently on mine I wish that wasn't true.

"Your lips are my new favorite thing," he mumbles against my mouth, so I kiss him more thoroughly. He settles in next to me on the couch and we spend the next two hours talking, laughing, and kissing. When he leaves, I do the thing where I close the door then lean against it, hand over my heart and sigh. I wish I could bottle the way I feel right now. This light, happy feeling in my heart is not something I ever expected, but now that I have it, I don't want to let it go.

It's not until I am in bed and almost asleep that I realize I didn't give him the book he came over for. I smile and turn into my pillow, happy I have a reason to see him again tomorrow.

* * *

By noon the next day the clinic is packed and I'm running from room to room. Dr. Potter doesn't want to hire another medical assistant because he says I am all he needs, but on days like this I wish he felt differently. I lean against the counter as the centrifuge spins down the latest batch of bloodwork. The phone lights up and Henny's voice comes through when I pick up.

"Sorry, dear, I put another one in a room. Little girl has a bladder infection and you know Doc is going to want a urine sample. I didn't want to make the poor thing wait," she says sweetly.

"No problem, I will go grab that from her now. Thanks for letting me know." I hang up and flip my stethoscope over my neck, grabbing a wipe and a sterile cup from the shelf. I hope she is old enough to do this with her mom's help, since Dr. Potter is a real stickler for seeing the urine under the scope. Most times he sends it off for a culture too, but if it's her first time having one, he probably won't.

I walk into the only vacant room and plaster on my smile. "Hi there! I hear we have a little girl with a bladder infection?" I address the girl sitting on the table, legs swinging. She looks about seven or eight and she is totally adorable.

"Yeah, it hurts to pee, to go potty, to urinate," she says, covering all the bases as she looks at her mom. I smile again and turn to mom to give her some instructions.

"Molly Sparrow? Holy shit. Molly?!" The woman says as she stands, her purse dropping to her feet. I stare at her trying to place her but come up short until she says, "Free Bird?"

"Lisa?" I set the cup on the counter because I can't hold something and hug her at the same time. We throw our arms around each other and rock back and forth as we hug. Then the flood of questions and *I'm sorrys* fill the room as we embrace like the long-lost friends we are.

"You're alive? I thought you died, or were killed, or moved. I guess you moved, have you been here since you were sixteen? I went by your trailer and you were gone. A week later a new family had moved in and they said they didn't know where you or your mom went. Did you come here?"

"Oh, no. I moved here about six months ago. Do you live in the area?" I ask. I glance over at her daughter and smile. She looks like Lisa did at that age.

"No, well, not far. We live in Willows, but came over for a little vacation, been here a few days. Krystal started complaining about it burning when she peed and I asked at the pharmacy where I could take her, and they sent us here." She pauses and shakes her head before saying, "I can't believe you're standing here in front of me right now." She pulls me into another hug. She whispers in my ear, "I really thought your mom killed you when she found out you were pregnant." She keeps her arms wrapped around me but leans back, her eyes shimmering with tears.

"Oh my God, no. I am so sorry you were worried. I have so much to tell you. Are you around long? Can we have dinner?" I ask her as Dr. Potter swings into the doorway.

"Molly, do you have that urine sample yet?"

"Oh shoot, no. Sorry Dr. P. Krystal and her mom will go do that now. I'll find you when it's under the scope," I tell him.

"Alright." He wiggles his fingers at Krystal in what must be his attempt of a kid greeting. I watch the little girl shift uncomfortably on the table. I grab the cup and hand it to her then tell her quietly, "He is a really nice man. Let's get your pee so he can take a look at it under the microscope, then we will get you some meds to make you feel better."

I give instructions on how to capture a clean urine sample, then wait outside the bathroom for them. I take the cup with my gloved hand when they emerge.

"Why is he going to look at it? Can't he believe me that it hurts?" Krystal asks.

"He likes to see the bacteria. He's super funny like that," I tell her and she giggles. Lisa takes her back to the room and once the urine is spun down and on the slide I go to find Dr. Potter.

"Looks like she has a raging infection from what the dipstick showed. It's under the slide now," I tell him once he emerges from a patient's room.

"I'll go take a look, is this her first one?" he asks as he waddles off to the lab. I used to think it was rude how he would ask questions as he was walking away from me, like he wasn't really interested in the answer. I've learned that's part of his quirky personality and since he does it to his wife too, I don't take offense anymore.

"Yes," I say over my shoulder, quickly ducking into the room close to the lab to clean it and get it ready for the next patient. When that is done, I check in with Henny and for the first time all day there isn't a patient waiting to be taken back to a room.

I walk back to where Lisa and Krystal are and overhear Dr. Potter explaining how the test showed a lot of blood and infection in her urine. I am grateful he didn't say pus like he usually does. It's not a word anyone wants to hear.

As they head to the front to check out, I follow them and grab a card jotting down my number quickly so I can hand it to Lisa.

"Here. Please call me if you can get together, or even if you can't. I would love to see you again. I've missed you so much." I press the card into her hand and she wraps her arms around me, pulling us together.

"I'm for sure going to call you. If you are free we can meet tonight! Paul can watch the girls for the evening. I need to see you, hear all about your life since I saw you last. God, Molly. I can't believe it's you." She is tearing up again and I am hit by a wave of love for my long-lost best friend.

Tom

"Conscience doth make cowards of us all."

I WAKE up with that quote bouncing around in my head. I scratch my hand down my jaw and reach for my glasses wondering why Shakespeare made an appearance in my dream. As I lie there I see snippets of images, none super clear. The one that stands out is of me on stage in some kind of costume, but the more I concentrate it fades further from my grasp.

I hate being onstage, and while I have never been in a play I have had to speak at large events during my ten years as an archeology professor. Before coming out here for the summer, I spoke in front of over a thousand people about the importance of securing grants in our field. It really bothers me that when a conference of all the best minds of anthropology and archeology, I am only sought out to talk about grant writing.

I sit up on my elbows and blink a few times to orient myself. Now it snaps into place. I was dreaming I was in a play. I was standing in front of an audience in nothing but tights and a ruffle around my neck. My shirt had gone missing and I think I was in trouble for that. But like most dreams, the more I try to force my memory, the more it slides back into the shadows. I sigh and push the covers off my legs and walk into the bathroom. I am taking a piss when the phone rings but whoever it is will wait. I saw the clock on my way in here and it's after nine, so I know it's not Molly. She's at work and no one else deserves to speak to me before my coffee.

I take a quick shower and as I am drying off, I can hear the faint ringing of the phone down at the bar ringing, then the one up here rings again. Damn it.

I wrap the towel around my waist and grab the phone on the kitchen counter grumbling out, "Hello?"

"Tommy?" a female voice asks and my legs instantly feel like they weigh a hundred pounds. I sink into the chair and clear my throat. "Laura, what's wrong?" I ask.

"It's Nick. He's in the hospital," she says and I wait for her to elaborate but she doesn't.

"Okay, are you going to tell me what happened or do I have to guess, because I can tell you I am thinking the worst right now," I say.

"Well, you wouldn't be far off I bet. He overdosed, and they think it was intentional." I can hear her pen tapping in the background and I can almost smell the cigarette she is puffing on.

"I thought you quit smoking," I say, because what else is there to say at this moment. We all knew it was coming and we've all prepared for this call. The only surprising thing is it's Laura who called me, so I ask before she can make a snide comment about her smoking, "Was he in New York when it happened?"

"No. I am at Mom and Dad's. They, um . . ." She trails off, so I wait.

"They didn't want me to call you until we knew something. The thing is, we aren't going to know anything, Tommy. He might wake up, he might not. It's all a fucking guessing game at this point, but I wanted you to know," she says. I can hear the strain in her voice, but that's only because I know her so well.

My mind is readjusting to put her at the kitchen table at our childhood home. The faded yellow floral wallpaper that had an almost metallic sheen to it, is behind her. Mom chose a bright yellow wall phone that had a cord longer than the whole block. We could take that handset down the hall to the bathroom that was off the kitchen, close the door and feel like we had some privacy. That is a valuable commodity when you are one of five children. That cord didn't have much curl left to it by the time I graduated high school.

"Should I come out?" I ask, as I close my eyes against her response.

"No, Tom. There is no need. What would you do? Read him boring books about ancient people?" she quips and I laugh.

"Maybe, wait, why do you assume it would be boring? He used to like that kind of stuff. We were going to dig our way to China that one summer. If Mom hadn't figured out we were using her big serving spoons we might've made it," I say, and this time she laughs.

"This is why I called you. You are the only one that remembers the good times. Well, at least you are the one that will talk about it." She sighs heavily and I can hear the chair scrape across the wood floor. I close my eyes and picture her there, probably trying to close the window now that her cigarette is out. Mom and Dad don't like her smoking and they sure as hell don't want it in their house.

"I can come if you need me. Lyle would understand. I can close up for a week or so?" I hate that I want her to tell me no, but I do.

"No, you made a promise to your friend, and this is your break. I've got it. Julie and Kimberly have been helping when they can, but you know how it is with them. It was my turn anyway. Kim had the last time and you were there two years ago when they found him down by the river." She sighs again before saying, "I feel like shit, Tommy. I just want this to be over, you know?"

"I know. I feel the same way. Nick doesn't deserve the life he was dealt, but he made the bad choices time and time again. We are all tired." I rub my hand down my face wishing I could go back to my nightmare about being on stage with only tights and a ruffle.

I spend the rest of my day working on the shelves for the bar. Lyle wanted to hang more wineglasses, so I cut notches and added a few little shelves on the sides for wine display. I'm happy with how it turned out, but mostly I am happy for the distraction from the image of my brother lying in a hospital bed.

By the time the bar opens my mind is in a better place. A few of the regulars keep me company and some tourists make things interesting. I pour drinks, smile and make it through the night like a guy who has no worries. Laura is right, we have all had our turn being the one who is there, talking to the doctors, comforting Mom and Dad, answering questions from the neighbors. Although the last part isn't probably true anymore. I think there are only two families on our street that would remember Nick. Everyone has moved on, moved away. I mean we all have, but my parents? Not so much.

Once I lock up, I climb the stairs to my little apartment and pull off my shirt as I toe off my shoes. I need a hot shower, but as I am heading to the bathroom I see the light flashing on the machine. I hesitate, almost afraid to listen in case it's bad news.

I blow out a breath and hit the message button.

"You have two new messages," the nice man says. I wonder who that is? Like did he have to audition for that job? Was there a lot of competition?

"Hey Tommy, wanted to let you know they have decided to intubate him. Mom and Dad think it's a good idea to give him every chance, but the rest of us were against it. Anyway. I'll call back if anything changes. Don't book a flight. It's fine. Stay there—"

The machine cuts her off and I expect the next message to be from her as well, but instead I hear Molly's sweet voice. It washes over me like the softest wave and I smile and close my eyes as I listen.

"Hey Tom! I wanted to let you know that I had planned on bringing you that Kent Price book today, but I actually ran into an old friend at work and we're going to go out to dinner and catch up. I will bring it by tomorrow I promise. I hope you are doing good. I'll talk to you soon. Bye!" The machine clicks and I hit replay so I can listen to her voice again.

I spend longer than I should in the shower, letting the warm water slide over my aching heart. I miss my brother. Not who he is now, but I miss who he was before the accident. I haven't gotten over it even after all these years. Nick is five years younger than me and I remember the day Mom came home from the hospital with him. I was so excited to have a brother I peed my pants. This is something that is brought up often at family gatherings, but I don't care. It was pure joy to see her climb out of the car with that blue blanket instead of a pink one.

I finally shut the water off when it's turned so cold that my balls start to crawl back into my body. I put on only a pair of briefs and climb into bed, wishing I had that book to read. I could stand a night of escape via Kent Price.

Instead of letting my mind wander to what Nick is going through, I think of Molly. I plan out a way to take her on a date before her son gets here. I know I need to make myself scarce during his visit. I have no intention of trying to insert myself into that, but I am curious what he's like.

I tuck my hand behind my head and without my permission my mind is flooded with images of Nick over the years, some good, most bad. I groan and roll to my side, frustrated and sad and so many other things. I am never going to fall asleep at this rate. I'm agitated. I feel like my skin is too tight and my brain feels itchy. I need to walk and stare at the ocean. It is the only thing I know to do when I feel this way, so I swing my legs out of bed and find some clothes.

As I step out into the night I take a deep breath in. Mendocino is quiet, with no one else suffering the same insomnia as me. I start toward the ocean and the dream I had this morning comes to my mind. Maybe the quote from Hamlet was trying to tell me something. Since learning about Nick I have shown nothing but cowardice. I know what I should do, and yet I remain frozen in my own fear.

Before I realize it, I am at the end of the lane with the ocean laid out before me. I step over the low barrier and out onto the bluff. There is an odd yet pleasing sensation standing alone with the waves. Their gentle nighttime sound is reassuring and provides my soul with something else to focus on. The push and pull of earth, water, time all meet here, and I am its solo witness.

As I stare out into the endless sea I think about time, and how it is something that has always interested me. I'm fascinated by how fast it can seem, zipping by without regard for your feelings, or so slow that each minute feels like a slow scrape across your skin.

I think back to the day I told my parents I wanted to be a teacher. Their first response, the one they spoke quickly and from their heart was to say, "You mean a professor."

I could have objected, but that's never been my role. My spot as the oldest in a line of overachievers was to say yes, then reach for the stars I didn't want. With Nick's injury I was trying not to cause any waves. So instead of becoming an elementary teacher like I wanted, I got my doctorate and went into higher education.

My father took me aside about a month after that initial conversation, Nick was doing rehab with the therapist and I had been his cheerleader, making him laugh and power through the hard stuff.

"Son, I want to tell you I am proud of your decision to become a professor like your mother and me. You will never regret getting your doctorate. It's not something everyone can do. I was thinking of a poem by Walt Whitman that I want to share with you," he said, then went on to quote the poem,

"There are those who teach only the sweet lessons of peace and safety;
   But I teach lessons of war and death to those I love,
   That they readily meet invasions, when they come."

I remember that I looked over at Nick who still had a nasty-looking black eye and stitches across his scalp and wondered if my father had lost his mind.

Now as I watch the waves gently rocking onto California's rocky coast I let that poem wash over me again. I think my father wished he had prepared us better for the bad times, I don't think he was quoting Whitman to inspire me to be a good professor, and yet that had not occurred to me until this moment.

Memories of Nick rush in to fill my heart, not the Nick that lies connected to tubes and IVs now, or the version of him high as a kite dancing naked on our front lawn. Blessedly I am given ten-year-old Nick racing me down the street on our bikes, hitting the corner at top speed just before the slight climb in the road that led to our driveway. If we slowed at all to make that corner safely, we couldn't get up the hill, but more times than he knew, I slowed to let him win.

Did he know? Did he see the little things I did for him before his accident? Did he understand how his choices after the accident hurt me? How they hurt the whole damn family?

I pick up a stone from the ground and toss it over the cliff, wishing it contained my worries. I turn to go back home, my mind a little calmer now. I glance at my wrist out of habit, but my watch is on the bathroom counter so I can only guess the time. It must be about three in the morning. I meander down the street and decide to go past Molly's so I can see her house dark and tucked in for the night, but when I turn the corner the lights are blazing.

I stop on the street in front of her home and smile at the sight I see. My sweet Molly is dancing in her living room wearing nothing but a T-shirt and underwear. I look both ways up and down the street to make sure I am the only creep watching her, then I shove my hands in my pockets and enjoy the view.

She is jumping and spinning with her arms open wide and I wish I was closer so I could see her face and hear the music. My heart beats faster when I realize I'm thinking of her as mine, yet I know that isn't entirely true. But as I stand here, in late June, there is nothing I want more than for that to be true. Will that fade by the end of August? I bet it won't, and that will make September first all the more painful.

I laugh as I watch Molly do a perfect rendition of the routine in *Flashdance* complete with the chair, no water of course, but when I replay this later in my mind I will add that epic splash. I adjust myself a little because watching her free and wild is a real fucking turn-on. That's what she looks like to me as she dances in her living room alone, free.

Maybe that's what she needs more than a summer fling. Maybe she needs to be free.

Molly

HOW IS it possible to feel both invigorated and exhausted at the same time? When my alarm goes off at seven that is exactly how I feel. I roll out of my bed and stumble to the bathroom in my T-shirt and underwear.

I brush my teeth and look at myself in the mirror to assess the damage after getting only about three hours of sleep. Dark circles are under my eyes, and I swear I've developed a few new wrinkles. If I did, they are born from laughter, deep belly shaking laughter, so I will wear them with pride.

It's funny, I didn't allow myself to miss Lisa all these years. I pushed pause on the cassette tape of our relationship because part of me knew deep down that I would see her again. Even when the letter I wrote to her on my eighteenth birthday was returned with "no longer at this address" scrawled across the envelope. I still knew. She said she knew too, and that made my heart swell.

Last night we met at a restaurant in Fort Bragg and talked and ate for so many hours, they had to ask us to leave. Then we sat in my car and talked until two in the morning.

She hasn't changed a bit, and yet she has changed so much. She said the same thing about me. The only time we cried was when she heard about what actually happened to me when I disappeared. Those tears didn't last long though, as we rapid-fire compared pregnancies and deliveries. She has two daughters. Krystal is her youngest. Her other daughter Tammy is twelve going on seventeen. All the attitude and none of the pimples to keep her in check. Apparently she is quite boy crazy and has sworn her true love to almost half the boys in her class. I died laughing at her description of flirty embarrassing things her daughter does on a regular basis.

She showed me a picture of her and I immediately told her to put her on birth control as soon as she gets her period. She is model pretty, tall and lean with big, round eyes and full, beautiful lips. Lisa laughed and said because of what happened to me on my sixteenth birthday, she had already planned on it.

Lisa's husband Paul is a general contractor and is in the area working on a few homes over in the expensive neighborhood right on the ocean. He does quite well for himself, so Lisa has been able to stay home with the girls. She's a regular PTA mom, bake sales, Girl Scouts and all. Exactly like she said she wanted to be. She met Paul in college at Cal State Sacramento. Her family moved north from San Diego right after she graduated high school.

We made plans to see each other often from here on out, and I promised to introduce her to my son when he gets to town. That one was a little harder to promise, but my therapist said I have a right to let him know who I was before him.

I drink my coffee and eat a piece of toast before walking down to the clinic. It's going to be a long day, but the conversation and laughter from last night will keep me going. Seeing her again was like finding the last piece of the puzzle and snapping it in place.

It's another busy day at the clinic. After getting patients ready for the doctor all morning I duck into the break room to eat the sad little peanut butter and jelly sandwich I brought for lunch. I'm two bites in when the phone on the wall rings with a call from Henny. She's pretty cool about making sure I get a lunch, so I know it must be important.

"Hi, Henny, what's going on?" I ask with the roof of my mouth coated with too much peanut butter. It will be a miracle if she understood what I said.

"You have something at the front desk," she says, then giggles. I cock my head and squint wondering if that is what I heard. I have never actually heard Henny giggle.

"Um, okay. I'll be right up." I hang up the phone and take a big drink of my orange soda before walking out front, praying that it dislodges the peanut butter. I freeze when I see the sales clerk from the lingerie store standing in the lobby.

It's happening. My worst nightmare is coming true.

At my work.

In front of my boss.

Do I run? Quit my job, sprint down the road and hurl myself into the ocean? That seems like the best plan. I could make it epic like that new blockbuster, *Thelma & Louise*. Me clutching my vibrator high above my head as I plunge across the barrier into a forever satisfied state of being.

"Hello, I don't know if you remember me, but I brought you something," the woman says when she sees me standing in the hallway contemplating my own demise.

I squeak out, "You did? Why?"

Henny laughs uncontrollably and scoots her chair closer because apparently she couldn't get the full effect of my shame from behind the counter.

"Well, the um—" she pauses and looks around nervously before continuing, "*item* I sold you was recently recalled and the information we received from the manufacturer was"—she pauses again and sighs—"quite alarming. I wanted to see if you were okay."

Henny snorts, then covers her laugh with her hand. I narrow my eyes at her, wishing she wasn't my boss so I could kick her. Or ask her to leave. Or both.

"I'm fine," I say in a clipped tone that I hope conveys *get the hell out of here, lady*. It does not.

The woman visibly relaxes and lets out a breath that sounds a lot like a pressure relief valve. "That's great, really good. So maybe you didn't use it yet? Don't. Don't use it. Ever. Seriously, I think they are making it against the law. That's not true, I—" she stops and wrings her hands together. "I just really don't want you to get hurt," she says, then adds, "I brought you something to replace it."

I don't want to make her suffer any longer so I talk over her saying, "I didn't use it. I'll throw it away if it's not safe. Thanks for coming by." I turn to go but she is pointing to a bag that is on the check-in counter and my brain registers what she said.

Henny stands up and holds her arms out like an old-lady version of Vanna White. Hands splayed and wiggling like she is showing off the car I could win if I can guess the seven-letter word for embarrassing.

"Oh, okay, sure. Thanks. You didn't need to do that," I say, looking over my shoulder to make sure Dr. Potter hasn't waddled out from a room.

"No, actually my lawyer said I did. So there you go. We are even." She wipes her hand across her forehead and makes a dramatic "phew!" sound. "Anyway, I have to get back to my shop. You'll find a gift card in there too so please come by anytime and I will help you find something perfect for that special evening." With that comment, she scurries out the door like someone who dropped a broken vibrator bomb on an unsuspecting medical assistant. My brain tries to think of a comparison, but it comes up short. There is nothing like this.

This is the worst.

I steal a glance over at Henny who is wiping her eyes and fanning her face. Well at least I made her happy. I grab the bag and stomp back to the break room to finish my sandwich.

The rest of the day is uneventful and as I walk past The Floppy Fish, I decide to pop in for a glass of wine before I go home. I told Lisa about Tom, leaving out the more embarrassing parts of his reason for coming into the clinic. That's not really my story to tell after all, and patients have a right to privacy.

My eyes take a moment to adjust to the dark when I push through the door of the bar, but when I can see, Tom's handsome face smiles out at me.

"Molly! What a nice surprise!" He throws a dish towel over his shoulder and comes out from behind the bar to greet me. He smells so good I want to melt into him as he leans in to kiss my cheek.

"Hi, I just got off work so I thought I'd bring you the book and have a glass of wine." I reach into my bag and pull out *Kent Price, Mission at Risk.* He reaches for it and laughs when he sees my bookmark.

"Clever, Molly. Very clever. You might not get this back," Tom says, holding up the red lace thong tucked into the book at chapter three.

"You have to at least use it until we are done with the book. Do it for Kent." I pat him on the shoulder as I make my way to the bar. I try and play it cool, like I give men my underwear often. I hear his deep laugh behind me and feel my face get hot. I have never known flirting like this.

I love that his whole face lit up when he saw me. I love that he came out from behind the bar to greet me, like he couldn't wait for me to reach him. I love everything about this and yet my brain keeps trying to remind me that it's temporary. He's leaving at the end of August and won't be back until next June. Could I do a long-distance thing with him? Would he even want that?

"Trying to solve world hunger?" Tom asks as he pulls a wineglass off the shelf. He reaches for my favorite merlot and uncorks the bottle, his forearm flexing in the most delightful way as he twists the cork free.

"Sort of. Trying to figure out how I will survive September." The words tumble out of my mouth before I have a chance to think and I cringe at how forward I sounded.

"I have been wondering that myself." Tom slides the very full wineglass to me and rests his arms on the bar. His gaze searches my face and it feels like he's touching me. "I don't suppose you'd be interested in moving to Connecticut?" he says, but he's smiling and his eyes are dancing with laughter, so I don't think he's serious.

"Well, let's see how things go. My son will be there for at least four years, so you never know." I wink at him hoping it looks fun and flirty, but inside I feel like throwing up. As much as I like Tom, something about moving across the country for a man feels wrong.

He smiles and winks at me before heading to the other side of the bar to help a customer. I wipe my hands on my scrubs because my palms think I'm running a marathon.

We chat off and on as I finish my wine and as I am about to excuse myself to go, Tom answers the phone before I can say my goodbyes. I wait so I can tell him I'd like to see him on Sunday, but his expression falls like a balloon losing its air. He covers his eyes with one hand and nods before saying something into the phone and turning his back to me. I see his shoulder rise and fall quickly and if I hadn't seen his face I would think he was laughing. Misty comes in from the patio and sees Tom and freezes in her tracks, like she's unsure what to do. We both watch as Tom hangs up the phone then stands stone-still.

"Tom? Are you okay?" I ask as I slide off my stool. I reach him about the same time as Misty and we each place a hand on his arm. He looks at her first, then me with blank, unseeing eyes. His skin is ashen grey, and sweat is forming on his upper lip. He takes his left hand and rubs across his chest before he speaks.

"I just found out that my little brother has passed away. I'm sorry. I'm going to close the bar for the night. I can't—" He stops and rubs his chest again.

"Tom, are you having chest pains?" I ask turning him toward me. I slide my fingers down to his pulse and am alarmed at the thready rapid beat I can feel.

"Well, yeah but isn't that what happens when you find out your brother died? It hurts. Here." Tom points to the center of his chest then takes a ragged breath.

"Help me get him to Dr. Potter's," I tell Misty as Patty walks up.

"What's going on? Tom, you look like shit." Patty sets her tray on the bar and joins us in staring at the very quickly deteriorating man I have come to care deeply for.

"He got some bad news, but I'm worried about his color and he's complaining of chest pain. Misty and I are going to take him to Dr. Potter's, can you hold down the fort?" I ask quickly shifting into Nurse Molly mode. I swipe my bag off the bar, never taking my hand off Tom.

"Of course, should I call someone?" she asks.

"No, let me get him to the clinic and I'll call the doctor if there's any problems," I say as Misty and I lead him around the bar and to the door. We don't look back amid the calls of concern and well wishes. I fish my keys out of my bag quickly when we reach the door to the clinic.

I turn on the lights and instruct Misty to take him to room one, then rush down the hall to grab my stethoscope and the EKG machine. When I get back to the room Tom is sitting on the edge of the exam table and under these fluorescent lights, he looks even worse.

"I need you to take off your shirt and lie back, Tom. I'm going to get an EKG and your blood pressure." I hold up my hand to stop whatever nonsense was about to come out of his mouth. Misty helps get his shirt off and I move quickly to his left side to get his blood pressure. The first reading is very high, but we did walk over in a rush and I'm sure I am making him nervous, but I see him shifting around like he can't get comfortable.

"Where is your pain?" I ask as calmly as I can.

"It has kind of moved to my back now, and a little bit in my left arm. My neck hurts too," he says.

"Misty, go to the front desk and you'll see by the phone a list of numbers. Call the first one on that list and if Doc doesn't answer go down the list until you reach him. When he answers tell him I have Tom here." I pause, then tell her, "Say the splinter patient, and he is having chest pain. Tell him I am doing an EKG and will draw some blood, but I want him here ASAP. If he can't get here we will call the ambulance."

Misty turns and runs to the front without another question or comment, and for that I am grateful.

"You think I'm having a heart attack?" Tom asks but I am busy getting the leads placed on his shoulders, chest, and legs. I grab the wires and start clamping them in place before I answer.

"I don't know, Tom. I want to be careful. Your blood pressure was elevated and I want to see what's going on, okay?" I keep my voice calm and level and Misty comes running back in breathing like she just ran ten miles.

"He's on his way. He was home."

Thank fuck. He doesn't live far and I know he will get here within five minutes, less if Henny is driving. That woman must have been a sprint car driver in a past life.

I pause and lower my face close to Tom's. "I want you to lie as still as you can so I can get this done before Dr. Potter comes. He will want to see this. Okay?"

He nods then lies still. I enter his name and hit start on the machine then wait as the paper starts to emerge with the details of what his heart is doing. Tachycardia, I knew that, but the rest of the read is clean, so the machine at least doesn't think he's having a heart attack. I blow out a breath in relief and Tom lifts his head.

"Is that a 'get the paddles' kind of sigh or a 'hey, he's going to be fine' sigh?" Tom asks as Dr. Potter rushes in.

Good Lord. What is he wearing?

"What have we got here, Molly?" he asks, reaching for the results from the EKG.

"Tom got some bad news and became diaphoretic and pale, and he complained of chest pain radiating to his back, arm and neck. His initial blood pressure was 180/110 but I haven't taken it again. I wanted to get an EKG." I rattle off the information and reach for the blood pressure cuff, but Dr. Potter puts his hand on my arm to stop me.

"Molly, he's not having a heart attack. It's okay. Let's take a deep breath and let everyone calm down." He turns to Tom and says, "Tom, your blood pressure is very high. Is that normal for you?"

Tom shrugs and I get a flash of that first day he came in. He left before I could check his vitals.

"When was the last time you had it checked? I'd like to know if this is a situational thing, bad news and all, or if you have been running around with a stroke on deck." Dr. Potter pulls his black rolling stool over and lowers his bare legs gingerly onto it. His robe, or whatever the hell that thing is, slips open and I see a very taut, firm belly that thankfully covers the short shorts he is wearing.

"Excuse me, I grabbed Henny's robe. We were in the hot tub when I got the call." Dr. Potter tugs at the edges of a pink little number that is lined with feathers. If I wasn't so worried about Tom, I would be on the floor laughing.

Tom gives a weak smile before answering. "To be honest, I haven't had my blood pressure checked in ages. I had a physical a few years ago and I don't remember the doctor mentioning anything about hyper-tension."

"Okay, well, I want to give you something to lower it for tonight then I want you back here fasting, tomorrow morning." Dr. Potter turns to me and asks, "Did you draw any blood yet, Molly?"

"No, I wanted to get the EKG first," I answer, no longer sure if I did the right thing by rushing Tom here.

"Okay, grab me a lab slip and when Tom comes in tomorrow morning we are going to do a full work-up." Dr. Potter stands and makes his way to Tom. "I want you to rest, not go back to The Floppy Fish and sling drinks, understand?"

Tom nods and I grab a lab slip from the counter and hand it to the doctor. Unfortunately for all of us, he walks to the counter to fill out the form and I see what looks like two hairy watermelons framed by shiny blue shorts and pink feathers. Dr. Potter must feel the chill on his ass cheeks because he straightens up and looks back at us. After tugging the robe down with not much success he says, "I'll take this to my office and grab that medicine. Stay put, Tom."

I walk to Tom and place my hand on his knee. He immediately covers my hand with his and takes a ragged breath. I search his eyes, hoping they hold the words he needs me to say. All I see is pain, so I step in and wrap him in my arms. He rests his head on my shoulder and we stay like that until I hear Dr. Potter coming down the hall. His flip-flops smacking on the linoleum make for quite an early warning system.

I step back and Tom straightens up but his face still holds onto his pain. I want to smooth the furrow in his brow, put the light back in his eyes, but I know I can't.

"Tom, I want you to take this, it's a blood pressure medicine, then like I said come back in the morning before you have anything to eat or drink. Molly will get some bloodwork, and based on that and how you respond to this medication, I will get you a prescription. Go home tonight. Rest." Dr. Potter places his hand on Tom's shoulder and looks into his eyes. "I mean it."

"I understand, Doc. Thanks." Tom takes the pill from the doctor and pops it in his mouth, swallowing before I can even get him a little cup of water.

"Molly, recheck his blood pressure, then get him home. No sex tonight, let the man rest," Dr. Potter says. He turns and leaves the room in a flurry of pink feathers and slapping sandals.

Tom

IF IT WAS any other day, I would be on the floor laughing.

Instead I hold out my arm and wait while Molly rechecks my blood pressure. I try not to think about my family, the pain and anguish on my mother's face. The relief my sisters must feel and the great divide between those two things. Instead I think about Dr. Potter's very tight and very large hairy belly. I may never stop picturing that.

"It's a little better," Molly says quietly as she pulls the cuff from my arm.

"Okay. Thank you. I guess I better get home." I stand up off the table and Molly grabs my arm to stop me. She wraps herself around me and I have to fight not to collapse into her. Instead I give her a firm hug, hoping it conveys that I will be okay. Logically I know I will. My heart isn't so sure.

Misty, who I didn't even realize was in the room, steps closer and places her hand on my arm. "Tom, I am going to go back to the bar, you don't have to close for the night. We can run it without you. Just get some rest."

I nod and give her my best smile.

"Come on, Tom. You are coming back to my place tonight. I want to keep an eye on you, and I don't think you should be alone." Molly is grabbing her bag from the counter. She takes her stethoscope off and sets it next to the lab order. Based on the number of little boxes I see checked, I will be donating all my blood tomorrow.

"That's a lot of tests," I say, pointing to the slip.

"It's standard, come on, Tom. Let's get you to bed."

"No sex," I say with a wink and Molly blushes.

"That is only the second most embarrassing thing to happen today." She laughs and I want to ask more questions, but I am ushered out of the clinic by a very no-nonsense Nurse Molly. We make it to her house and once inside I feel the weight of that phone call start to hit again.

As if Molly could sense that, she takes my hand and leads me back to her bedroom. She pushes on my shoulders gently, so I sit on her bed and watch as she gets on her knees to take off my shoes and socks. The sight of her down there makes me think of what I'd like to do with her tonight.

"No sex, Tom." Even with the teasing tone, her sweet voice wraps around me like a caress.

"Then you need to get up, because seeing you on your knees between my legs like that is *not* good for my blood pressure."

She smirks and stands, holding out her hands to help me up. She starts unbuttoning my shirt then grabs at my 501's to undo the buttons. I place my hand over hers and shake my head.

"I am not going to be able to follow doctor's orders if you unbutton these. Let me do it." My voice comes out gruffer than I intended but my quickly hardening cock is doing all the thinking.

"Let me get you something to put your contacts in for the night. I'll be right back."

Molly ducks into the bathroom that is attached to her room and comes back empty-handed a few minutes later.

"I put it on the sink with a toothbrush and some toothpaste."

"Thanks."

After I get my contacts out and brush my teeth, I go back in to find Molly in bed with the covers pulled back welcoming me in. God, what a lovely sight she is. I think, out of self-preservation, I pushed pause on my grief. I can feel it slipping back in now, threatening to take me under. I cross the room quickly and climb into bed next to the most beautiful woman I have ever known in real life.

"Do you think you'll be able to sleep? I'm here if you want to talk, but if silence is what you need, I can do that too," Molly says as she strokes my arm gently. I tuck my arm under my head when I roll to my side and she quickly mirrors my position.

"I don't mind talking. I want to thank you for taking care of me tonight." I smile at her but she looks worried and she reaches up to cup my face in her hand.

"You are such a sweet man, I don't like seeing you hurting."

I let out a sigh and close my eyes for a moment before I continue. "I am going to assume since I no longer have a high-pitched ringing in my head, that my blood pressure has come down. I am grateful you made me go in. Hearing about Nick was just—" I trail off not sure how to describe what I am feeling. It's not entirely grief. That is, of course, the first layer, but under that it's the guilt for being glad that Nick's tortured life has ended. Then under that is the pain for my mother and father, who never got over the hope that Nick would rally and lead a better life. In fact, last Christmas my mom had decided that if Nick could find a good woman to love him, his life would turn around. None of us had the heart to tell her that wasn't going to happen. An unemployed drug addict wasn't really going to draw in the high-quality women my mother was picturing for her son. That is probably what hurts the most right now. His pain and suffering are over, but for my mother it's just beginning. She will have to face it now, that he never fully recovered from his head injury and turned to drugs to ease the pain.

I realize that I've gone quiet for a long time, lost in my thoughts, but Molly hasn't moved, she's waiting patiently for me to continue.

"My sisters and I knew this day was coming, and as cold as it sounds, I feel a sense of relief that he is at peace now. My parents, on the other hand, are going to mourn and grieve like the last twenty years haven't happened. In their eyes, Nick was just going through a phase, about to get clean, about to land a good job. It was like a never-ending well of hope was at their feet. For me and the girls, that hope dried up a long time ago." I close my eyes again, surprised at the depth of the fatigue I feel.

Molly's sweet voice softly breaks through the haze I'm feeling. "I think as a parent, you always have hope for your children. You have a love for them that is boundless and instant. At least that is how it should be. Some parents don't get that memo, but the good ones do. It sounds like your mom and dad are good parents. All that hope they felt, I'm sure was tempered with reality, but Nick must've felt their love. In the end, that's all that matters."

I nod, unable to open my eyes, and I drift into a deep and peaceful sleep. I dream of Nick and I racing on our bikes over endless green hills, and I wake up with the sound of his laughter wrapping itself around my heart creating a protective layer I know I will need.

A gentle hand is on my shoulder and I open my eyes to see Molly's smiling face. "Good morning, Tom. I let you sleep because I don't know how you feel about missing breakfast. I have to be at work soon—do you want to walk down together?"

I rub my hand over my face and manage a smile. "Thanks Molly. Yeah, let me get dressed and I'll be out in a few minutes."

We walk in silence to the clinic and I debate telling her the ringing in my head is back, but I decide against it. I kind of want to see if what I have grown so used to as background noise over the past few years is a warning my blood pressure is too high.

Molly unlocks the clinic and leads me back to the same room we were in last night. She takes my blood pressure in both arms then instructs me to lie down. I watch as she walks to the door and turns off the lights. When she comes back to the table she places her hand on my shoulder and quietly says, "It's still pretty high. I am going to have you lie here and I'll get your blood before Dr. Potter gets here. Do you have any issues with getting your blood drawn?"

"I don't particularly like it, but if you are wondering if I'll faint, then no. I'm okay." I give her a weak smile and she gets to work taking every drop of blood from my body.

I watch as she writes my name on the millions of tubes. I hope the doctor gets the information he needs from all that, but most importantly I hope my body can make more.

We both hear the doctor and his wife laughing just outside the door, then what must have been a kiss and a swat to an ass before the door swings open. Molly scurries out with a nod to Dr. Potter. Thankfully she took the blood vials with her, since I didn't want to admit they were making me woozy.

Dr. Potter picks up my chart and glances at the numbers Molly wrote down then he sits on the black rolling stool and scoots himself closer to me. "How are you feeling, Tom?"

"Not great. I have like a ringing in my head, not my ears. Do you know what I mean?" I ask.

"Yes. Your blood pressure is really high. How long have you had that ringing sensation?"

"A few years off and on. It happens more when I am back in Connecticut teaching." I rub my forehead remembering how bad it was last year when I returned.

"What do you teach? Please don't say anything in health care because I would be very disappointed." He narrows his eyes at me and I laugh.

"No, I am a professor of archeology at Willmore University," I explain.

"Ah, that's a fine school. They have one of the top cardiac research teams in the nation. Do you know Dr. Gentry?"

"No, I have met a few of the professors from the medical school at fundraising events, but that name doesn't sound familiar."

"Well, I am going to put in a call to him and while you're back at work, he will follow you. He's the best. Don't waste your time with anyone else." He stands and takes the stethoscope off his neck, putting the earpieces in, then tapping the flat bell. He listens to my heart in several places then moves up to my neck, listening to both sides. That isn't something I've ever had done, and the scientist in me is curious. But before I can ask anything he moves to my back and listens some more before asking me to take a deep breath and hold it several times.

"Okay, ideally I would like you to have a full cardiac workup, but the hospitals around here aren't the greatest. When will you be back in Connecticut?" He flips his stethoscope over his neck and leans against the counter.

"I have to go back tomorrow or the next day for my brother's funeral. That was the bad news I got last night. He lost his battle with addiction and he passed away. I need to go help and be with my family." I instantly see the concern cross his face and I am starting to understand why Molly likes him so much.

"Okay, I see. I am sorry to hear that. I lost a cousin to addiction; it's a devastating disease that can ruin whole families. Was it just you and your brother?"

I shake my head. "No, I have three sisters."

"I'm glad you're going home to be with them. I'll put a call in to Dr. Gentry, and if you can find the time to see him while you are there that would be a good thing. In the meantime I am going to give you a prescription for some blood pressure medication. Molly will call that in for you, then I'll let you know when the blood tests come back. Molly will make sure to send Dr. Gentry the results as well."

We continue to talk for another twenty minutes at least, and I start to worry that other patients are being neglected. I am about to say something to that effect when we hear a light tapping on the door.

"Come in," Dr. Potter says.

"Sorry to interrupt, I have a guy in Room 10 that needs stitches. He cut his finger trying to pry open a shell. I have it all prepped," Molly says, and I notice how different her tone is. It's authoritative and kind of sexy.

"Right, well I guess I better get back to work, Tom, it was great talking to you. I'll make those arrangements like we discussed. Leave your Connecticut number with Molly so I can get ahold of you there. Safe travels." And with that he is off.

Molly gives me a small smile before saying, "I have to get in there to help him, can I see you after work?"

"Sure, I have to make arrangements to fly back to Connecticut, and find someone who can manage the bar for a week or two. I'll be at The Floppy Fish, please stop by." I want to pull her into my arms, but this is her place of employment and I think she feels uncomfortable with Dr. Potter knowing we're dating.

"Okay, I'll see you then." She turns and rushes off before I can say another word.

The rest of the day is spent on the phone with airlines and my sisters. Mom is down with a migraine, but Dad seems to be holding up okay. They're all happy to hear I'm coming back, even if it's only for a week.

I called Lyle and told him what was happening, and he suggested I ask Jasper to help out with the bar. Apparently, he uses him a few times a month when he and Jill want to have a date night.

With all my plans set and a few hours until I have to open the bar, I lie back on my bed and start reading *Kent Price, Mission at Risk* while clutching the red lace panties Molly used as a bookmark. It's nice to let my mind be somewhere else for a while, and pretending I am Kent chasing Fernando across the European countryside is the escape I need.

Molly

IT FEELS WEIRD WITHOUT TOM. He's only been gone a week, and I remind myself that come September, I won't see him at all. My heart aches at the thought.

How did I let this happen? I haven't gotten through my whole list, something that I thought would be done by the time I let myself get involved with someone. Like completing that would signify to the universe that I was ready for a healthy relationship. Something Allen Saunders said, in an old *Reader's Digest* my mom had, keeps running through my head: "Life is what happens when you're busy making other plans."

On Monday I sent the letter to Grant detailing my address and saying I'm filing for divorce from his dad. My attorney will also be sending one to make sure the Densworths understand they are not to contact me in any way. Both letters should arrive in San Diego on the same day.

I let out a sigh, feeling caught between relief that it's finally here and dread that Isaac will try to come see me. I love the life I have made for myself here. I don't want him to ruin that with his cold, angry scowl.

I unfold my list and stare at it, wondering if I will ever be brave enough to find my mother, Martha. I don't know what I would say to her if I did find her, but part of me wants to at least know where she is. When I stopped along Hwy 1 two days after I left San Diego, I thought I saw her in a parking lot. The woman, who looked a lot like my mom, was arguing with a man who was quite a bit older than her. I was too far away to hear what they were saying or know for sure it was her. Before I could get up the nerve to walk closer, she climbed into a beat-up Chevy van and sped off.

King City is a pretty small town and Sparrow isn't that common of a last name. I pick up my phone and dial 411 before I can give it too much thought.

"Hi, I am wondering if you can see if you have a number for a Martha Sparrow in King City, California?" I am surprised how calm I sound.

"Yes, one moment please." I hear the clicking of a keyboard then she comes back on and says, "I have two in that area, would you like those?"

My mouth goes dry instantly and I croak out, "Yes, please."

I jot down both numbers, then thank her before hanging up. Jesus, I didn't think it would actually work. Now what? Do I call?

My fingers are dialing before I know it, and the line rings twice before a recording picks up. "We're sorry, the number you have reached is no longer in service or is out of order. Please try your call again."

Okay, so it's the other one. I dial that and wait through three rings before I hear, "You have reached Martha Sparrow. I can't come to the phone right now, so leave me a message and I'll call you back. If you actually want a call back, then speak slowly so I can write the damn number down for fuc—" the machine cuts off and I hang up quickly.

I blink a few times trying to clear my head. I wasn't sure it was her at first, but the cussing at the end clinched it. It's her.

My mom.

I have my mom's number.

Holy shit. She's been in King City this whole time?

My hands are shaking as I cross number three off my list.

~~#3 Find Martha~~

That was all I agreed to in therapy, find out where she is. I don't have to call her again, or talk to her. I blow out a breath and set the phone down. My mind racing to that time in my life where I felt like I was abandoned. I guess it wasn't just a feeling, after all. She did leave me, but I don't know why. Was she that disappointed in me?

I need to make something to eat, since I feel all shaky and I have the start of a headache coming on.

I start pulling out ingredients to make pasta when the phone rings. I freeze. Shit, what if it's her? What if she did that thing where you can call back the last number that called you? What do I say? I can't let it go to voicemail—she'll know it's me when she hears my message. Damn it. I dive for the phone and answer before my machine can pick up.

I grumble out a hello hoping my voice sounds different enough that if it was her, I could throw her off.

"Molly? Are you okay?" Tom says with a laugh.

I clear my throat and place my hand over my heart to calm myself down before I answer. "Hi Tom! Sorry, yeah, I must have had something caught in my throat. How are you doing?"

"I'm okay, I was calling to tell you I'll be here another week."

"Oh, sure. Okay. I understand." My heart doesn't understand, it feels all pinchy and tight.

"You can tell Dr. Potter that I was able to get in to see his friend. I am staying a little longer because he wants to run some tests, and to be honest, my mom and dad are not doing very well with all this."

"I can imagine. I'm glad you are staying then. Can I ask what test the doctor wants to do?" I saw Tom's bloodwork when it came back so I have an idea, but I'd like to hear more about what the doctor there is thinking.

"He's going to do an echocardiogram and a stress test. He also wants a sonogram of my carotids. Apparently I have astronomically high triglycerides and cholesterol." Tom chuckles then says, "I thought that all the red wine I drink would help keeps my pipes clear. Isn't that why Italians live so long?"

"I think it has more to do with the things the eat than the wine they drink, but that's a nice theory." I smile, picturing Tom leaning back in a chair with his ankle crossed over his knee, glass of red wine in hand.

"I also called to check on you. Grant must have your letter by now. Have you heard from him?" Tom asks. I am surprised he remembered with all he has going on.

"No, but he might have written me. I am going to check the mail in Fort Bragg tomorrow." I pause, debating whether to tell Tom about finding my mom, but I decide against it. It's still too new and scary to share.

"If you get a letter from him, call me here at my parents' house. I am staying here, okay? I want to know what he says. You haven't heard anything from your ex or his family, have you?" I can hear the concern in his voice and it only makes me miss him more.

"No, not yet. The attorney said the papers were served yesterday though, so it's too early to know if I'm in the clear. I wish I could say that Isaac will be happy he is free from me, but as bad as our relationship was, he felt like I was his. Does that make sense?"

"Yeah, when we had our first date I couldn't understand how anyone had let you go. Maybe he isn't ready for whatever you did have to be over."

I laugh at that. He's probably right as much, as I don't want him to be. Isaac hoarded things and I was one of his things, nothing more.

"How is your mom doing? How was the service? I wanted to call but I didn't want to intrude." I really want to change the subject but more importantly I want to hear his voice. I want him to talk so I can press my ear into the phone and picture him beside me.

Tom sighs before saying, "As we expected, she's just now figuring out that her son was indeed a drug addict. My sisters are doing most of the heavy lifting, especially since they found out I have high blood pressure. I am allowed to comfort but not get too stressed, whatever that means." His low, deep rumble of a laugh fills my ears and shoots straight to my heart. "The service was nice, quite a few of his old friends came. I think that was good for Mom and Dad, you know, to see that people still cared."

"How is your dad holding up?" I ask, my voice low. I don't want to break this bubble of warmth I feel at hearing his voice wash over me.

"Dad is Dad. He has mowed the lawn three times since I've been here and talked to all of us about getting life insurance policies. I did find out that he developed hypertension in his late thirties, so I have him to thank for new fun health adventure. I hope that the tests all come back normal and all I need is this pill every day."

"Me too, are you feeling better?" I ask.

"Yeah actually. I feel a lot better, that ringing feeling is totally gone and I am sleeping much better, well—" he stops and I wait for him to finish.

"I sleep best when you are beside me. I know that has only happened a few times, but hell, I miss you, Molly."

I love his honesty, his confidence to tell me how he feels. My stomach flips before I can answer, "I miss you too. When you say things like that it makes me feel all warm and fuzzy, Tom. No one has ever made me feel warm and fuzzy."

My admission makes me uncomfortable, but Tom doesn't leave me hanging in the wind. "You make me feel all kinds of things, Molly Sparrow. When I get back, I want to show you exactly what you do to me."

My stomach feels like I am on a roller coaster, and I feel my face flush. Is this what I missed out on all these years? "That sounds like something I can look forward to. Did I tell you that the lady from the lingerie store stopped by the clinic?"

"No! Why? Did she tell you that vibrator was being recalled for being defective?" Tom laughs and I can almost see his handsome face as he does. I wish I had a picture of him that I could stare at while we talk on the phone. I need to make sure to get a few pictures of him before he leaves in the fall.

"Yes! You are exactly right actually. Henny just about wet herself, she was laughing so hard. I guess the company declared that particular model dangerous."

"Molly, you have no idea how happy I am to hear that. I really wondered if I would be able to match your desires if that was your kink."

"No! Tom, oh my God." I cover my face with my hand and laugh. "I can't imagine a woman who would enjoy that kind of violence." I pause and consider my options, but my desire to keep him on the phone for longer makes me brave, so I continue. "She gave me a replacement. A different kind, of course."

I hear him take in a quick breath and a chair scoots across what sounds like wood floors. I wait for his response and hear nothing until I hear a click of a door. "What did she give you, Molly?" he asks in a lower voice than before.

I giggle and ask, "Did you duck into a private room or something Tom?"

"Busted. The phone in the kitchen is a dangerous place to be in this house, so I pulled the receiver with me into the hall bathroom. I'm not going to lie, I feel like I'm in high school again."

"Are your parents home?" I ask, feeling time transport me as well. Before Isaac, I talked to a few boys on the phone, attempting to flirt and failing miserably.

"Yeah, but it's late here, I'm sure they are asleep. My worst night-mare is having my parents catch me with my hands down my pants though, so I'll hide in here. Now stop stalling and tell me all about your new toy."

I laugh and pull the bag off the coffee table. "Well, to be honest I haven't looked at it, so if you can keep it in your pants a little longer, I will check it out!" I am laughing as I reach into the bag and pull out the box. This one is even less descriptive than the one I purchased. "So far it's not very exciting, Tom, it's a plain brown box."

"The suspense is killing me." He laughs as he says that and I try again to picture him.

"So are you sitting on the toilet?" I ask as I slide my fingernail over the tape that is protecting the flap from a hurricane. Jesus, I am going to need scissors.

"Nah, this bathroom is kind of strange, but with five kids it was the selling feature for my parents. I am sitting on a bench that faces a wall of mirrors. There are two sinks, so we could almost all get ready in here with some elbows and shin kicks to be in front of the faucet. All three of my sisters and probably every friend they had did their makeup in here. I am told the lighting is very flattering."

My fingernail finally slides through the thick tape and I pull back the flap. "Sounds like a magical place, Tom. Every girl likes good light-ing." I pause then say, "Okay, I got the damn box open finally. Are you ready?"

"So ready," Tom says, another chuckle falling from his lips.

I put my hand in and pull out a small thing a little bigger than a lipstick. "Huh." I stare at it, totally confused.

"Well? Is it a thruster or a flicker?" Tom asks.

"I'm not sure. It, well, okay there is a button and—" I bite my lip out of frustration because this thing is not big enough to be pleasurable. I don't understand these things at all. I hit the button and it turns on, vibrating rapidly.

"Jesus, I can hear it from here!" Tom says, then after laughing for a full minute he asks, "How big is that thing? Sounds like a jet engine."

"It's small, like if I put it inside me I may never get it back, kind of small," I say.

"Oh, it's for your clit, Molly. You put it right there and let it do its job, preferably when I can watch."

"I don't know about that, Tom, I am not that brave," I whisper, fumbling with the toy to turn it off.

"Of course, Molly. I didn't mean to make you uncomfortable. I just —" he starts but I cut him off.

"I want to be that kind of woman. I want to be wild and free and sexy. But I don't know how," I admit, and as soon as the words leave my mouth, my shoulders relax. It felt good to admit that.

"Molly." Tom says my name like a breath and I squeeze my eyes shut to fight off whatever he might say next.

"Molly, the first time I laid eyes on you I thought of what Kent Price said in the first book when he met the flight attendant."

"The girl in the bar?" I laugh, because I know exactly what he is going to say. I reread that line many times imagining what I would say to such a smooth pick-up line.

"Yes, I wished I had the confidence to lean over and whisper in your ear, 'You make me wish we were alone so I could get to know every curve and dip of your beautiful body. I would map it with my hands first, then to be sure I knew every inch, I would start over with my tongue.'" He chuckles then says, "I am going to admit something to you, Molly."

"What's that, Tom?" My voice cracks a little as I respond.

"I left the clinic that day because I knew I wasn't going to be able to control myself if I saw you again, and you had seen me at my most vulnerable. My fear of rejection won out."

I let out my breath and smile. "Tom, I saw what you have to offer, up close and personal. If you had asked me out, I would have said yes," I say, my voice still low and hushed, like someone might overhear me.

"Well, that is very good to know. Can I ask you a personal question?" Tom says. I notice he has lowered his voice too and I am back to feeling like a teenager again.

"Yes."

"Have you ever touched yourself in front of someone?" His voice wraps around me like silk and in that moment if he was here, I would do anything he asked.

"No, have you?" I am curious and try to picture him on his knees on my bed gripping his length. It's a beautiful sight in my mind and I bet it's better in person.

"No, but I have always wanted to do that. Is that something you'd consider with me, Molly?"

Without hesitation I say, "Yes. I want to see that. I want that more than anything."

"Can I tell you something?" he asks, his breath faster now.

"I think I know, but I want to hear you say it, Tom."

"I am so fucking hard right now. I need to take care of it. Will you stay on the phone Molly? Will you talk to me?"

"Yes," I say and it comes out like a whoosh of air.

"I want you to touch yourself too, make yourself feel good. You don't have to use the toy."

I don't tell him my hand is already dipping into my underwear but when I touch myself and feel how wet I am, a moan escapes.

"Fuck, Molly, tell me what you're doing."

"I just slid my hand into my underwear, and God, Tom. I am so wet. I feel like I am about to explode and I wish you were here."

"Me too, baby, do me a favor and spread yourself open. Tell me what that feels like."

"I ache. I feel empty, Tom," I say and my hand starts to move, small quick circles.

Tom moans and curses, "Jesus Christ, Molly. I just about shot my load picturing you spread out for me. Do you like to finger fuck yourself?"

"Sometimes," I pant. I slow my hand, not wanting this to end. "Tell me what you're doing?"

"I had to get some lotion so I could imagine I was sliding into you, all hot, wet, and tight. Fuck, I bet you are so tight, Molly. Aren't you? Your pretty little pussy would strangle me, wouldn't it?" I can hear Tom's grunts and pants and I imagine his rock-hard cock in his hand as he works himself.

"Yes, it would, God, Tom, I am not going to last much longer. I can't—"

He cuts me off. "Go ahead and come, baby, I am right there with you, but when you do I want you to picture me pounding into you so deep you forget your own name."

I explode with that image of Tom above me thrusting hard, long, and deep, over and over. My orgasm rips through me and seems to go on forever and when I yell out, "Oh God, Tom!"

I hear his release through grunts and growls. "Jesus, Molly. I've never come so hard in my whole life. Hold on. I have to set the phone down."

I lean back on the couch and close my eyes. My breathing is still labored and I feel aftershocks between my legs so I gently place my hand back over myself. A few more little strokes and I am coming again, softer this time but still delicious in the way it makes me feel. I moan in pleasure right as Tom picks up the phone.

"Jesus, Molly, your little moans are so fucking sexy. Did you come again?"

"Yes," I say. I close my eyes and pull my legs up onto the couch. "I wish you were here, but that was incredible. I have never done anything like that."

"Never had phone sex, Molly?" He laughs.

"No! Have you? Oh my God, Tom, do you call those nine hundred numbers?" I sit up, shocked at that visual.

"I do not! No, that's not something I have ever wanted to do, Molly. In fact, I haven't ever done that with another woman. I have never been so turned on by a woman's voice that I felt I needed to take care of things. It's you. You do that to me." His voice is low again.

"I'm glad to hear that. I like that we have a first together. I didn't think I'd get those at my age."

I hear a door click open and Tom gasp before saying, "Hey Dad, I hope I didn't wake you. I tried to be quiet, you know taking the phone in here." I can hear a muffled voice respond but miss what he says.

"Sure, yeah, I can do that in the morning. Get some sleep, Dad. Yeah, love you too."

"Oh my God! Was that your dad?" I whisper, as if his father can hear me through the phone.

"It was. He came down for some milk. I am so glad I wasn't at the kitchen table with my cock out," Tom whispers back.

I laugh so hard at that image it takes me a moment to respond.

"I should let you go. Please call me after your appointment with Dr. Gentry. I want to know what he says, okay?" I am trying not to worry too much but I am starting to care very deeply for this man, and it's hard not to be concerned.

"I will, and you call me when you hear from your son. I bet Grant is going to love your place." I hear Tom yawn and I do the same quickly after.

"I promise. Good night, Tom."

"Good night, Molly."

Tom

I WAKE up early the next morning and drive down to the gas station to fill up the cans for Dad. He seems to be mowing his way through his grief and needs more gas to accomplish that. I hope that he has a plan to take care of the neighbors' lawns because our grass doesn't grow fast enough for this kind of therapy.

After I have all four cans filled to the top, and returned to the shed, I take myself out to breakfast. There is a small café down the street from the university that is so busy during the school year I can't even get a table. Today it's pretty empty.

When the waitress comes with my coffee I lean back and contemplate the new unidentifiable feeling that has settled in my chest. I really needed that phone call from Molly last night. This past week has been so awful. The funeral was hard of course, but the worst part for me was going by Nick's sad little apartment. The one thing my parents did to stand up for themselves during the throes of my brother's addiction was to make him get his own place. He had stolen several high-value art pieces from them and that was apparently, a line in the sand.

When I climbed the steps to the "apartment" above the garage I had a feeling what was on the other side of that door was going to stay with me. I wish I had been wrong about that but I wasn't. The only piece of furniture in the whole place was a twin mattress that was stained and ripped. I didn't look in the fridge. I couldn't bring myself to check if my brother had food. The sink and counter were littered with grease-stained paper plates and empty beer cans, but the thing that got me was the photo album next to the mattress. I wondered if Mom and Dad knew he had it. It was his, so he had the right, but I know how precious that album was to my mom. On the cover it said, Nicholas F. Hemingway. As I ran my finger over the name I laughed at how many times we told him the F stood for Francis.

I would have looked through it right then if the owner of the garage hadn't come up demanding I pay for the rest of the month. I wrote him a check and tucked the only good memories my brother had under my arm and returned to my parents' house. I didn't tell my mom and dad about the photo album, and instead I slid it in where it had been for years, safely nestled among his siblings.

Usually when I return from Mendocino my stress wraps around me like a scarf that's too tight. Today I see the green trees and full bushes that surround this small building as the beautiful things they are. The way I used to see them as a kid. I guess it could be Molly that has lightened my heart, but I don't think that is the only reason. I don't think I realized how Nick lived in the darkest parts of my mind.

I order oatmeal instead of the bacon and eggs I want, and mentally pat myself on the back for my healthy choice. I glance at my watch and wonder what Molly is doing. Is she just getting up, or is she lounging in her bed thinking about last night? I swallow hard and shift my mind elsewhere so I won't have to walk out of this café with my pants too tight. Nobody wants my boner with breakfast.

I have all weekend to kill before my appointments on Monday. Part of me wishes I was back in Mendocino, working on Lyle's projects. But then there is this new calm.

I know part of it has to do with Nick's death. I don't have that suffocating worry about what will happen next. I don't dread the next phone call or wonder if he's suffering. He is no longer here physically but he is also not in pain anymore and that gives my heart a little lift. Instead I wander around the small town that borders Willmore University with my newfound peace. Most of the professors live on the other side in the bigger city of Hamlet. I prefer Storybrook with its small-town feel but big-city views. The river runs right past the town and was the reason it was settled. I love the history of this place, if I am honest, the amount of time I spent digging in the soft soil looking for artifacts as a kid was probably the same amount of time other kids played baseball. I guess it makes sense that I became a professor of archeology. I have that thought as I pass our high school. Storybrook High graduated only about a hundred seniors a year, but most have gone on to great things. We have congressmen and senators among our alumni as well as a movie star or two.

I stuff my hands in my pockets and close my eyes trying to imagine my life if I had chosen to teach high school here. Would I have been a better influence on my brother, more available? The what-ifs dance in and right back out. I have played that record too many times. Ultimately Nick made the choices that led him to the life he had, I know that, but as I walk the streets where we grew up I let the memories of my childhood lead me. I walk past the tire swing where I had my first kiss, and the baseball field where I learned that I have zero hand-eye coordination.

I haven't been staying at my place, since it seems like my parents need me and I don't have the desire to even go see my place. I'm happy wandering around, and even happier to be there for my parents.

I stop outside the little bookstore that my brother and sisters and I would frequent on allowance day. I love that it is still here, even if it has new owners that can't seem to remember my name. Walking in the door and hearing the little jingle of the bell, makes a smile pull across my lips.

Nick loved books. He loved to be read to, to read himself, and before his accident he loved to write. From the age of ten until he was injured at twelve he wrote short stories and even some poems. I wonder if Mom kept them? That is something I'd like to have.

I wander up and down the rows of books and stop in the mystery section where I see the entire collection of Kent Price books. I gather up all twelve books and carry them to the register, effectively ending my walking tour of the town.

When I head back up the hill to my parents' house, I see my sisters' cars in the driveway and feel my shoulders relax a little. They have been great through all of this, and even though I'm the only one with summers off, the girls have really stepped up. No one asked me to cut my summer short, not even my mom who loves having me over every Sunday for dinner during the school year.

I walk in the front door and drop my bag of books on the table that holds years of scratches, pen marks, and a few teeth marks from a crazy orange cat we had.

"We are in here, Tommy," someone calls from the den at the back of the house.

Laura has spent more time here than in New York the past few weeks and a bit of guilt tugs at me. But when I hear them arguing, that guilt slides away.

"I did not tell Jeff Grand that you thought he was cute! That was Kimberly!" Julie yells, but Laura is in full attorney mode, cross-examining them both.

"If that were true, and I don't believe for a second that it is, then why did I find a note in your bedroom that said and I quote, 'Do you like my sister Laura, check yes or no' with his yes check mark and signature?"

When I round the corner, I laugh at the sight playing out. Kimberly and Julie are sitting at the round oak table and Laura is pointing a wooden spoon at them. My father is asleep in the recliner and I notice the green-stained shoes by his chair. Mom is watching the whole thing while taking notes. She always gets roped into being the court reporter/judge/jury. God bless her.

"Don't laugh Tommy, I am getting to the bottom of this before I go back to New York." She points the spoon at me and I hold up my hands like I am surrendering. She spins back around and says, "So Julie, do you have an explanation for said note?"

Julie smirks, then elbows Kimberly in the ribs, but shakes her head no. "I will never change my story, because I have the truth on my side."

I catch her dropping her hand and crossing her fingers. I smile but don't let on that I saw. There must be more to this story, but I can't even remember a guy named Jeff.

"Who is Jeff Grand? I don't remember him." I lean over and give my mom a peck on the cheek before I settle into my chair.

"I wish I didn't remember him. He's a partner at my firm and he loves telling everyone how my sisters slipped him a note to see if he liked me!" Laura's voice raises a few octaves and my dad snorts in his sleep. Mom does an automatic shush to quiet us and my whole world shifts back twenty-five years. Funny how being in your childhood home can do that to you.

"Oh wait! I do remember him! Was he the kid that ate all those worms on a dare?" I ask.

Laura groans and drops into her seat. She covers her face with her hands. "Everyone called me Mrs. Wormbreath."

We all laugh, including Mom, which surprises me. "So he works with you at Fenny and Grand?" I ask. Then it hits me. "Oh no! It's his father's firm, isn't it?" I start to laugh and so does Julie. Kimberly is holding it together, but only barely.

"His uncle, not father, but yes. I unfortunately share a secretary with Worm Breath, so I get to see him a lot. So much actually, and since he remembers that one of my sisters told him I had a crush on him, he and his horrible toupee have become insufferable."

The entire table erupts into laughter, and my father wakes up like he got dropped out of a helicopter into Saigon. Crouched and ready for action, his only weapon, an empty Diet RC. God help us all.

Sunday is spent with cards, and an entire afternoon-long game of Monopoly that ends only when Kimberly "accidentally" knocks the board over. That evening the photo albums come out along with laughter and tears and hugs. I say a silent thank-you that Nick's album is where it is supposed to be. The pain in my heart at the thought of my brother looking back at his childhood alone in that awful apartment is soothed a bit by my sisters and parents talking about all the good times we were lucky enough to share.

There was of course the obligatory and unavoidable conversation with Kimberly about what uncontrolled hypertension can do to the kidneys. I promise to forward any and all blood work her way, and she makes me promise to keep seeing Dr. Gentry. Apparently he really is the best. Not that I thought Dr. Potter was wrong, but the sister seal of approval means more.

By Monday I feel better—emotionally at least—than I have in years. Laura is heading back to New York today and we have plans to see a

Broadway show together in the fall. I almost ask if I can bring Molly, but I decide against it. They know I have gone on a few dates with her, but I don't want to get my hopes up that there will be a Molly and me in the fall.

I make my way to the cardiac wing of the hospital that is attached to Willmore University. Thankfully it seems fairly quiet. I had unreasonable fears of running into our department chair, but she is rumored to be on a dig in South America.

A medical assistant who is nowhere near as cute as Molly takes me back to a room and gets my vitals. She retakes my blood pressure while I am lying down then again when I am standing up, never once giving me any indication that there is cause for alarm. Since I have been feeling so much better, I'm confident he will say that I'm wasting his time, then we will talk about some Willmore University gossip and I'll be on my way.

"I am glad you came in today, Tom. Tell me, are you having any chest pain today?" Dr Gentry comes in and gets right to it. He is a tall, thin man with black framed glasses and I want to ask if he has a cape tucked under his lab coat.

"No, I haven't had any pain since that day I saw Dr. Potter," I explain.

"Good, that's good. Well, your blood pressure is pretty high today," he says and I am so surprised by this revelation that I interrupt him.

"But I don't have any ringing in my head anymore, and I feel great."

"That's why it's called the silent killer, Tom. Most people have no symptoms at all. I'm glad you came in." He pauses and looks directly at me to ensure I am listening. I nod and he continues, "I got your blood work from Dr. Potter and the EKG that was taken. We are going to have you go down the hall and get that echocardiogram and then the stress test. I want you to let the tech know if you have so much as a pinch in your chest okay?"

"Okay." I deflate. Damn, I thought everything was better. I go through all the tests, then am told to return the next day for the sonogram of my carotids. Dr. Gentry calls in new medicine for my blood pressure and I drive by the pharmacy to pick it up before going back to my parents' place.

Molly

THE NIGHT before Christmas is a magical time. I grew up poor, knowing we couldn't afford much, but for that one special night, the possibility of what could be wrapped around me like the softest of blankets.

As I stand at my front window peering out to the street I have the same endless hope coursing through my veins. The thought of seeing my son again in person after six months is twisting me into knots. When he was younger and would go off to summer camps, and the few times he went to Paris with his grandfather, have nothing on this moment.

He called me after I spoke with Tom and told me when to expect him. When I told Dr. Potter I would need some time off, he didn't bat an eye, in fact told me to take the week. As he pointed out, I haven't been even a minute late since I started here. So I have five whole days to devote to Grant.

The black BMW pulls to the curb, and I suck in a breath and step away from the window. My hands have decided to sweat like they have never sweated before, so I walk to the kitchen and wipe them off on a dish towel while I wait for the inevitable knock. As I stand at the sink, I hold my breath and count to three before I let it out slowly, then I do it again, hoping it gives the same effect as it did when I was in therapy.

The gentle knock on the door rattles me to my very soul. He might as well have pounded with all his strength. I laugh a little at how nervous I am. I smooth down my skirt, my hair, and my nerves then pull the door open.

"Hey, Mom!" Grant smiles with his father's dimples and my slightly crooked front tooth and my heart melts.

"Grant!" I grab him and pull him to my chest.

"Ow, hey, easy there," he says, but buries himself in my arms.

"God, Son, I have missed you so much." I kiss his shoulder since that is all I can reach in our current state of embrace. I would literally stuff him into my heart right now if I could. I have never missed another person more in my life.

"I missed you too, Mom. You cut your hair off!" he says as he pulls back. He looks at me and I instinctively put my hand up to brush my hair out of my face. I haven't done that in a long time but it's muscle memory and it was a nervous habit of mine.

"Yeah, I uh, I needed a change," I explain.

"I like it. It looks great on you!"

I smile and probably blush, then step aside so he can come in. He immediately kicks his shoes off and puts them next to mine under the bench. Then he stands up straight and looks around. I watch him take in my small oceanside cottage. His eyes bounce from one thing to the next but then settle on me.

"I like your place," he says as he stuffs his hands in his pockets.

I can't tell if he's nervous or uncomfortable, but I have a moment of panic that I made the wrong decision inviting him here. I take a deep breath and steady my voice, "Yeah?"

"Yeah, it's like getting to know you." He looks down when he says that, as if he doesn't want me to see he is struggling with how to react to all of this. I want to make it better, explain away all the doubts and questions he must have, but I don't. Maybe that is selfish, but I can't do anything except take in the sight of him, here in my home. That is what I want to focus on, to burn into my memory for when he's gone.

"I hope you can get to know me better now. I hope my leaving didn't cause—" my voice catches and I pause before I say, "I hope we're okay."

"I don't totally understand why you left, but Grandmother and I have talked a lot, and I think I know some of the story. She said I needed to hear it from you." He looks at me like I might spill all the years of pent-up secrets and anger while we stand by my front door.

"Oh. Well, I um, I don't know what she told you so it's hard to—" I stop and wipe my hands on my skirt again. "Do you want to sit down? Or do you need to use the bathroom or anything?"

"Nah, I'm good. We can sit." He walks over to the couch and I watch him, feeling a mix of excitement and dread. He has gotten taller since I left. Have his shoulders always been so broad? I cross to sit next to him.

"You look great. Was graduation fun? I am sorry I missed seeing you walk across the stage. I won't miss your college graduation. Do you know what you want to study?" Have you had a chance to see the college? Did Grandfather take you?" My words come out like someone opened a fire hydrant on a hot summer day.

Grant smiles at me and places his hand over mine. "My graduation was okay. I am not sure what I want to study, but I have some ideas. I haven't seen Willmore yet, but I think Grandfather and Grandmother are meeting me there to help me get settled."

I want to ask why his father isn't going, but I don't. I nod and fight my urge to apologize to him, instead I ask him more questions to catch up on his life.

We spend the day walking around Mendocino, going into the small shops and walking along the beach. He seems calm and happy and infinitely more mature than most eighteen-year-old boys. As we head back to my house, we pass The Floppy Fish, and my heart squeezes a bit. I miss Tom. I want to introduce him to my son, but that is a line I'm not sure I'm ready to cross. I don't know what Tom is to me, or how much I mean to him. Would it be weird for him to meet Grant?

"You okay?" Grant's voice pulls me out of my thoughts.

"Oh yeah, I'm fine. I have a friend that works there, but he's out of town at the moment. He is actually a professor at Willmore. He teaches archeology."

"Are you guys dating?"

I blink a few times and consider saying no, but I don't want to lie. I need to let Grant into my life and let him get to know me. This is who I am. A single woman who dates. God, that sounds lame in my own head, I am not saying that to my son.

"Yeah, we have gone on a few dates. But he is only here for the summer so it's not serious."

"Did you cheat on Dad? Is that why you left?" he blurts out.

I wince at that. "No. Absolutely not. I left because I didn't love him. I never did and I felt like I was suffocating in that house, in that life. Grant, you were the only—" I stop, not wanting to air out our issues on the sidewalk.

"Let's go back to my house and have this conversation. I need to tell you the whole story."

"About time," he mumbles as he stuffs his hands in his pockets. I guess his calm demeanor didn't mean he was totally okay with all of this.

We walk in silence to my place, and he excuses himself to use the bathroom, so I take the opportunity to turn on the oven so I can put in the enchiladas. When he comes back he takes a seat on the couch and rubs his hands on his legs.

I sigh and steel myself for what he might say. No way to get past this without going through it so I start. "I met your father on my sixteenth birthday. He was at a party at the beach and I thought he was my age. He never said how old he was, and I never asked. I didn't ask a lot of questions to be honest, and we had unprotected sex that night. It was my first time, and he told me it was his too." I pause because Grant had scoffed at that.

"And you believed him?"

"I was young." I shrug.

"And dumb," he says quietly.

"Yes. Well, I can only assume that I got pregnant that night although your father and I saw each other a few more times before I realized I was pregnant. When I told him, he said he would take care of it, then the next thing I knew I was at your grandparents' house and they took custody of me."

"What? What does that mean?" His confusion is laced with something else, pain maybe? I might be projecting that because telling this story is bringing up all my feelings.

"Well, they offered to take care of me and the baby, and I found out later they had given my mom a check. That was the last time I saw her. I learned after that how old your father was. I think they were afraid we would press charges."

Grant blows out a breath and shakes his head. I fight the panicky feeling in my chest. He may not believe my side of the story since I have no idea what his grandmother told him. I stand and get the enchiladas out of the fridge and put the pan in the oven. I need a moment to collect myself before I can continue.

"I stayed with them while your dad was finishing college, they hired a tutor, and I graduated from high school because of them. They also arranged for me to go to college. I owe a lot to them." I stop short of saying that I felt trapped, and wished I could escape.

"That part I knew. Grandma told me that you and Dad were really young and he wanted to get his degree, so you moved in with them. I didn't know the rest." He looks down at his hands for a moment before saying, "How old were you when you guys got married?"

"I was eighteen. Your father was twenty-two by then." I answer him honestly.

"Did you love him when you married him at least?" he asks quietly.

"No. I am sure that is not what you want to hear, but I didn't. I had nothing, I had no way of taking care of you by myself and I had lived with them for two years, I saw what they could offer you. What kind of a mom would I have been to take you from all that to a homeless shelter?" I don't tell him that I could have left him with the Densworths because even though I knew on a logical level I could walk away without my son at any time, I couldn't do it. I loved him so deeply and I wanted to be with him.

"Okay. That makes sense. I'm glad you stayed, Mom. I can't imagine what our lives would have been like, but God . . ." He pauses and rubs his face with his hands. "I bet you could have left me there. That was a choice, wasn't it?" He looks at me and I nod. "You missed out on so much. Because of me."

That wasn't something I had ever considered, and I tell him that. "Grant, no. I wanted you. I would give it all up again to see your chubby little hands and kiss your sweet face when you fell trying to learn to ride your bike. That stupid cobblestone driveway that your father insisted on, wasn't the best place to practice," I say.

Grant laughs. "No, we should have gone out to the street. But see, that's what I mean. I don't have those memories of Dad. He was never around, always off on a business trip or something. At first I thought that was why you left, because you were lonely."

"God, no." A laugh bubbles out of me. "Sorry, I was grateful that he traveled a lot for work. I didn't have to see him as often, and I had you all to myself for the most part. I did have to share you with your grandparents, but that was okay. I could tell how much they loved you."

"Did you know about all his girlfriends?" Grant asks. He sounds almost accusatory, like I should have done something if I did know.

"Yes." I don't elaborate. There is no need.

"Mom, how could you let him treat you that way?" Grant pushes up off the couch and jams his hand into his hair. He spins to look at me, and I can see the hurt in his eyes. "I hate him. I hate him so much. Do you know the weekend I found out I got into Willmore he was in Vegas with one of his whores?"

"Grant!" I stand up and reach for him, but he pulls away.

"After I learned that, I started asking him more questions and once I went to the office to see if I could catch him, you know? Like I wanted so badly to believe he wasn't a cheating bastard." He takes a ragged breath then says, "But he is. He was fucking his secretary, and I had the misfortune of walking in on that."

I shudder at the thought of what Grant must have seen and try again to reach out to him. This time he lets me.

"Honey, I am so sorry you had to see that. I am also sorry I wasn't more honest with you. I didn't want to turn you against your father, I thought you had a good relationship with him, well, at least when he was there." I slide my hand down his arm and try to hold his hand, but he pulls away.

"Yeah, well Grandmother said the same thing. How could you both have thought that I had a good relationship with him? He was never fucking there! When he was home he was in the den smoking a cigarette and drinking his whiskey. He didn't come to my track meets because 'work' always got in the way." He makes little air quotes when he says the word "work." "He never helped with homework—that was you or Grandfather. I thought he was working hard to provide for us, to make a name for himself in the company. Do you know how many excuses I made for him?" He's pacing now in my small living room area, and I wring my hands wishing I knew how to help him.

I was not expecting his anger towards his father. I would have gone to my deathbed with Isaac's infidelity. No child needs to know that about their parent. I think once Isaac realized I wasn't going to play the role of doting wife in the bedroom, he started seeing other people. Grant was probably four of five the first time Isaac called to let me know he was working late and wouldn't be home for dinner. I remember rolling over in bed the next morning and realizing that he'd never come home. The relief that washed over me was like a hint of freedom.

"I wish I could make this better. I hate that you are hurting," I say, because through all the other noise, that is the bottom line. I can't change what happened, or who his father is.

"I hate that you spent so much time with him. I'm sorry, Mom. I wish we could have left. Grandmother would have helped us." My eyes fly open wide at that statement.

"Oh, I don't think so, Grant. She was part of why I stayed. She made it very clear what she wanted from me that first night I met her, and I can only assume she feels the same way now."

"I don't understand. What did she want?" Grant says. He sinks into the couch again and I'm glad he's sitting, because his pacing was making me nervous.

"She wanted you. She wanted an heir. If I am being totally honest I think she wanted a do-over," I say before I can give the statement much thought. Now that it's out there I watch Grant's face for a reaction, but I can't read the expression I see.

The oven timer goes off so I leave Grant on the couch to pull out our dinner. I set the table and start working on the salad. He's quiet, but that was a lot of information to digest. I am not going to push him. He looks so much older. I know that's silly, since it's only been six months, but he is a man now. I search his face for my little boy and see only hints of the child he was. He's so handsome and for a moment I have a pang of regret that my mom didn't get to see him as a child. I wonder what would have happened if she had been at home the day I stopped by.

"Think you can eat? I made my enchiladas." I watch as he takes a deep breath and stands.

"Yeah, thanks. I have never recovered from the ones Jasmine tried to make after you left." His smile is back as he takes a seat and we eat and chat about nothing important. He tells me about prom and some of the crazy things that happened. Apparently, the girl who was crowned prom Queen had been in the bathroom throwing up her vodka dinner while her King was passed out behind the stage with another girl in his arms. The chaperones were pissed and both kids were sent home to even angrier parents.

The Bishop's School where Grant went to high school is an exclusive private school in San Diego. Parents spend a lot of money to send their kids there. The diploma is like a ticket to any college, unless apparently you get wasted at prom. Neither kid got to walk at graduation and Grant said they both took a "gap year" to get back on track.

I feel bad that gossip about other people is making me feel so much better, but it is. We spend the rest of the night talking and laughing and I wonder if that was the worst of it. Grant has always been mature and thoughtful. I can count on one hand the times I have seen him melt down over something.

"I need to grab my bag out of the trunk." Grant stands and stretches.

"Okay, you're sleeping in my room. I'll take the spare room," I say and he shakes his head like he is going to argue with me. He won't when he sees the bed in there. Dr. Potter and Henny gave me that bed when they learned I didn't have a bed for my second bedroom. I agreed when they offered because I thought it was an actual bed, not a folded mattress that was sewn with hatred by angry demons. The metal frame that contains the beast is so stiff I have to use pliers to slide the latch that opens the damn thing.

The first time I opened it I laughed my ass off picturing that scene in the *Peanuts* Thanksgiving special where Snoopy tries to open his lawn chair. That was very similar to my experience.

Just as Grant comes back in the front door my phone rings. I think about letting the answering machine get it, but I know it's Tom. I miss him desperately, so I answer.

"Hello?"

"Molly, God, I am so glad you answered. Am I interrupting anything?" His deep, smooth voice comes through the line like a balm to my soul. I point down the hall when Grant holds up his bag.

"Hi! Just a second," I say, then I yell out to Grant, "No other door. You won't fit on that bed. Take my room. I'm only going to be a minute."

I settle into the kitchen chair and say, "Okay, I'm back, Grant was bringing in his bag. How are you?"

"Oh, if your son is there we can talk later. I was, well I was missing you," Tom says, sounding all kinds of shy and adorable.

"I miss you too. Are you hiding in your parents' bathroom again?" I ask.

He chuckles. "No, I'm at my house now. They kicked me out after my sisters went back home. I think my dad wanted freedom to mow in peace."

"Is he still taking out his grief on the neighborhood lawns?"

"He is. His shoes are green now. Kimberly has started calling him the Jolly Green Giant."

"Oh dear. How are you? How were the tests? Did Dr. Gentry tell you anything yet?" I pick at the woven placemat trying to ease my nerves a little.

"The treadmill test thing was fine, and so was the scan of my carotids. I don't know about the Holter monitor yet. I just turned that in, so it might be a few days."

"Did you have any incidents while you were wearing it?" I ask

"One or two. Nothing serious, Molly. I'm okay. How is your visit with Grant?" He drops his voice like maybe my son can hear him.

I glance over and see Grant leaning on the wall near the hallway. He has a soft look in his eyes and a smile on his face. He blows me a kiss and turns to go to bed.

"SORRY, are you still there? Grant was saying goodnight."

"You aren't going to make him sleep on that metal death trap, are you?" I say with a chuckle.

"God no, I am sleeping on that, he gets my bed." She sighs and I think she sounds happy. I wish I could see her face right now, so I would know for sure.

"You're a good mom, Molly," I tell her, then quickly add, "And don't argue with me on that."

She laughs, and asks, "So Dr. Gentry said the other tests were fine?"

"Yeah, he added another medication because even though I was feeling better the day I went in for the testing, my blood pressure was really high again."

"That's why they call it the silent killer, Tom," she says.

"You sound like Dr. Gentry. But yeah, I am realizing that. My dad said his was really bad and they only found it when he went in for a vaccine he needed to travel. It's funny I would have been about nine or ten when that happened and I don't remember him or my mom saying anything about it."

"Well, you were just a kid. Maybe they talked about it but you didn't understand?"

"Maybe. I hope this last test is clear and I can get back to Mendoci-no." I pause then say what's on my mind. "And you. I miss you, Molly."

I hear another sigh and close my eyes, hoping she feels the same way. This past week has been such a time travel for me and it's confusing my feelings. I'm acting like a lovestruck teenager but I don't know how to stop.

"I miss you too. We were walking around town and we went past The Floppy Fish, and I guess I stopped and stared at the place. I didn't even realize I had done it until Grant asked me about it."

That makes me smile.

"I told him about you," she says so quietly I almost don't hear it.

"You did? What did you say?" My heart swells with hope.

"I said we were dating. I hope that's okay. I don't want to pressure you, I don't have a lot of experience with this sort of thing so I—"

I cut her off, "Molly, I would very much like to meet your son. We are dating. I'd like to ask if we can be exclusive but that doesn't seem fair since I am only a part-timer in Mendocino."

"I might consider that," she says quickly.

I like that more than I should and I feel like a selfish prick for only about three seconds before I smile. "That makes me happy."

We talk until almost one in the morning, then I lie in my bed and think about all the things I want to do to her when I get back to Mendo-cino. Never in my life have I thought about a woman like this. I have dated, even had a couple of long-term relationships. Do we count high school for those kinds of things? I was with Ronda for like a year and a half, but we didn't even have sex, so really, how serious were we? Then in college I met Diane. She was my first and we were together almost three years. I never thought about taking the next step and eventually she figured that out. It was easy and comfortable but not exciting. I tried that too, dated a girl who was so exciting she almost got me arrested. That didn't last. I'm not that fun.

Since then I have played it safe, found a few women who will attend fundraisers and don't mind the occasional late-night call. It's been at least a year since I called on any of them though and now, with my thoughts so focused on Molly Kristen Sparrow, I doubt I will ever call them again. I fall asleep thinking of the merlot on Molly's lips.

* * *

The phone wakes me up and I glance at the clock before I answer. "Hello?"

"Tom? This is Dr. Gentry. Listen I wanted to let you know your Holter showed some changes in the ST segment, that tells me you have a bit of angina. Based on your symptoms and bloodwork I am going to assume at this point it's stable. I am going to prescribe some nitroglycerin. It's a little bottle of pills you'll keep in your pocket at all times. You have pain, you take one of those, okay?"

I sit up and rub my eyes before answering, "Okay, is that a serious thing?"

"No it's manageable. Your blood vessels are shrinking down and causing that pinching pain feeling you have. The nitro opens that all up and should give you relief. Come see me when you are back for the semester. We will repeat your blood work and see if that cholesterol has come down. Keep eating that oatmeal instead of bacon okay?

"I will, thanks, Doc!" I hang up and dial the airline right away to book a flight out for later today, then jump out of bed and pack before I call my parents to tell them the news.

When I finally land in San Francisco I am too tired to make the drive up the coast, so I get a room close to the airport and drive up the next morning. The traffic out of the city is light today since most people are on their way to work. Suckers.

During the summer I like to pretend I don't work and I like to make fun of those who do. I wonder if I am the only teacher who does this. I don't count what I do at The Floppy Fish, because that isn't work, it's fun.

The two-and-a-half-hour drive up drags on even in light traffic because I want to be in Mendocino more than I want air to breathe. I know I have to tamp that down a bit since her son is still in town, but I need to see her.

Not want.

Need.

I park around the back of The Floppy Fish and walk to the front of the building just as Dr. Potter is locking up the clinic. I wave and he hurries over to me. Well, hurries might be an exaggeration. Shuffles with purpose is more like it.

"I got the notes from Dr. Gentry. How are you feeling?" He asks as soon as he reaches me, so it comes out a bit winded.

"I feel good. No problems with the new medication he gave me and I haven't had an episode of chest pain since I got the diagnosis. Hopefully they will be few and far between."

"I hope so as well. I have to get going. Henny is waiting for me, but I wanted to see how you were!" He heads off in the direction of the ocean and I look around for Henny, but don't see her. I glance at my watch and see it's only two in the afternoon. I wonder why he closed the clinic midday? I hope Henny isn't sick or anything.

I fish my keys out and unlock The Floppy Fish, breathing in deep as I open the door. I love the smell of this place. Beer-soaked oak planks mixed with the pine oil and something I have never quite been able to identify. I feel my shoulders relax as I step in and let my eyes adjust to the dark space. I walk past the bar to the stairs leading up to my place. I need to dump my bag and then go find Molly if I can. Maybe I should call her and let her know I am back in town. I don't want to interrupt her son's visit, but I feel on edge. That doesn't really describe it, it's like a buzzing, swirling feeling. I felt it when I landed in San Francisco and as I drove up here it only intensified. If I see her, even for a short time, I know it will go away.

At least I kind of hope it does. Living like this, with this constant want, can't be good for me. My sisters drove home the point over and over that I needed to learn how to relax, be calm and not let things build up. I am sure they meant stress, but the buildup of longing I have for Molly is actually getting kind of stressful.

I dial her number and laugh when I hear her answering machine message. I love that song too, and I love that she finally feels free to be herself.

"Hey Molly, it's Tom. I wanted to let you know that I am back in town. I, um, have to work tonight. If you want to stop by with Grant, or whatever, that would be fine. You don't have to, of course, I was just hoping to see you. Okay that's all I was—" I hear the click of the machine cutting me off. Jesus, she needs to make the incoming message time a little longer. A guy can't fit in all the words that fast.

I unpack quickly then call my parents to let them know I made it back safely. Dad isn't home since he's apparently learning how to change the blade on the mower down at the local hardware store. Mom seems pleased with his new hobby, so I don't comment when she says she's hoping he'll get a weed-whacker obsession next.

At three thirty I head downstairs and start getting ready for the night. The place is spotless and I make a mental note to thank Misty, Jerald, and Patty for taking care of the place while I was away.

When I flip the sign at four, it's only a few minutes before the locals start trickling in. I am pouring beers and setting them on a tray when the front door opens. The bright light coming in behind the person makes it impossible to see their face but there is only one person shaped like that.

"Hello, Dr. Potter!" I say. I toss the bar towel over my shoulder and press my hands into the worn wood of the bar top, leaning forward to greet him with a warm smile.

"Hello, Tom. Mind if I kill some time here?" He makes his way to the tall barstool and I watch, wondering how he will manage to get up on the thing.

"Not at all, what can I get you?"

"How about whatever you have on tap? As long as it's Sierra Nevada's Pale Ale." He eyes the stool warily but manages to climb up with only one or two grunts.

I pour him a nice full mug of beer and expertly slide it to him. "You closed up the clinic early today, I noticed. Everything okay?"

"Fine, fine. Molly took some time off to see her son, so Henny and I decided to play a little hooky." He wiggles his big bushy eyebrows at me before saying, "She's getting a little something special ready for me at home so I told her I was coming here. Glad to see you back." He tips the beer to his lips and in one slow motion drains the entire glass.

I blink at him, not sure I really saw that. His glass is empty and he's staring at me like he didn't just chug a pint. I decide not to mention it and instead ask him what his plans for the evening are, but immediately regret it when he tells me.

"Well, Henny and I went over to Secret Notions, and she picked out a few things. We want to try some new role-play tonight. I'm going to be a businessman and she's going to be a lady of the night." He winks and me and I swallow hard.

Not at all what I expected him to say.

"We've done the pirate and wench thing, that was fun, although Henny didn't appreciate the hook as much as I thought she would. I thought it did a good job of holding her leg up, but she got hamstring cramps and we had to switch positions. Then we tried boss and secretary but that felt too close to our real life, you know?" He's acting like we are talking about the weather and I can't move my feet. I am glued to the floor by some invisible force that wants me to suffer through this.

"Now my all-time favorite was stamp collector and shop owner. The places I licked her that night—"

Misty walks up and asks for three drinks and I have never wanted to make a Harvey Wallbanger more in my life. I am even happier when I see the orange juice is almost out and I have to go into the kitchen to get more.

I lean against the counter after I grab the juice from the fridge and contemplate hiding in here for the rest of the night. What the hell? Hopefully by the time I go back out there he will be gone or he'll want to talk about something else.

I mix the drinks for Misty, trying my best not to look Dr. Potter's way, but he's sitting there with his hands folded waiting patiently for me to return to his little shop of horrors.

When I have no more excuses to avoid him, I walk back over and ask if he wants a refill. My second mistake of the evening.

"No thanks, one is enough for me. Did you know that men can experience erectile disfunction after drinking? Beer can make it difficult to get an erection because alcohol affects hormone levels and circulation. It also affects the nervous system, you know that lovely numb feeling you get after a few drinks. I don't want anything to get in the way of my plans for the night." He smiles at me.

"Right, well, that makes sense, I guess. Thank you for that information. I will keep that in mind," I reply, not sure what else to say to this man who seems to like to overshare.

"Tom, let me ask you a question." He pauses but not long enough for me to object. "When you and Molly have been together have you tried any role-play? She seems a bit uptight, not that I should be commenting on that because she is a damn fine employee, but I do wonder if she can cut loose when she needs to."

"Uh —" I freeze, unable to say anything, because what the hell?

"No wait, don't tell me. I hope you can help her sort that out. Did you know the vibrator was invented to help women release some of their stress? Doctors used to perform pelvic massages to completion of course, but so many women were coming in, the doctors became fatigued. All that fingering and manipulating was difficult." He shakes his head and chuckles.

My eyes must be the size of bowling balls, but if they are, he doesn't seem to notice or care. I swallow hard again and pray for another drink order to end my little nightmare.

"Well Tom, thanks for letting me kill some time here. You are a delightful bartender. Watch out for those ass splinters." He pats the bar and wiggles out of his chair. I don't breathe again until the door to the bar swings shut.

Jesus Christ.

The next two hours are a mix of reliving that strange encounter with Dr. Potter and watching the door in hopes that Molly and her son will come in. We get busy around seven thirty and I am filling the tray for Patty, so I miss the front door opening. When I set the last drink on the tray and Patty nods her thanks I glance up and my breath catches in my chest.

How did I forget how beautiful she is? She is standing off to the side by one of our high-top tables, wearing a dress I have never seen before. It's a stunning blue color and hits her just below her knees. The neckline is a simple scoop like a tank top but Molly makes it look sexy, with her ample cleavage peeking out the top.

She is wearing flats and I think that must be why her son is towering over her. She is tall, but Grant must be about six three. He says something and she throws her head back and laughs. His eyes crinkle with delight at her. He's wearing a Willmore University T-shirt and a pair of jean shorts. He has dark hair styled perfectly and I can see some of his mother in him. The rest must be Isaac. That makes me uncomfortable for some reason, and for a moment I wonder if I made a mistake asking them to come here.

As soon as she turns and sees me, however, that feeling drifts away like a leaf in the wind. Those big stunning eyes go even wider and a smile spreads across her face. I feel my heartbeat speed up and I quickly grab the towel off my shoulder and wipe my hands. I set the towel down on the counter, but then pick it up and toss it on my shoulder. A move I have done a million times since I started working here, and yet I miss and the towel goes flying behind me.

I can't take my eyes off her. She tucks a piece of hair behind her ear, but since it's so short it pops right back out. Her hair is longer, making me feel like I was gone too long.

"Hi. You made it." I step closer and she does too, but we stop short, both of us unsure how to greet each other in front of her son. I clear my throat and try to swallow but I have suddenly become a one-man desert.

"Hi, yeah, we did. We would have been here earlier but we got to talking and lost track of time." She wrings her hands in front of her and looks at the floor.

"It's okay, it was busy earlier, a little quieter now." My gaze hasn't left her face so I see the pink spread across her cheeks. She snaps her head up and looks over at her son. "Oh! I'm sorry, Grant, this is Tom. Tom, this is my son Grant."

I hold out my hand and he meets mine with grace well beyond his eighteen years. "Hello, my mom has told me a lot about you. It's nice to finally meet you."

I smile and say, "I've heard a lot about you as well. Thanks for coming down. Can I get you a Coke or something else to drink?" I glance back over my shoulder at the bar to make sure Misty or Patty aren't waiting on me.

"A Coke sounds great," Grant says and steps past us to go sit at the bar. I turn to Molly and give her a small smile that she returns.

In between serving I'm able to visit with them a little. I learn that Grant is going to Willmore with an undeclared major and he really has no idea what he wants to study. I assure him that it's okay and a lot of young people are unsure of their path. He's charming, insightful and really, really smart. I forget many times that I am speaking with a teenager. He has asked me a bunch of questions about my field and why I chose to teach instead of going on digs. Misty ended up getting her own drinks a few times when I was distracted by a story, but she didn't seem to mind.

People start to slowly leave and I glance at the clock, surprised to see it's almost closing time. I gather the empty glasses left on the bar and put them in the tub, then excuse myself to take them to the kitchen. Patty comes in after me with a full tub she carried in from the outside area.

"Is that Molly's son?" she asks without looking at me. She's stacking the glasses in the huge industrial sink and I wait for her to finish so I can add mine.

"Yeah, he's here for a few days before he heads off to college."

Patty nods and smiles at me before saying, "You really care about her, don't you?"

"It's that obvious?" I ask.

"It was obvious that first night she came in. In all the years you've been coming here, I have never seen you interested in someone. I thought you were married or something." She shrugs and turns on the faucet to start washing the glasses.

I laugh, "No, not married. I guess no one ever got my attention before. Hey, you don't have to do that. I can get it after we close."

"No, Tom, you need to walk Molly and her son home. I got this." She gives me a small smile and a nod then gets to work without another word.

When I walk back out to the bar Molly and Grant are standing by the front door. The clock above it says it's just past midnight.

"Mind if I walk you home?" I ask, looking at Grant.

"No that would be great. I wanted to ask you about the grant writing thing, if I could. It kind of had me thinking."

"Really? Sure we can talk about that. Your mom doesn't live that far from here, maybe we can talk more at breakfast?" I open the door and wait for them to step out before following them. I lock the door so Patty doesn't have to worry about a stray drunk coming in while she is alone in there, and we head off.

The night air is cool and crisp and I notice Molly shivering a little as we walk along. I drape my arm over her shoulder and pull her into me while Grant explains about the charity work he did his senior year of high school. This kid is seriously impressive. I wasn't doing anything like that when I was in my senior year, of course I kind of knew I was going to get into Willmore. Maybe Grant had to do all this extra stuff to earn a scholarship or something. I don't want to ask since I made Molly angry when I assumed it might be a financial burden.

We walk the few blocks to Molly's and when we reach her house I stop and let my arm slide off her shoulder, wishing I could pull her in for a kiss. To be this close to her all night and not taste her lips has been torture.

"It was great talking with you, Tom. I am going to head in, let me know what time we're doing breakfast and I'll be ready. I have to leave the day after tomorrow, so I hope we can spend some more time together." He reaches out to shake my hand and I smile at him while extending mine.

"I would love that, Grant. I know you haven't seen your mom in a while, so thanks for sharing her tonight." I squeeze his hand a little when we shake. I have to fight the urge to pull him into a hug. It's too soon for that, I'm sure.

Molly

AS SOON AS Grant is inside my house, Tom turns to me and places his hands on either side of my face. He doesn't pull me in like I expect; he just holds me.

"Molly." He says my name like it's a whole sentence, and I feel my stomach dip as the world seems to stop moving.

I try to reply but I can't. Words are swirling around but none can capture what I want to say to this man. Instead my eyes well with tears. I am afraid of the strong emotions gripping me, but I have nowhere to go.

"I have missed you so much. More than I thought I would," he says as he runs his thumb across my cheek, capturing my tear that slipped free.

"I missed you too Tom."

He steps in closer and moves one hand to the back of my neck, sliding up into my hair. "Your hair grew while I was away."

"Yes, it grows pretty fast. I might let it grow out again," I say, watching his face inch closer to mine. I wonder why I'm telling him this and I will myself to stop talking.

"Okay." He breathes out and steps even closer. He lets his lips graze mine gently and I sigh.

"Fuck," he whispers, and pulls me in with urgency, kissing me more thoroughly. His hand snakes down to my hip and he grips me there like he's holding me in place, stopping us from taking this too far in front of my house. I let my mouth dance over his, our tongues tangling as the cool sea breeze moves between us. My heart expands and my stomach drops and twists as I feel the need to mold myself to his body.

I step in and move my hands to his back pulling him into me, relishing how warm and solid he feels. I pull back and whisper, "God, I missed you so much, Tom. You feel so good. I wish I could invite you in, but—"

His mouth moves over mine, silencing me. We kiss like that for what feels like hours, his hands roaming all over me, gently exploring, remembering, learning.

He gives me one final slow sweet kiss then steps back, breathing hard and rubs his hand down his face. "You better get inside, Molly. I won't be responsible for what happens if you stay."

The look on his face is something I will remember until the day I die. No man has ever looked at me like that. Like I am all he wants, all he needs and he will stop at nothing to have me. It's intoxicating and addictive.

"I want to find out very soon what it would be like to disobey you, Mr. Hemingway." My chest rises with a ragged breath and I watch his gaze drop, and he drinks me in. His tongue peeks out and runs across his lower lip.

"Good night, Molly," Tom says as he steps back. It feels wrong to let him walk away right now, but I don't have a lot of choice in the matter. I don't want the first time he takes me to be behind a bush on my street.

"Good night, Tom. Breakfast tomorrow? Where we had our first date?"

"Perfect. I'll walk over here at nine. See you then." He shoves his hands in his pockets and steps back again. His gaze is so intense I find it hard to look away. So I don't. We stand there locked in each other's eyes, a million words unsaid between us. I want to memorize every bit of his face, the way his thick blonde hair hangs longer on one side of forehead. His strong firm jawline that supports the best smile I have ever seen on a man. The slope of his shoulders down to his muscular arms, the arms I want wrapped around me. He has nice thick thighs and a solid ass. Not every guy looks good in Dockers, but Tom can wear the hell out of them.

"See you in the morning," Tom says quietly, breaking me from the spell. He turns and walks back towards The Floppy Fish with my heart in his pocket.

* * *

I expect to be the first one up in the morning but when I wake up I smell coffee brewing. I smile. I don't think I knew my son liked coffee or knew how to make it. I wrap myself in my favorite robe and walk out to find Grant at my small table, mug in one hand and the book I got about Connecticut in the other. He hasn't heard me come in so I can take a moment to enjoy seeing my son. I'm so proud of the man he has become. Seeing him with Tom last night did things to me. It's like I got to see Grant through someone else's eyes.

He must feel me watching him because he turns his head toward me and grins. "I hope I didn't wake you. I planned on walking down to the ocean but then I saw this book, and well, I'm still here." He gives a little shrug with one shoulder and I get a flash of him explaining how he needed to finish *The Lord of the Rings* because he wanted to read *The Hitchhiker's Guide to the Galaxy* before it was checked out of the library again.

"Books have always been kind of like a flytrap to you," I say with a small laugh. I walk to the coffee pot and pour myself a cup then I join him at the table.

"Tom said he will be here at nine. Are you still okay with the plan to go with him to breakfast? If not, I understand, I know this must be—"

"Nice to see you happy?" he says, setting down the book and his coffee.

I swallow hard, not sure what to say to that.

"I really like Tom. He's easy to talk to," Grant says as he studies my face. "You never looked at Dad like that. But do you know what I noticed more than that?"

"What?" I say barely above a whisper.

"Dad never looked at you. I can't say I ever saw him even notice when you came into a room. I hate that. I hate the way he treated you." His voice has pitched up and his hand curls into a fist. "Why didn't we leave when I was little? When you first left I admit I was mad, but the more time I had alone with him the more I understood. Then seeing you here in . . ." he waves his hand around the room and adds, "this place is like finally getting to know you. I didn't know you liked small cozy cottages, or that your favorite color is yellow. Why didn't I know that?"

"I guess I didn't ever tell you, it wasn't important." I look down at the table, unsure what to say. I don't want to be the reason he and Isaac don't get along. I don't want him to hate his grandparents like I do.

"You're important, Mom. You. Did you know all my friends were jealous of me because I had the best mom?" He asks, his voice sounding more and more angry.

"No, that doesn't sound true, the other moms were—"

He cuts me off. "Alcoholics? Addicted to pills? Cheating on their husbands? Traveling the world on their husband's dime, not giving a flying fuck if they missed their kid's tenth birthday. Do you remember Davey Simple? He and I spent about an hour after his party talking about what a piece of shit his mom was for not bothering to come home for his party."

"Is that the boy who had a live band at his party?" I ask trying desperately to picture the kid he is talking about.

Grant laughs. "Yeah, Journey came and played a few songs. His mom thought maybe he wouldn't notice that she wasn't there if his favorite band was. Too bad she got the band wrong."

"Oh no! Who was his favorite?" I cover my mouth with my hands to hide the smile forming. I think I do remember this kid now.

"A Flock of Seagulls," Grant says, a tiny grin appearing on his lips.

"Oh my God, I do remember Davey! He had the hair! He looked like, who was the lead singer?" I ask, openly laughing now.

"Mike Score, I think. Yeah, Davey had the hair down perfectly. He was over in Liverpool when the band got big and came back to the states for school that year with the hair. I was so jealous," Grant says.

"Really?" That makes me laugh even harder.

"Oh man, you have no idea. We all thought he was so cool."

"How is Davey now?" I ask.

"I'm not sure, last I heard he was going to join the military to piss his parents off. They wanted him to take business classes so he could slide into a desk job and eventually take over for them when they retire. He turned eighteen during our senior year so he was hardly ever in school."

"Oh, I see." That makes me both sad and impressed with Davey.

"You were always so nice to my friends, and you *came* to things. All the things, no matter what it was, I knew you'd be there. I was the only one who had that, Mom." Grant sounds so sad. I reach across and cover his hand with mine.

"You were my world, Grant. I wouldn't have missed a moment of anything you did."

"When you asked me to come with you, I only said no because I didn't really believe that you'd leave." Grant says as he slides his hand out from under mine. He runs it through his hair and looks out the window. I wait, not sure if he will elaborate.

"Grandmother told me about how you and Dad met. When you left, she said she was surprised you lasted as long as you did."

My back straightens at that. I have vowed not to ruin his relationship with them, but I am sure they do not have the same courtesy for me. I take a sharp breath in before I ask, "What did she tell you?"

"Let's see, I believe her exact words were, 'my piece of shit son didn't bother asking your mom's age before sticking his dick in her.' And then she went on from there." He takes a drink of his coffee like that was the most natural thing for her to say.

I gasp, literally gasp, because that woman didn't so much as blink improperly, so to hear she used language like that shocks the living hell out of me. "She did not say that!"

Grant smiles at me and says simply, "I think I know a very different version of her than you. Did you know she gave me my first drink of alcohol when I turned fifteen?"

"What?!" I yell and stand from the table.

Grant laughs and says, "Yeah, Grandmother was quite the rule breaker. She gave me cake for breakfast once too, said if you asked I was to tell you I had eggs and milk and bread. Technically I wouldn't be lying."

I sink back into the chair feeling like my world has tipped on its end, but not in a pleasing way like with Tom. This is not the woman I knew. The woman who kept me at arm's length even when I was scared and crying. I shake my head in disbelief but then look up at my son and narrow my eyes before saying, "It makes sense now."

"What does?" He cocks his head, genuinely confused.

"Why you like her so much. I never got it. I never understood why you'd ask to go to their house. Was Grandfather secretly fun too?" I ask, totally puzzled.

"Oh no, he really is as boring as he seems, but Grandmother was all that and a bag of chips. She was careful who saw that side of her. She said she liked it that people were a little afraid of her."

"Does she know you call her that?" I ask. I shake my head because none of this makes sense. The Vivian I knew was a well put together shrew who ran the family business with an iron fist, and her family with an even firmer hand. Nothing was done without her approval. To hear that she is this completely different person with Grant is very confusing.

"Yeah, I tried calling her Grandma Chips but she wouldn't allow it." Grant laughs and I'm about to ask another question but there is a knock on the door. I glance at the clock and see it's only eight. My stomach tightens with worry and it must show on my face because Grant stops laughing and glances back at the door.

"Are you expecting Tom?" he asks quietly.

"Not this early," I say. I stand and tighten my robe before walking to the door. Before I can open it however, Grant is beside me. He puts his hand on my arm and I step aside, letting him be the one who opens the door.

"Good morning! I know I'm early, but I brought donuts." Tom says sheepishly. He's holding a box from a store in Fort Bragg so he must have gotten up very early to go get them.

Grant opens the door wider and motions for Tom to come in. As Tom is toeing off his shoes Grant relieves him of the donut box, his grin wide across his face.

"How did you know Grant likes donuts?" I ask, trying to slow my son's progress to the small table. "You need to share!" I scold him as he hurries past me.

Tom laughs and steps in to kiss me on the cheek. The moment his lips touch my skin my nerves settle a little. I am so shocked by Grant's account of his grandmother I may not recover.

"Save me the sugar one, the rest are up for grabs," Tom says as he makes his way to the coffeepot. He pours himself a cup and swats Grant's hand away from the one and only sugar donut. He grabs it and takes a big bite while Grant tries to reach for it.

Grant laughs and says, "I always ask for three or four of those when I get a box. They are the superior donut."

"I knew I liked you," Tom says then turns to me and asks, "Whose car is that out front? I was worried when I saw it that it might be your ex here bothering you"

"The convertible 325i? That's mine," Grant says with a mouthful of chocolate glaze.

I watch as Tom's eyebrows raise then furrow. Grant explains that's his graduation gift from his grandparents and Tom gives a weak smile. I guess he has figured out that Grant won't need a scholarship to attend Willmore.

"I told them it was too much, but they insisted. I do like the way it drives so I won't complain." Grant shrugs like he's not talking about a car that cost over thirty thousand dollars. Way more than I made my first year working as a medical assistant, that's for sure.

"Oh, sure, that makes sense. Are you driving it out to Connecticut?" Tom asks, recovering quickly.

"Yeah, my grandparents are flying out to help get me set up in my place. I have a friend at UC Davis, so I want to stop and see her before I head out." Grant grabs a napkin from the little holder I have on the table and wipes the chocolate off his fingers.

"I don't like the idea of you driving all the way out there by yourself," I say immediately, putting my hands on my hips. Grant blushes a bit and I regret sounding so stern.

"Well to be honest, um, the girl I am going to see in Davis is coming out with me. We've been talking a lot and she wants to take a trip before she starts classes. We have a whole route planned. It will be fun, and safe. I promise." Grant smiles and looks at Tom, maybe for help.

"I've made that drive a few times. It's not bad. I can give you the name of a few cool places to stop along the way if you'd like. You have to go through Reno so you can see Lovelock Cave. I can show you on the map if you want." Tom still has his mostly uneaten donut in his hand like he's forgotten he's holding it.

"Let me go get my maps from the car! I would love to see if the route we planned will be good. I'd take any advice you have. I've never driven that far and I really want to make sure we have fun and not just drive for eight hours a day, you know?" Grant says as he stands.

"Sure! We have time, you don't mind, do you, Molly?" Tom asks and my shoulders relax a little. A warm feeling spreads across my chest at him asking me, and maybe more so that they seem to get along so well.

Grant and Tom pore over maps for the next hour, giving me time to take a shower and get ready. Hearing their laughter and conversation from my room gives me such a full heart I feel almost giddy as I walk out to the living room.

"Yes, if you go this high route then you'll see some of the places we talked about, but you can—" Tom's voice trails off as I walk in the room. His eyes lock onto mine and then I watch as his gaze drops, taking in my yellow tank top and denim shorts. I'm wearing my sandals and I hope I don't look too casual for brunch.

He clears his throat and sets the pen that he was holding onto the map before stepping toward me. "You look lovely, Molly. I like the scarf thing," he says, motioning to my hair.

"Thanks." I nervously glance at the ground as Grant agrees with Tom.

"Looks great, Mom. I really like your short hair. I'm getting used to it at least. You were always so easy to spot with your long curly hair, but it looks good short too."

"Are you guys ready for breakfast? I'm ready whenever you are." I shift uncomfortably on my feet. I am not used to this much praise and I want to change the subject from me.

"Yeah, I need to use the bathroom real quick." Grant walks past me and I shift my gaze to Tom letting the butterflies take flight in my stomach.

181

Tom

WHY CAN'T I ever seem to remember how beautiful this woman is? Every time I see her it's like a punch to my gut, knocking the wind out of me. She has a yellow scarf tied in her hair like I've seen my sisters wear, but on Molly it's sinfully sexy. She looks like that picture of Rosie the Riveter.

I step closer and my heart rate spikes as she moves closer as well. My hand reaches for her and then she is in my arms, melting into my embrace like this moment is all she has wanted. That may be my wishful thinking, since holding her close to me is all I have been able to think about since getting back to Mendocino.

We don't speak. I just hold her close to me, fighting the urge to bend down and kiss her. If I start, there will be an uncomfortable moment for all of us when Grant emerges from the bathroom.

We both laugh silently as Grant makes more noise than necessary as he comes back out, saying, "All done, and boy am I hungry!"

We step apart and I smile at Molly who is looking at me with misty eyes. I cock my head in question, but she shakes her head.

We all walk down to the restaurant on the cliff, talking easily like the three of us have done this a hundred times. I marvel at the comfortable feeling I have as we all walk into the restaurant. The last time I felt this way was when I was back home, surrounded by my family.

Molly asks if we can sit on the patio and the waitress leads us out to the large deck that overlooks the ocean. I spot him before Molly because she is talking to Grant about the lobster quiche.

Dr. Potter and Henny fresh from their night of role-play are seated right next to where the waitress is taking us. I move my hand to wave as Dr. Potter leans over and cups Henny's face in his big meaty hand. "I wish I could kiss you, but it's too personal," he says and I immediately recognize the line from that new movie *Pretty Woman*. My stomach tightens at the thought of interrupting their role-play. Maybe he won't see us. Of course that is ridiculous, since our table is right next to theirs.

"Molly! So great to see you! This must be your son!" Dr. Potter pushes himself out of his chair and steps closer to us with his hand held out to Grant.

Grant doesn't miss a beat, reaching for Dr. Potter's outstretched hand as if he is seasoned at meeting adults. This kid is so polished.

"Hello, I'm Grant. Nice to meet you."

"So great to meet you! We have heard so much about you!" Dr. Potter motions over to Henny. She wiggles her fingers at him in a little wave and smiles.

"How do you know my mom?" Grant asks and I see Molly stiffen and suck in a breath.

"She works with me. I am Dr. Potter, or you can call me William or Bill." He puffs out his chest a little and I look over at Molly watching as she runs her hands down the front of her shorts.

Grant turns and looks at his mom like he is seeing her for the first time. He turns back to Dr. Potter and asks the next logical question as Molly holds her breath.

"What does she do for you?" Grant's head is tilted like he's trying to process this new information.

"Your mom is the best medical assistant and X-ray tech I have ever had. You should be very proud of her," he says.

Henny chimes in, adding, "We have decided to close the clinic when she can't work. We have gotten so dependent on her." Henny is beaming at a very uncomfortable Molly. Has she never told her son about her job?

"Really? Wow, that's great. I had no idea. When did you start doing that?" Grant pivots to Molly, who has taken one of the seats at the open table. I quickly move to sit next to her, leaving Grant and Dr. Potter to stand and figure this out. I slide my hand under the table and rest it on Molly's leg that is bouncing all over the place. I give her a little squeeze and she settles down a bit.

"I've been a medical assistant for about five years. I got my X-ray certificate around the same time," Molly says quietly. Grant is staring at her like she grew a third eye.

"We were lucky she moved here, Henny is right, when Molly isn't at the clinic it's just not the same. Probably isn't fair to the community to shut down a lot though, so Molly, don't make a habit of this!" Dr. Potter throws his head back and laughs as Henny titters behind her hand.

Molly's leg starts bouncing again as Grant says, "Well, it sounds like I have a lot to talk to my mom about, if you'll excuse us?" He sounds so controlled and polite, I again marvel at how refined he is for his age.

"Of course. We were just leaving actually. Come dear, let's finish up our little game at home. See you on Monday, Molly!" Dr. Potter reaches for Henny who slides out of her chair and tucks herself under his arm.

As soon as they are out of earshot Molly leans over and asks, "What game are they talking about?"

"You do not want to know. I beg of you, please stop. No good can come from this line of questioning." I stare into her eyes with what I hope is an urgent warning kind of stare.

She slides her glasses up on the top of her head, but her scarf gets in the way so she bends and tucks them in her purse instead. I think she is trying to stall the inevitable questions from her son.

"So while I was in school, you took classes? I don't understand how you have a whole career I knew nothing about. Christ, Mom, I feel like I don't know you at all." Grant is glaring at Molly and all my instincts tell me to stay out of it, but Molly's leg starts bouncing under my hand again and I can feel how nervous she is.

"Grant—" I start but Molly puts her hand over mine, silencing me.

"I planned on telling you today, but I didn't know how to bring it up. I wanted something that was all mine, you know?" Molly is holding onto my hand like I am preventing her from falling off a cliff.

"Does Dad know you had a job? Does Grandmother?" Grant's voice is pitched a little higher but I see him slump into his chair a little, like maybe he is starting to calm down.

"No. I paid for the school with cash I had, and then my paychecks went into a bank account that they didn't know about. It's how I could afford to move here," Molly says and I feel her straighten up a little bit. She blows out a breath and continues, "I needed to figure out what *I* wanted, Grant. Your grandmother picked my major for college because she paid for it. I didn't get to make decisions about my own life. When you were twelve and got busy with school and all the clubs and stuff I looked into different classes. The medical courses seemed interesting and they turned out to be something I really enjoyed. I don't feel bad about any of it, except not telling you sooner. I can't really explain how important it was to me to have something that was all my own. I hope you can understand, if not today, then someday."

As soon as she has said her piece, her leg stops jumping and her grip on my hand loosens. I don't want to let her go though, so I hang on to her and give her a supportive smile, which she returns.

"Okay. This is a lot to process. Jesus, you make it seem like you were a prisoner or something. Was it really that bad for you, Mom?" Grant asks, his voice sounding so sad.

Before she can answer the waitress comes over with three waters and our menus. "Sorry about that. I saw you visiting with Dr. Potter and didn't want to interrupt with these. I'll be back in a few minutes to take your orders."

She's gone in a flash so we all pick up our menus even though I am pretty sure we all want the lobster quiche. My mind is racing with all the questions I want to ask but know I shouldn't.

As soon as we set our menus down on the table, the waitress is back to take our order. Molly surprises me by ordering a bowl of oatmeal with fruit, Grant gets the quiche, and I decide to copy Molly. We all sit in silence for what feels like a year, but then Grant breaks the tension.

"So you probably could have x-rayed my foot instead of that weird guy at the hospital?"

Molly almost spits her drink out of her mouth, but recovers quickly by grabbing her napkin. "Oh my God! I forgot about him! Yes, I was certified by then and I have to tell you it took all my strength not to smack him with the film cartridge. He did so many things wrong!"

"He did? Great, my foot will probably fall off or something," Grant says with a chuckle.

"No, but he shouldn't have had to take it as many times as he did, and I have no idea why he felt like he needed to drape your entire body with the lead aprons." Molly starts laughing.

Grant turns to me to explain. "I stepped on a nail and they thought a piece of it broke off in my foot, so they made me get an X-ray. The guy was in scrubs but nothing about him seemed like a normal medical person. He was covered in tattoos and wore a ring on every finger. He had these little things, like taped to his shirt too, right Mom?"

Molly snickers and jumps in, "Those are the markers, you know, left and right? They get placed on the cartridge and they show up on the film once it's developed. They help the radiologist to not review the film backwards. You only need one of each, but he had like ten or twelve taped to his scrub top. I've never seen anything like it."

"So, did you have some of the nail in your foot?" I ask.

"No, I told them the other bit of the nail was still in the board, but they didn't believe me," Grant says. I notice his more relaxed state and it calms me as well.

"They did the right thing by checking that. Oh, if that was your last tetanus shot you should come by the clinic and let me give you another one before you leave. Tom needs one too." Molly winks at me and I chuckle.

After we are done eating, I walk with Molly and Grant down to the beach, but I have a feeling I should make an excuse to leave so they can have some time alone.

I hate lying so I say what's on my mind. "I have really enjoyed meeting you, Grant. I hope I can see you when you are at Willmore. Your mom has my phone number there. Please feel free to call if you have any questions or problems."

He smiles and sticks his hand out for me, so I shake it, then pull him into a quick hug. He isn't stiff or uncomfortable and pats me on the back as he says, "I'd really like that. Thanks, Tom. Thanks for making my mom so happy. She deserves the best, you know?"

I nod. "Yes, she does."

Molly blushes and rolls her eyes a little but a smile forms on her lips. I lean over and give her a little kiss on the cheek before saying, "Call me when you're free and we will go to dinner or something."

"Okay, thanks Tom," she says before turning to her son and motioning him to keep walking with her. I watch as they continue down the beach, shoes in hand, a heavily needed conversation bouncing between them.

Molly

GRANT and I walked until there was no more beach. The rocks that jutted out into the ocean impeded our progress but made for a good place to sit and finish the conversation that was long overdue.

I lean back on my hands and tip my face to the sun, waiting for another question. It hasn't been as bad as I feared, Grant is more curious than angry now.

"Do you think Dad will come here?" he finally asks.

"I really don't know. I hope not. I don't think he was happy being married to me, but he liked that I was there, you know?"

"Not really. I thought I understood things, but since coming here I kind of feel like my whole childhood was—" he stops, shakes his head before he continues, "I don't want to say a lie, that's not the right word. Illusion? That sounds more accurate. It was all smoke and mirrors, wasn't it?" He sounds so sad and I look over at him and give him a small smile.

"I'm sorry I wasn't more honest with you. You were a kid, I didn't want my feelings about your dad or grandparents to tarnish the things in your life."

"But what about you?" he says again. He has asked that particular question more than any other. I wish I had an answer for him that didn't sound self-deprecating.

Thankfully by the time we walk back to my house the conversation drifts away from our dysfunctional family and onto his plans for the drive out to college and his friend. Apparently when they went to prom he had a little crush on her, but she made it very clear she wanted to only be friends. He accepted that and they kept in touch as she packed and moved to Davis. He has called to check on her and their friendship has grown. He says he really isn't sure if this trip will change things between them, but he promises he's happy either way.

He is up early the next day eager to reach Cathy and start their road trip. I hug him like I've wanted to every day for the past six months, and he promises to call often and send me postcards from all the places they stop. When I walk back into my house it feels different somehow.

I look around and smile. It feels more like my home than before, because it held laughter and love and even a few tears. I cross to my couch and flop down, my only goal to just breathe. I let my mind wander never really settling on any one thought, like flipping through the pages of my favorite book. I pause and chuckle at something I remember Grant saying or Tom's enthusiasm about places along the way to Willmore.

I couldn't have asked for a better visit with my son, and for that I am grateful. The phone ringing snaps me out of my thoughts and my stomach flips in hope.

"Hello?"

"Good morning, Molly. Am I correct in assuming Grant has left for Davis?" Tom's deep, smooth voice comes through the line and my face grows red.

"Good morning. Yes, he left about twenty minutes ago." I'm about to invite him over but the line goes dead. I pull it away as I hear nothing, then a dial tone. That's weird. He must have hit the receiver by accident. I hang up and wait a second, assuming he will call me back. When the phone doesn't ring right away, I call him, listening as the phone rings and rings with no answer. I get a moment of panic as I picture Tom clutching his chest or something, but before I can decide what to do there is a knock at my door.

I cock my head and laugh quietly before setting the phone down and walking to my front door. When I open it I find him trying desperately to catch his breath. He's bent at the waist and his chest is heaving but when he looks up and sees me, he straightens and takes a settling breath.

"Hi," I say with a smile.

He doesn't speak, but steps into my house and kicks the door shut with his foot. He toes off his shoes and kicks them under the bench, which makes me laugh because I can feel the passion and tension between us, but he's still being thoughtful. He steps closer to me and places his hands on my face and pulls me in for a kiss that I will never forget.

It's soft at first but quickly becomes frantic and I welcome it. I whimper as he slides his tongue along my lips wanting in, wanting more. I push him back a little and tug at his shirt, and he reaches for it as well, helping me take it off. His chest is rising and falling and I take a moment to appreciate what I am doing to him.

"Bedroom, Molly. Now. I can't wait another minute. I need you. I need to wrap you in my arms with nothing between us. I need your skin on mine, I need—"

I cut off what I'm sure would have been a great speech by grabbing his hand and pulling him down the hall to my room. Our clothes are off in a flash and then he is guiding me as I walk backwards to my bed. He presses himself against me and the feeling of his hot skin on mine is delicious. I step back feeling for the edge of the bed then I sit and stare at him, eye level with all he has to offer. I reach for his hardened length and smile when a moan escapes his lips.

I want to take him in my mouth, but I have only done that once and it was eighteen years ago. His hand on the side of my face tips my gaze up to his eyes.

"You don't have to, Molly," he says, and the look in his eyes is like nothing I have ever seen. I believe him, but more than that, I know he would understand why I am hesitant.

"I really want to do that for you, I just haven't. I mean I did once, but it was a long time ago. Can I try it and stop if I don't like it? Or if you want me to stop I can."

He shakes his head and his eyes crinkle with his smile. "Open your mouth, Molly, nice a wide. I'll be gentle." The rasp in his voice is the sexiest thing I have ever heard.

I open for him and he steps forward, grabbing himself for some control. I expect him to push in but he doesn't, he gently rubs the tip over my lips and takes a sharp breath when I dart my tongue out to lick at the head. There is a little bit of precum leaking from the tip and I swipe my tongue across it then open wide for him.

I feel the head slide past my lips so I close around him and suck a little earning a moan and a thrust.

"Sorry, Jesus, Molly. That's fucking fantastic, just like that," he says. I look up at him and love that he is watching everything I'm doing.

"You look so beautiful right now. Fuck, your lips around my cock is the most amazing thing I have ever seen." He moans and his head tips back, his hips thrust forward a little. I open wider and slide my hands to his ass pulling him in closer. His dick is hitting the back of my throat, so I swallow to fight off the gag I am feeling and Tom cusses.

"Fuck, Molly, do that again. Christ that—" he stops talking for a moment as I swallow again pulling him further into my mouth. I do that over and over and his hips start to move quicker, and he's moaning every time he hits the back of my throat. I love it. It's sexy and powerful and I never want to stop.

"Oh my God, no I can't, Molly, stop, fuck I'm going to come if you don't stop." His voice is strained and I take it as a challenge rather than a request.

I pull him closer and slide my tongue over his length letting him pull out to the tip, before I suck all of him that I can, back into my mouth. I feel him tighten and he jerks then pulls out of my mouth and grabs his cock giving it a few firm pumps. His come shoots all over my neck and chest as he shudders through the longest orgasm I have ever seen. Well, the only orgasm I have ever seen. I will never forget this. The look on his face, his tight stomach and thighs, his shudders as he pumped his release all over me.

He puts his hand on my shoulder to steady himself as his breathing starts to slow. I wait. Looking up into his handsome face and I smile when his eyes meet mine. "How'd I do?" I ask innocently.

"Molly. Jesus, are you okay? That got away from me." He looks at the mess he made and his smile grows. "You do look beautiful like that, but let me get you cleaned up." He turns and goes into my bathroom and returns quickly with a warm wet washcloth. He wipes my neck and chest with such care I feel a lump forming in my throat and I swallow hoping he doesn't notice my sudden wave of emotion.

"I'll be right back." He takes the washcloth back into the bathroom and returns, picking up his jeans before he gets to the bed. I watch as he fishes his wallet out of his back pocket. I cock my head wondering what he's doing then I see him pull out a condom. He tosses it on the bed next to me and steps between my legs.

I wrap my arms around him, burying my face in the soft dusting of hair on his stomach. His hands are moving over my hair and tickling my ears. I feel his cock jump and glance down. "I must not have done a very good job, you didn't even go soft."

"I did, it's coming back to life because you are touching me. And my cock really likes you touching me, Molly."

I laugh and scoot back onto the bed and Tom follows me, lying down over my body, caging me in. The weight of this man's body on mine feels better than anything I have ever experienced. I sigh and spread my thighs a little to let him settle between my legs.

"I want to kiss you everywhere, touch you everywhere. There isn't enough time in a day to do what I want to do to you, Molly Sparrow." His lips find mine and he kisses me thoroughly. I feel his cock nudging me and he reaches down and rubs the head through my slick flesh.

"Jesus, you're so wet," he rasps out then does it again.

"You don't have to use the condom. I'm clean, and I'm on the pill. Please Tom. I want to feel all of you, just you."

"Are you sure? I'm clean too but I want you to be comfortable."

I tilt my hips and open my legs wider as I grab his ass. He slides in like he's made for me. I arch and moan as he pushes in further, and when he is seated as far as he can go, we both freeze, relishing the moment. I could stay like this forever and I want to tell him that but I'm not sure if that would freak him out, so I pull him down so I can kiss him.

His lips move over mine in slow languid strokes and I love that he is taking his time. This kiss, while he is inside me, is as passionate as the night on the street when he first got back. I have never had kisses like this, ones that are a part of the act and not just foreplay. I feel lost and found all at once. I am on fire from his touch but it's not a flame I want to douse.

"God, Molly, I can't get enough of you." Tom moves his lips to my ear, kissing softly along my neck and down to my shoulder. He pulls up and adjusts my legs to wrap around him. He is on his knees now and there is nothing soft or sweet about how he is slamming into me. I fucking love it. My big heavy breasts are moving back and forth with each thrust of his hips. He places his hands over me and squeezes each breast gently, kneading them as he moves in and out. He slides one hand slightly and pinches my nipple, then rolls it between his fingers.

I gasp at the shock it sends through my body as I feel myself clench around him. "Oh God, Tom. That feels so good," I manage to say. I can feel a slow build of an orgasm but that can't be. I have never had an orgasm during actual sex. I didn't think it was possible for me, to be honest.

He does it again to the other nipple right as he pushes in hard. I feel a warmth start to spread and I moan as I arch into him, wanting more. He slides his hand down my stomach and without missing a beat starts to rub his thumb against my clit as he slides out. With two more thrusts I scream as pleasure rips through me.

"That's it, Molly, give it to me. God, I can feel you tightening around—" his sentence stops and he arches his back and groans as he comes, his hips jerking and thrusting without the same measured rhythm as before. He stills and looks down at me with an expression I have never seen. "Molly," he whispers and he folds over me, wrapping me in his arms.

We stay like that, tangled and sweaty until both of our breathing resumes a more normal pace. I stroke his back and run my fingers up into his hair, then repeat their journey.

"If you keep doing that I'm going to fall asleep. That feels so good."

"Do you have somewhere to be?" I whisper, not stopping my hands.

He gives a subtle shake of his head and I feel his whole body relax. His full weight on me is pure heaven. I close my eyes and drift off into a blissful dreamless sleep.

Hours later I wake to Tom's sweet kisses all over my chest with occasional gentle tugs at my nipples. I arch up to meet his mouth and he chuckles. "You are a very sound sleeper, Molly. I've been doing this for a while now."

I pull him up so I can kiss him. I sigh when his mouth finds mine and he slides his tongue along my lower lip. He nibbles at it mumbling something about merlot, but then he stops and says, "I never want to stop doing this, but my stomach has other plans. Would you object to ordering in? I'd take you out, but I am feeling like a selfish bastard at the moment and I don't want to share you with anyone." He doesn't wait for an answer, just moves back to his earlier position of worshiping my breasts with soft gentle kisses.

I turn my head slightly and see that it's a little after one and as if my stomach realized the time too, it rumbles loudly. Tom laughs and pulls up, looking down at me with delight he says, "I'm going to take that as a yes, let's order in?" His eyes are crinkled with the smile that has taken over his whole face.

"Chinese? Or pizza? Or that little deli a few streets over. I can walk over and pick it up if we call it in," I offer. All of that sounds good. I wonder if he would laugh if I suggest we order something from every place. I am ravenous.

"Chinese, because I know they deliver," he answers. "Do you have a favorite dish or should I get a little of everything?" Tom asks as he slides down my body kissing me softly on the stomach. I tense a little and I hope he doesn't notice.

I have never had anyone touch me this way, it's hard to process. I feel like a goddess or something, the way he caresses me with his hands and mouth. The way his gaze travels over every inch of my body with such reverence makes me feel like I actually deserve this.

He makes a humming noise as he slides his hands under my ass lifting me up a little to kiss each hip. "I need to get the phone, but you are distracting me."

"I'm just lying here," I say innocently. I'm not about to stop this wonderful man from whatever he has planned, even if it means waiting a while longer for food.

Tom

⟡

AFTER WE EACH had another toe-curling orgasm, I finally pulled myself away long enough to get the cordless phone from the kitchen and order Chinese food. I decided to wait on the porch for the delivery, because Molly said she wanted a shower. The thought of warm water sliding over those perfect breasts, and hips was too much, so outside is safer if we actually want to eat today.

I rub my hand down my face and try to recall another time I was this overwhelmed by a woman. I come up short, because there has been no one in my life like Molly Kristen Sparrow. It's like the most beautiful soul was wrapped inside a perfect body, and all of that was topped off with a face that could stop a thousand wars. Or start them, I really can't decide which. I am so far gone for this woman that I don't hear the delivery boy's bell the first time.

"You okay, mister?"

I look up and see a boy about twelve years old holding out a bag to me. I smile at him and apologize. "Oh sorry, yeah, I'm fine. Thank you for bringing this." I hand him the cash and point to the five-dollar bill on top. "That's your tip, okay?"

"Really? That's awesome! Thank you!" He takes the cash and I lift the bag out of his hands, smiling at how heavy it is. I am starving, and I bet Molly is too.

I walk back into the house and make quick work of finding plates and silverware. When Molly comes out I have everything plated and ready to go. I turn to make a gesture at the table, but my breath catches in my throat at the sight of her. She is wearing some silky matching top and shorts that hug her curves like I want to. Jesus, she is so beautiful.

"Molly," I manage to say, with my throat dry and my heart racing.

"How do you do that?" she asks shyly.

I step forward and reach for her hands, intertwining our fingers so I can pull her into me. "Do what?" I say as my gaze searches her face.

"Say my name like that, how do you make it sound so sexy?" She places a gentle kiss on my lips and we both freeze in place. My whole body flushes hot at her touch and my heart squeezes in my chest.

"I don't mean to, it's just, look at you, Molly. How could I not?" I trail my finger over her cheek and brush a small curl behind her ear. "You are quite literally the most beautiful creature I have ever laid eyes on."

She tries to look down but I slip my finger under her chin and hold her so she can't. "Molly," I say again, quieter this time hoping she feels the weight of it.

Her eyes shine with tears but she doesn't pull away or try and look down, she holds my gaze and whispers my name. "Thomas."

I blink slowly soaking in the feeling that shot through my heart. Pure joy, mixed with hope and longing. I swallow hard and lower my forehead to hers. "Are you hungry? I ordered enough food for an army."

"Starving," she says, giving me a quick peck on the lips before stepping out of my grasp. "You need to let me eat or you will meet grumpy Molly. I tend to need food after being ravaged for hours."

I laugh at that and motion for her to sit. "I hope this is the first time you are experiencing a sex-induced starvation, Molly." I raise an eyebrow at her hoping she hears the teasing nature of my comment.

"I can honestly say yes to that. I've never felt like this before." She stiffens a little after she says that, so I reach across the table to grab her hand.

"I haven't either, Molly." I squeeze her hand, hoping she believes me.

She pulls her hand away and color flushes her cheeks before she says, "I'm glad to hear that, Thomas." Then she laughs. "I can't do it. You are not a Thomas to me." She's shaking her head but a smile is on her lips.

I laugh and say, "I like to hear you say Tom, especially when it's all breathy." I wiggle my eyebrows at her and pluck a wonton from my plate.

We both eat in comfortable silence then pack up the leftovers before moving to the couch to sit and talk. Seems safer than returning to the bedroom, where I know I wouldn't be able to keep my hands to myself.

"How was the rest of your day with Grant? Was he really angry at you for not telling him about your job?" I ask. Her legs are draped over mine and I'm tracing a pattern on her thighs, enjoying the goosebumps I'm causing.

"He was, but the more we talked, I think he came to terms with it. He said that he doesn't know how to be around his father anymore and I hate that."

"His relationship with his father is *his*, Molly. Don't take on that burden."

She sighs and tips her head back to rest on the throw pillow. I can't help but stare at her exposed neck as it slopes down to her chest. She's not wearing a bra and the silky tank top she's wearing stretches tight across her breasts. I watch her nipples as I trace my fingers higher up her thighs and smile when I see them harden.

"I know I shouldn't, but I made it my personal mission in life to not come in between my son and Isaac or his parents. I was so grateful for everything they were doing for him, how could I turn him against them?"

"But you didn't feel the same love they were giving your son, did you, Molly?"

"No, not even close. I felt like an outsider, sometimes I felt like Grant wasn't even mine. They hired a nanny as soon as he was born and I had to fight to hold my own son. I was so young and scared, I didn't know how to deal with that."

"Jesus, Molly, I'm so sorry." It makes me so sad to hear about her past, but I want to know it, to know how she became the woman she is now. The woman I seem to be falling head over heels in love with.

"It's okay. I mean, really to anyone else I was lucky. Isaac could have driven off that day and never returned. My mom and I would have struggled to deal with a baby, but I would have made it work."

"I have no doubt that you would have. That must've been hard to see your own mother leave when you needed her most. I wish she would have fought for you, or at least stuck around."

"Did I tell you I found her?" Molly sits up suddenly when she says that, her eyes wide.

"No! How?"

Molly recounts seeing a woman she thought was her mom in a town along the way here, and taking a chance to call information to see if she had a listed number. I marvel at her as she tells me, and feel proud when she says she hung up without leaving a message.

We talk more about her mom and the conversation flows to my parents and all the ways I feel I let them down over the years. She asks questions about my sisters and Nick and I love that her face lights up when I talk about the chaos that was my childhood. I think when you're an only child you have no idea what it's like to have that kind of insanity. I also don't know the peace of knowing if I left a cookie on the counter to get some milk it would still be there when I returned.

We return to the Chinese food we had for lunch sometime around seven and adjourn to the bedroom eventually. I don't want to assume I can stay over but at this point she will have to tell me to leave.

* * *

"Tom? Are you awake?" I hear a sweet voice close to my ear and my already hard cock twitches.

"Only if you're naked," I mumble and earn a giggle.

"I have to get to work. You can stay as long as you like, just lock the front door and pull it shut tight when you leave," Molly says causing me to sit up and look over at her clock. Jesus, I didn't mean to sleep so late. It's almost eight.

I look at her and she's wearing the same pink scrubs she wore the day I went to the clinic with my enormous splinter. I grab her and pull her back into bed with one firm tug and she laughs.

"Those scrubs do things to me, Molly. Did you know that?" I kiss her neck as I run my hands down to her full, perfect ass. Jesus, this woman is going to be the death of me.

"You like them? They aren't very flattering," she says.

I thrust my hips to show her how flattering I think they are and she giggles, but it quickly turns into a moan. "God, Tom, that feels so good. What are you doing to me?"

"Hopefully this," I say as I reach between us and untie the strings at her waist.

"Okay, yes, we have to be quick," she says as she pulls her top off and undoes her bra, tossing both on the floor. I help her out of her pants and she straddles me, rocking her center against me.

"Do you always wake up like this, or can I take some credit?" Molly asks as she rotates her hips over my painfully hard cock.

"This is all for you," I say as I grab my length and guide it into her.

She settles all the way down, taking me into the place I have come to know as my heaven. She stills and leans forward a little placing her hands on my chest before she starts to move back and forth a little, then up and down, finding her rhythm. Her big, full breasts are on display and I think I have found my favorite position with her.

I reach up and hold her breasts as she bounces and twist one nipple gently between my finger and thumb. I feel her tighten around me and I look up into her face and see the same intensity I feel reflected back at me. She leans forward a bit and I guide her breast into my waiting mouth, sucking and pulling on her nipple.

"Oh my God, Tom, please. Don't stop, that feels—" her words stop and her hips move more frantically as I feel my balls tighten, I try and hold back so I can feel her fall apart, but it's too late. I shatter right along with her, tumbling down the cliffs into the waiting sea.

I hold her tight as we both gasp and shudder out the remains of our pleasure. She pulls up enough to press her lips gently to mine, and I kiss her. I kiss her like it's the first time, like I am reborn and she is my god.

"How will I let you go, Molly?" I whisper as we finally pull apart. Her eyes are sparkling with tears.

"I have to go to work, Tom," she says quietly, and we both pretend
that is what I meant.

201

Molly

I HAVE HAD MORE sex in the last week than I have in my entire adult life. I went so long without it and had no idea it could be so good that now, at thirty-three, I feel like a teenager.

He is all I can think about, his kind heart and wonderful sense of humor. I also can't seem to stop thinking about his cock and the magical things he can do with it. Thank God he seems to be as ravenous as I am when it comes to sex.

I tap my foot anxiously as Dr. Potter explains in vivid detail how to collect a stool sample to our last patient of the day. That is usually my job, but this is the third time Mr. Jensen has tried to bring me his poop in a zip-top baggie.

"Now George, repeat after me—" Dr. Potter starts, but I step out of the room before he can finish. I double-check that all the bloodwork is bagged and placed in the pick-up box that hangs on the back door. I turn all the lights off in the rooms except of course where Dr. Potter is still droning on about poop protocol. Henny is finishing up the filing for the day, so I lean on the counter and smile at her.

"Did you already send the phone to the service?" I ask, clutching my purse out of her sight. I hope she's okay with me leaving, I hate to ask, even if it is after five.

"Yes, I did. You can get out of here, Molly. I think we can manage if you want to get over to see Tom." She winks at me and I give her a small grin. She's really nice, but something I didn't know about Henny until I started dating Tom is that she loves to talk about her sex life. She has told me things that will haunt me until the day I die, and asked me questions that are probably illegal for an employer to ask.

"Thanks, I am going to Willows tomorrow to see my best friend Lisa, so Tom was hoping I could stop by tonight," I explain. I have found that if I am talking, she isn't, so my new defense against learning things like how Dr. Potter likes to have his testicles tickled with a feather, is to talk constantly. With no breaths. Never pause, or I learn what flavor of lube he likes.

"Well you can hurry on over there, and Molly, please remember to ask him if he would like to try that cock ring. I have extra and I don't think—"

I wave over my shoulder and hurry to the front door before she can finish. As soon as I step out onto the sidewalk I shudder and hoist my purse back up on my shoulder. Thank God Tom works close by, and I can see him in just a few steps.

I freeze at that thought, because that won't be true for nine months of the year. I squeeze my eyes shut and blow out a breath. Nope. I am not going to dwell on that. Live in the moment, cry later. My new motto. Maybe I can get a bumper sticker that says that?

I push into The Floppy Fish and let my eyes adjust. Tom is nowhere to be seen and there is already a good-sized Friday night crowd. "Hey, Jerald," I say with a wave.

"Hey, Molly. Tom's upstairs, he said to tell you to go on up." Jerald thumbs over his shoulder in the direction of the stairs.

"Thanks." I smile at him and head up the narrow staircase, finding the door open at the top. I can hear the shower going so I make myself comfortable, kicking off my shoes and climbing up on his bed.

He starts singing and I cover my mouth with my hands to muffle the laughter. I would pay a lot of money to have a recording of him belting out "Free Bird." He's not half bad, but when he gets to the bye-bye line his voice cracks like a teenage boy.

I stand and cross to the bathroom door and knock. "Tom? I wanted to let you know I'm here. Great singing, by the way."

I hear him laugh, then he says something I can't hear, so I crack open the door. "What?" I ask.

"I said, it sounds better in here. Why are you out there?" He peeks his head out of the shower curtain to wiggle his eyebrows at me.

I laugh then ask, "You want me to join you? Seriously?"

"Yes," he says with confidence as he pulls the shower curtain open further then does some weird hip maneuver that causes his cock to swirl in a circle.

I burst out laughing and pull off my scrub top. "You don't have to ask me twice if that kind of cock-robatics is happening in there."

I take the rest of my clothes off and step into the shower with Tom. I glance down at his now very hard cock and ask, "Can it still spin?"

"Not as much, but it's still entertaining," he says as he reaches for me. I have gotten so comfortable with him, I no longer have that unease at him seeing me naked in bright lights. It is something I never thought I'd have with someone and I love it. I love that I feel just as comfortable in front of him as I do when I am alone.

He pulls me into him and lets his lips gently connect with mine. It's slow and measured, everything I want and yet not enough. I whimper and pull him closer, loving how hard he feels against my stomach. There is something I have learned about Tom since we started having sex: He loves to be in control. I have taken the lead once or twice, but I found out that I really like it when he is the one calling the shots.

"On your knees, Molly," he says with his lips very close to my ear. I close my eyes and relish the warm rush that I feel at his words.

I drop slowly, keeping my eyes directed up to his face the whole time. I've learned he also likes that. I looked back at him once when he was behind me and he came so hard he almost blacked out. I love that I have this kind of effect on him. I have never felt more beautiful in my life.

I grasp his hardened length and rub the tip across my closed lips, which earns me a deep moan from Tom. I smile and dart my tongue out to circle the head. It jumps in my hand and I watch as Tom lets his head drop back, his hand going flat on the shower wall.

"Fuck, that feels so good, Molly," he says. "You are a very quick learner. It's never felt like this."

I try and take that as a compliment and not picture other women on their knees for him. We haven't talked a lot about his past love life, but he knows about the two people I have been with. I don't even realize I have paused until I feel his hand caress my cheek.

"Are you okay?" Tom asks with such kindness in his voice I feel myself blush with embarrassment.

I nod my head and hollow out my cheeks giving him one good long suck as I let his cock spring free of my lips. I stand and turn so my back is to him, loving that he immediately wraps me in his arms. I let my head fall back to his shoulder and he reaches for the soap and washes every part of me he can reach. It's not sexual, but loving, and my eyes sting with tears.

"Molly, what did I say?" he whispers in my ear. I thought I was hiding it, but apparently not.

I turn and loop my arms over his shoulders, pulling him closer. I kiss him softly trying to regain my confidence before I tell him what happened. I should have continued, instead of making such a big deal about this. This is more embarrassing than if I had ignored the comment.

"I just—" I blow out a breath before I continue. "I worry that you've been with women who have more experience than me, who know what they're doing, you know? I want to make you happy."

"Molly," he says in that way he does, and he places both hands on my face making me look up at him. "No one has ever pleased me more."

The intensity of his eyes and the gentle grasp on my face makes my tears form. One slips free and he gently presses his lips to mine. Nothing exists outside of this warm little shower, where Tom is kissing me like I am the only woman he has ever kissed. Like I am the only woman who matters.

"There are things I want to tell you, Molly, but it isn't fair. You need to be free. It's like if I were to try and capture the wind and keep it to myself. I don't have the right." He kisses me once more before reaching back and turning off the water.

We dry off in silence. My mind is spinning with what he just said, unsure if he means he is letting me go. Do I want that? We only have one more month together. Should we stop whatever this is?

He pulls a T-shirt out of a drawer and hands it to me as I reach for my scrubs. "I took the night off, Molly. Put this on or stay naked. Your choice." He gives me that smile with the dimples and my stomach forgets about the what ifs and tumbles down the hill.

I pull his T-shirt on and let out a sigh at how soft it is. It's just a plain white T-shirt, probably one he wears under a button-up, but I love it more than anything I own. It smells like him and it hangs on me, making me feel small and dainty. I didn't realize how much I would love that.

We climb into bed and he pulls me up so that my head is resting on his chest. As he strokes my hair, gently running his fingers through the wet strands I want to purr. It feels so good.

"Are you okay now?" he asks. He bends and kisses the top of my head.

"Yes, I'm sorry. I didn't mean to derail our shower sex."

"Shower sex is highly overrated if you ask me. I prefer this." He traces his finger up and down my arm.

"Me too."

"I didn't mean to compare you to other women. I wish you knew that there is no comparison, Molly."

I give him a little squeeze wishing I felt that with all confidence. "I don't know how that can be true, Tom, but thank you for being so kind."

"Come to Connecticut. Come visit your son, come see me. There is usually a parent weekend the second weekend in September. Please say yes. Please make plans with me." He says the last part so quietly I almost miss it.

I turn so I can look up at him before I ask, "You want that? You want to see me after you leave?"

"Yes, but that is what I meant earlier, Molly. You deserve to be free if that is what you want. I know what your life has been. You have worked really hard to get here, to this point, and I don't want to swoop in and steal your freedom."

"I have never thought of what we have like that, Tom," I say, then quickly elaborate. "I don't feel like I need freedom from you. I have really been enjoying whatever this is, and I'm struggling with the fact that you are leaving soon. Does that sound too needy?" I huff out my exasperation. "See that is what I mean, I don't know how to do this, I don't want you to think I am—"

Tom cuts me off with a gentle kiss. It's soft and sweet and I expect him to stop, but his hands start moving and my mind settles a little knowing we don't have to talk any more.

This is what I need right now. I need to feel him around me, holding me, touching me like I am all that matters. When he rolls me onto my back and cages me in with his strong arms I let him love me because he is all that matters.

* * *

"Okay you are going to need to explain that again. She offered you a cock ring?" Lisa slaps the table and snorts a laugh, making me almost spit my root beer out of my nose. I rub at the bridge trying to ward off the stinging feeling that I know is coming.

"I am not kidding. She has told me things, Lisa. I need therapy."

"God, I missed you," she says reaching for my hand across the table. I squeeze her hand and smile.

"I missed you too. I don't know how it's been over eighteen years. When I look into your beautiful face it seems like yesterday."

Lisa blushes and pushes her hair out of her face. "You are sweet. Sometimes I feel like I'm in my fifties instead of my thirties. Paul loves me and my kids are happy, so I shouldn't feel that way. Can I tell you something, Molly?" she asks, and I nod.

"I miss having small, firm boobs. I miss being able to bend over and not having my tits look like someone dropped golf balls into a pair of tube socks."

I snort and push my soda away, afraid to take another drink while she's talking. I forgot how funny she is.

"I miss being able to wear a pair of pants that don't double for a push-up bra. Why is the waistband so high? I shouldn't have to lean back to get my tiny boobs out of the way when I button my pants!"

"We don't have the same problems, Lisa." I wipe a tear from my eye but then lift my T-shirt and point to my jeans that are a good inch above my belly button. "This waistband doesn't stand a chance against my boobs. I swear everyone said I'd have a smaller chest after nursing. That is the opposite of what happened. I got huge. Maybe that would've happened anyway, since I got pregnant at sixteen maybe I was always destined to have a huge chest."

"Okay, listen, we've had a great time talking about all the things wrong with our thirty-year-old bodies, but I want to hear more about this Tom guy." Lisa stares at me over her soda.

I stall not wanting to say what is really on my mind, but eventually I have to tell her. I don't know why it feels like I'm doing something wrong, but it does.

"He's really great. I like him a lot, more than I probably should."

Lisa raises her eyebrows at me and cocks her head before asking, "Why do you say that?"

"Because, Lisa, I just got out of a bad marriage, out of a situation where I felt trapped. I have no business falling in love with somebody else."

Her eyebrows shoot up to her hairline, and she takes a drink of her soda before she says, "Love? Hoo boy, you move quick."

I wince at that. This is what I was afraid of. Maybe I am jumping in too soon and maybe this isn't love that I feel. I'm so screwed up because of what happened when I was young. I don't even know what I want now.

I stare back at Lisa, wondering what it was like for her when she met Paul.

"How did you know Paul was the right guy for you?" I ask.

"I'm not really sure," she says. She twirls her straw a little before continuing. "I think I realized that my days without him were worse than my days when he was around and, he was always around. He fell first." She laughs at the smile I give her then continues, "I took a little convincing. Every time we were together I laughed and felt so happy. I guess I realized eventually, that that was love. Do you feel that way about Tom?"

"Yes? I mean I think so. I really don't know, Lisa, I love spending time with him and we have so much in common, but there are so many things in the way."

"Like what?" Lisa asks.

"Well, the biggest thing is that he doesn't live here year-round. He lives in Connecticut and he comes out for the summer to help his friend Lyle run the bar."

"Well, that does seem like a big deal. Do you want to move to Connecticut?" Lisa asks.

"Move? God, I don't know, Lisa, we have barely started seeing each other. He's the first guy I have ever really dated, you know? Isaac doesn't count. That wasn't dating." I roll my eyes and laugh but Lisa just gives me a thin-lipped smile.

"Sounds like you have a lot to think about," she says.

"I want more time with him, Lisa, without him leaving hanging over my head, you know?"

"But you can't change that, so why not embrace it? You said Grant will be there, right? If he takes all the right classes he will still be there for at least four years, so you do have time to figure this out. Maybe stop worrying about what comes next? Just enjoy what you have."

I nod at her, amazed that after all this time she still knows how to make me feel better. It makes me sad that I missed out on all this for the past eighteen years. Not just sad—if I'm being honest. I'm angry. When I first met with my therapist I dealt with a lot of this bottled-up rage, and I thought I had a grasp on it, but now I know I have only a slight hold. Right now it feels like trying to hold onto Jello.

"What does Grant think about Tom?" Lisa asks.

I shake my head a little to clear my head before I answer,

"They got along great. Grant is old enough now to understand what a moron his father is." I try to make it seem like a joke, and thankfully Lisa laughs.

"I wish I could remember him a little better, I just have a like a glimmer of a dark-haired guy with those aviator shades, oh and that hair! Remember we thought he looked like Elvis?"

I bark out a laugh. "No, I thought he looked like James Dean! The way he dangled that cigarette off his lips was the sexiest thing I had ever seen." I pause then add, "That actually should have been my first clue that he was older than me."

Lisa lifts a shoulder in a little shrug and smiles. "I know this isn't going to be helpful or even what you want to hear, but he was really smitten with you."

"I do remember that." I pull my drink back in front of me and take a long pull from the straw.

"Did that last at all?" Lisa asks with sadness laced through her words.

"I don't really know how to answer that. He wasn't mean or anything, but the whole time I was pregnant he was gone. Finishing his degree, or learning the business with his father. I didn't see him very much."

"So you lived with his parents?" Lisa's eyebrow lifts and she pushes her empty plate away.

"Yes, until I was eighteen. Once Isaac and I got married we moved into our own place," I explain, even though we have talked about this before. I guess I didn't answer all her questions.

"God, Molly, I'm sorry I couldn't help you. I have to tell you your story haunts me." Lisa looks down at the table, like she can't bear to look at me.

"I'm okay, really. It's not like I was locked in a dungeon or anything. I got my high school diploma, then I went to UC San Diego. I mean, none of that would have happened without Isaac's family." My heart squeezes at that, the old familiar guilt I have for accepting everything they offered.

"What was your wedding like?" Lisa asks, and I force a smile.

"I think there are some pictures in *People* magazine if you really want to see."

"What? Are you serious?" Lisa's eyes go wide and she leans in. "Why? Is his family famous or something? I know they are rich, but is that enough to make *People* magazine show up at your wedding?"

I laugh and duck my head before explaining. "Isaac went on a date with Farrah Fawcett before he met me. They spun the whole thing like I stole him from her. She had just got that role in *The Six Million Dollar Man*, so they wanted to dig up something. I think there is a picture of her and her husband sitting on the groom's side as I walked down the aisle. I guarantee she was not upset at all about Isaac getting married. To be honest I don't believe it was even a date. I think she felt bad for him and agreed to go out for a drink. I'm pretty sure Vivian orchestrated the whole thing so the press would come."

"That sounds like something she would do." Lisa nods her head like she is now an expert in all things Densworth.

"She was, and still is, all about the appearance of things. I guess if you have a billion-dollar empire, it's important to make the public think you have your shit together." I shrug and attempt a smile. I need to put the feelings I have back in perspective. My life has changed so much, and the path I am on now is all for me. Vivian doesn't get a say in my life anymore and neither does Isaac.

We spend the rest of the day catching up, talking and getting to know each other all over again. It's so weird that so much time has passed and yet there are moments with her that feel like we haven't missed a beat.

As I drive back through the windy roads to Mendocino, I think about something she said. I don't know if she meant it the way it came out, but it made me think. She asked me when I was going to start living for me. I paused at that, because I felt like the last six months have been completely for me. The job I have, the house I bought, and all the things I have done since I moved away, have been an expression of what I've always wanted. But Lisa sees something different and I'm trying to understand that as I make my way home.

I know she is going off things that sixteen-year-old me said and did, but I had forgotten a lot of what she brought up. I had forgotten my own dreams.

MOLLY SEEMS different after her visit with Lisa, but I can't quite put my finger on what's changed. She and I have spent almost every night together and while I have enjoyed the hell out of having her near me and under me, I worry about how I will survive when I go back to Willmore for the school year.

"So Grant is all settled?" I ask Molly over dinner at her place on Sunday night.

"Yes, he sounded happy when he called. I wish I could have gone out there to help with that, but I'm sure his grandparents had it covered."

The edge I hear in her voice gives me a momentary pause. Is that what has changed? She's angrier? That's not quite the right term, she's not mad, just like, feistier.

"Does it bother you that they're still a part of his life?' I ask. I pour her a little more wine, then lean back and wait for her to answer.

"No. Yes. Not really, but also so much I want to find a way to roundhouse kick my ex-mother-in-law." She pauses and looks up at me. "Does that make sense?"

"Completely," I tell her. I have to fight the smile I feel creeping in.

"Sorry, Tom, I feel like I've been on edge lately. I've had a lot on my mind."

"I noticed, but I figured if you wanted to talk about it you would. I don't want to pry."

I see her face soften with my words and that tugs on my heart a bit. I've noticed that with her, that she tries to act tough but there is a part of her that needs this. Needs me. I like that more than I should.

"Tom, you aren't prying. I love having your input. I haven't ever had that before. That's the other thing I am struggling with, if I can be completely honest."

"Please, Molly. I hope you know you can tell me anything." I reach for her hand and give her a little squeeze.

"I was married to Isaac for about sixteen years. It was never more than an arrangement to make his mother happy. We weren't in love, hell, most days we barely spoke." She pauses and takes a drink of her wine then flips her hand over, so I rest my palm on hers. Her soft skin is such a drug to me. I let my eyes close briefly as I trace my finger across her wrist.

"There was a time when Grant was about five that Isaac and I tried to make something of our marriage. He brought me flowers and we went on dates, both of us trying for the first time to make an effort. It was nice, until . . ."

I wait, hoping she doesn't say he hurt her, because I really don't want to go to jail for murder and I don't know if I could hide a body like Kent Price does so often.

Molly blows out a breath and shakes her head a little like she is clearing a memory. "Until we both realized we had nothing in common but our son." She lowers her voice to almost a whisper before saying, "Isaac is what my mom used to call, one slice short of a loaf."

I try again to fight the smile forming on my lips but it's no use. Molly sees it and soon her beautiful smile makes an appearance as well.

"Not bright?' I ask, and she laughs.

"Dumb as a box of rocks, Tom." She shakes her head again and her beautiful laugh tickles my soul.

"We all have our shortcomings. Maybe he has street smarts, or a good head for business?" I release her hand and finish my wine.

"We were talking about politics and he asked me if Jimmy Carter was president of just California, or the whole United States. Apparently he voted for him because he thought he was picking a leader for California. It's like he had zero understanding of our government." She tips her wineglass back, finishing it off.

"Well, that certainly is—" I pause, unsure how to continue.

"Dumb, Tom. It was dumb. He got mad at me for letting Grant read *The Hitchhiker's Guide to the Galaxy* because he said no son of his was going to hitchhike!"

I laugh at that, unable to help myself. "So what does he do for work, or does he work? I get the feeling his parents are wealthy."

"Ridiculously so, but yes, he works." Molly makes little quote motions with her fingers when she says the word *works*. "He has a title within his parents' company, but honestly I don't think they give him actual responsibilities. He's more like a figurehead."

"I see. So Grant got his good looks and brains from you then?" I ask. We have finished our wine and dinner, so I gather the dishes and place them in the sink. Molly turns in her chair to watch me rinse the dishes before loading them in her small dishwasher.

"You know, I never thought a man doing dishes would be so incredibly sexy." She rests her chin in her palm and her eyes dance with mischief.

"I aim to please, Molly. Perhaps one day I could perform these tasks in the buff for your viewing pleasure?" I waggle my eyebrows at her, earning that glorious laugh of hers.

"Oh yes, please! I think I would enjoy that very much, Tom."

I hit "start" on the dishwasher and dry my hands with the towel she had placed neatly on the counter. My eye catches on a stack of papers with a list of colleges on the top. I cock my head and move closer to read it, before realizing she might not want me to see it.

"I was going to talk to you about that," She stands and crosses to me, twisting her hands together like she's nervous.

"Are you thinking of going back to school, Molly?" I ask.

"Yes, well I am looking at my options." She stops and gently places a hand on my arm before continuing. "I think I want to get my RN license. I've called around to these schools and they are sending me more information about their programs."

"Molly, that is incredible! What brought this on? I thought you loved your job?" I take her hand and lead her to the couch so we can sit and be more comfortable.

"Lisa. I mean I guess I started thinking about it on our first date, if I'm honest." She sits on the couch and immediately lifts her legs to my lap. She knows I love to run my hands up and down her thighs, so she gets in position without me having to ask.

"I'm going to need more of an explanation, Molly," I say squeezing her knee. She jumps a little and swats my hand away.

"Lisa said I was settling. That she expected I'd be a charge nurse in the ICU, not a medical assistant at a walk-in clinic." Molly rests her head on her arm and sinks into the couch some more as I gently massage her legs.

"Why would she say that? What you do has value. I told you that on our first date, if I remember correctly."

She smiles at me, her eyes crinkling. "You did say that, I appreciated it then and now."

"But you want more?" I ask.

"I want to be challenged. At first this job was amazing because I was still learning, but I find myself getting bored now and I don't want to live like that. Can I tell you something?"

"Of course." I give her another squeeze but higher this time, enjoying the way her eyes flutter shut for a moment.

"The day you came in with that impressive splinter was the most interesting day I had in such a long time. I felt, I don't know how to describe it really. I guess I felt alive?" she says, her voice going quiet at the end of her sentence.

I hold it in for as long as I can, which is about three seconds. My head tips back and I laugh. A deep, shoulder-shaking belly laugh.

"What's so funny?" Molly says, pushing my shoulder. She is smiling as I turn a little on the couch to face her.

"I'm glad I could provide you with some excitement, Molly. I'd volunteer to do it again, but I might not be as lucky the second time."

She pushes my shoulder again but then leaves her hand there a moment before letting it trail up my neck and into my hair. I sigh and lean into her touch. "You make me feel alive, Molly."

I watch as her skin turns that lovely shade of pink and she casts her eyes down. She traces circles at the nape of my neck and I wish I could purr. I have never enjoyed a woman's touch as much as I do hers. I could lie down and let her run her hands all over me and it would be almost as good as sex with her. Okay, that might be a stretch, but it's close.

"So you think it's a good idea? Me going after my RN?" she asks with such vulnerability it hurts my heart.

"I think that whatever brings you joy, or makes you feel alive, I will support a hundred percent."

She leans forward and places a featherlight kiss to my lips. I fight the urge to deepen it, letting her set the pace. I want her to know what's in my heart, what I have realized, but I don't want to muddy the waters for her. She needs to make decisions that will benefit her, not us. Not for me.

She continues to kiss me, teasing and delighting me as she moves to straddle my lap. Her hands are on both sides of my face now, softly holding me in place. It's unnecessary—I'm not going anywhere.

"Tom?" She has pulled back enough to look me in the eyes and I feel my breathing hitch a little. She is so beautiful like this, close to me, on me. I run my hand up and into her hair.

"Yes?' is all I can manage because at this moment I can't read her. That is unusual. I feel like in the short time that I've known her I've been able to see what's in her heart. She is nibbling on her lower lip like she did in the bar the first night.

"Can I be honest with you?" she asks but dives in for a kiss before I can answer.

We kiss like we are learning each other again, slow and sweet. Her full, beautiful lips are my drug and I take hit after hit knowing there will never be enough of her kisses. I pull her closer to me, suddenly missing her, even though she is right here.

She comes to me, her chest pressing against mine and I feel the rise and fall of her breathing, the rapid beat of her heart. I memorize this moment, etch it into my soul so that when she is gone I will have this to hold onto.

"Wait, I really need to tell you this, sorry." She pulls back but stays on my lap. I let my hands rest on her hips and drop my head back to the couch cushion.

"Go ahead, Molly, you have my attention." I give her hips a little squeeze and earn a giggle.

"I'm glad, and I hope that what I'm about to say doesn't change that or scare you away. I've given this a lot of thought and it seems fair to let you know, so you have all the facts." She takes a deep breath and I try not to laugh, I can see how nervous she is and I can't imagine why, or what has gotten her so worked up all of a sudden.

"IthinkImightbefallinginlovewithyou," she says and it comes out like a word, not a sentence. Then she jumps up off my lap and starts to pace back and forth. She shakes out her hands, then wrings them together. "I know maybe it's too soon to say something like that, and I want you to know I don't need you to say it back. I mean that would be great if you also felt that way, but I get it if you don't. I just don't know where I'll be going to school and if I'm not here next summer when you come back, I wanted to tell you I think you are amazing and I am so grateful I had the chance to get to know you." Her words continue to spill out of her like the little pills in a bean bag that has ruptured.

She pauses and I contemplate standing and going to her, but then she launches into another speech. I feel the smile on my lips growing with each word.

"I mean, listen you have to know what a catch you are, and I am sure there are women at Willmore who have thrown themselves at you in the past. I am under no delusions that will stop. So that is part of the reason I wanted to tell you how I feel. You know, in case that makes a difference. I can't possibly ask you to wait for me while I go through the nursing program. That is what, at least a few years, maybe longer?"

I scoot to the edge of the couch cushion and hold out my arms, waiting for her to see me. She spins, ready to launch into another one-woman discussion about her unrealistic feelings for me. She takes a sharp breath when she sees me.

"Come here, Molly."

The expression on her face is a mix of longing and fear and I can barely wait until she is in front of me. I place a hand on each hip and curl my fingers in. "Kneel, Molly."

She drops willingly and quickly to her knees before me and I widen my legs to accommodate her. I move one hand slowly up her body until

I reach her beautiful face. She leans into my palm and closes her eyes. I take a moment to study her. I have never seen a woman so utterly breathtaking as her, and to have her on her knees before me is almost too much to bear. I lean forward and press my lips to hers, breathing deeply as I do. She whimpers as I pull away.

"Molly," I say on a breath, then steal one more kiss before I tell her what I have kept close to my heart for a while now.

"I don't *think* I am falling in love with you, Molly Kristen Sparrow. I *have* fallen over the cliff and into the deep beautiful sea that is you. You pulled me in and under and I am but a small ship hoping you will take mercy on me and let me love you."

I watch her eyes fill with tears, and like before, as one spills over, I catch it with my thumb. I love how easily her emotions reveal themselves. There is never a moment when I have to wonder how she's feeling. I can see it, feel it. I kiss her again with a new emotion growing in my heart. I will let it sit for now because confessing our love to each other is enough for today, I don't need to tell her I want to marry her. That might be more than she is ready for.

* * *

I wake to soft kisses on my eyelids, my cheeks, my neck and finally a quick one on my lips. "Bye, Tom," she says as she smooths her hand over my hair.

I try to pull her back into bed where she belongs, but she must've been expecting it because she is just beyond my reach.

"Not again, Tom, you need to give me some time to recover from that marathon last night. I feel like I ran a hundred miles, my legs are so sore." She laughs but I groan because I am picturing her riding me last night, those big, beautiful tits bouncing as she chased her pleasure.

"Where are you going?" I manage to mumble. I roll to my stomach hoping to sneak close enough to grab her, but she must be a mind reader because she has moved farther away from the bed and my grabby hands.

"Work. I have to talk to Dr. Potter today about the fact that I'll be leaving if I get into a nursing program."

I open my eyes and push up to see her better. She's wearing a pair of pale blue scrubs and has a matching headband holding back her growing hair. The look of worry etched across her face has me sitting up. "What's wrong, Molly?"

"What if he gets mad, or won't give me a letter of recommendation? He and Henny are constantly saying they can't run the place without me, what if they won't support me in this? I can see it happening Tom, that is a real possibility." Her voice has pitched up a little higher and she's back to pacing and hand-wringing.

"Molly, I am sure they will support you," I say, but really how could I know that? Dr. Potter closed the clinic when Molly took time off to see her son, so maybe they would make this hard for her.

I stand and cross to her, placing my hands on her shoulders. She looks into my eyes and her shoulders relax a little. I seize the moment to lean in and kiss her, then rest my forehead against hers. "It's going to be okay either way, Molly. You are living for *you* now. Isn't that what you told me last night?"

She nods but the worry is still in her eyes. "I may have been more confident because telling you that I was in love with you went so well. What if this blows up in my face?"

"It's not like he can force you to stay, so really you don't have to worry. I know you are hoping for a letter of recommendation but if your grades from college were good, I can't imagine it will be a problem for you to get in."

She nods and I can see her relax a little bit. "Right. I got good grades. You're right, Tom. I don't think I realized how much I wanted this until I told you about it. Now, it's like I won't be able to function if this doesn't happen."

"Then let's make sure it happens." I kiss her and then wrap her in my arms hoping she can feel the belief I have in her.

Molly

I HAVE CHICKENED out every day for a week. I promised Tom last night that this week would be different, that I would talk to Dr. Potter about nursing school. I've heard back from both Sacramento State and Chico State and they are sending me applications. I requested my transcripts from UC San Diego so I'll be ready.

I stand outside the clinic and blow out a breath trying to find the courage I have when Tom and I talk about this. It's so easy with him. I feel unstoppable. I take a deep breath and whisper "you can do it" to myself a few times.

I have always arrived before Dr. Potter and Henny. Every day except the first day I started here, but as I turn my key in the lock on the front door I know today isn't going to be like any other day. The first indication of that is the white 44DD bra that is draped over the check-in counter. The second are the sounds I hear coming from the file room.

"Oh, Madame Henny, your crystal ball was right, I do like that. Tell me what do the spirits say about coming in the back door?"

"The spirits say yes, oh God yes. Fill me with your seed!"

Nope.

No.

No thank you.

Absolutely not.

I exit quickly and quietly then walk around the block and down to the ocean to try and clear my head and possibly my soul. There are a few people out on the beach picking up shells and Mr. Kendal is doing his Tai Chi. I watch his slow gentle movements and ponder joining him, it looks peaceful. I could use some peace after what I was subjected to just now. I deserve a raise, and if I wasn't planning on leaving, I would leverage my misfortune of walking in early. Instead I close my eyes and let the gentle breeze bring me the subtle scent of the ocean. I have never lived far from the sea, and it occurs to me that I will have to move inland if I get into any of the nursing programs I am looking at. I let that feeling wash over me with each gust of wind opening my eyes only when I hear a seagull nearby.

Lisa called me out on this when we were talking about my escape from San Diego. Besides pointing out that I had stopped believing in myself, she very plainly showed me I wasn't as brave as I had thought. I hugged the California coast like it was a lifeline. The farther north I got the more I panicked. That's why I really stopped here, even if I didn't realize it at the time. I was never going to make it to Canada. I didn't have the courage to keep going then. Do I now?

Can I jump into the unknown with both feet and let go of the ocean that has been the soft soundtrack of my whole life? I blow out a breath and glance at my watch. It's been fifteen minutes since I left the little sex shop of horrors. They have to be done, right? I shudder, then turn and walk very slowly back to the clinic.

Both Dr. Potter and Henny act completely normal when I loudly enter, saying, "Sorry I'm a little late." I hurry past them to the back to put my purse and lunch away.

Thankfully we are busy. I think every parent in town decided to get their kids' sports physicals done today. On top of all of those we had a patient with a laceration and another with a broken finger. I have never been so happy, even if I know once the patients are seen, I am going to have to talk to Dr. Potter.

At a little after five Henny is busy checking out the last patient of the day and I have the lab cleaned and all the rooms ready for tomorrow. I walk past Dr. Potter's office a few times before I get the nerve to go in.

"Dr. Potter? Can I talk to you for a minute?" I ask from the doorway. My feet feel frozen in place.

"Of course Molly, come in and sit. I'm just finishing up these charts." Dr. Potter waves his hand over his desk, like maybe I had forgotten how busy we were today.

I step in and take the chair across from him. I can do this. I repeat that in my head a few times before I start. "I wanted to let you know, I've decided to start looking into nursing programs. I want to get my RN."

Dr. Potter slowly removes his glasses and sets them on the desk. He stares at me for a bit before running his hand down his face. "I'm surprised it took you this long, Molly. Where are you looking to apply?"

"I've asked for information from Chico State and Sacramento State. I'm looking at UC Davis too but that will be harder to get into and more expensive."

"I see. So you want to stay in California?" he asks.

I shrug. "I'm not set on that. To be honest I picked schools I had heard of, I probably need to widen my search so I have a better chance of admission."

"Why stop at RN? Why not med school?" Dr Potter asks. He leans back and is tapping his pen on his chin like he does when he's analyzing a patient's complaints.

"Med school? Oh no, I couldn't —" I start but he cuts me off.

"Molly, you have a mind for medicine, and a heart for patients. I've only worked with you for a few months, but I have never seen a medical assistant with more competency. To be honest with you, if you hadn't brought it up, I would have."

I blink at him a few times, unsure what to say next. "Thank you, Dr. Potter. I . . ." I pause and take a deep breath before continuing. "I don't think I can do med school. I am a worker bee, not the queen." I immediately cringe at my weird analogy but he just smiles.

"What about nurse practitioner? You'd still be a nurse but have the freedom to see patients on your own with the oversight of a physician." He narrows his eyes then shakes his head. "At least consider that. You'll have to get your RN first anyway then get into a master's program to get your clinical time. I have a few schools I can recommend."

"I'll think about that. It's not something I had ever considered, but maybe I should. Dr. Potter, would you be willing to write me a letter of recommendation?"

"Of course, Molly. You know I consulted a psychic recently and her crystal ball—"

"Thank you, Dr. Potter, I'm sorry but I have to meet Tom at the bar. Thanks again!" I hurry off before he can continue down whatever weird path that sentence was about to go. I do not need to relive this morning unless it's in therapy, or after a few drinks.

It's early so there are only a few people at the bar, a tall guy in a cowboy hat who might be on a date. He seems awfully dressed up for a Monday night. I think he's with the cashier from the bookstore, but she has her back to me so I can't be sure.

I spot my favorite seat by the wall and climb up onto the barstool and set my purse next to me. My smile spreads easily across my face as soon as Tom walks in. He has a keg lifted up on his shoulder and as he swings it down I get a nice view of all his muscles. He hasn't seen me yet so I take the opportunity to watch him. I know this Tom so well, and I wonder what he is like when he is back at the university. Is Professor Hemingway different? I try and picture him in a lecture hall standing in front of a hundred students. I of course decide that he's wearing a tweed coat with leather elbow patches. None of my professors dressed like that but it was UC San Diego, it was rarely cold enough for a tweed coat. Tom would wear tweed.

"What's got you smiling like that Molly?" Tom says as he sets the keg down.

"You, in tweed."

He glances down at his T-shirt and then back up at me, confusion clear on his face. "I'm going to need you to elaborate a little bit more."

I wave my hand, dismissing him, and lean forward. I point to my lips and say, "I require a kiss hello then I will tell you about the wild day I had."

Tom doesn't hesitate and his lips are on mine quickly. Soft, warm and my absolute favorite thing. Well, the thing I can enjoy in public.

"So tell me, did you summon the courage to tell Dr. Potter?" Tom asks and I am about to answer him when we both hear a woman gasp.

"Jesus, Dylan, no." Tom is shaking his head and I cover my mouth with my hands as we watch the tall, well-dressed cowboy get down on one knee and propose to his date.

"That's sweet," I whisper.

But Tom shakes his head. "It's their first date."

"Oh." I put my hands back over my mouth to cover the laughter that is about to bubble up. The woman is now frantically looking around and I see I was right. That is the cashier from the bookstore. She slides off her stool and grabs her purse before saying something quietly to Dylan.

I'm confused by the look on his face since he seems happy, and as she holds out her hand to him and they walk out giggling I must assume she said yes.

"That was not what I was expecting," Tom says. He leans back over the bar and kisses me gently.

"I guess everyone is having a wild day today," I say after a few more luxurious kisses from my handsome bartender.

"Interesting day at work? Anything like a doctor telling you that you'd make a great nurse and you have his blessing to pursue that career?"

I laugh at Tom leaning on the bar with both hands, expectant look on his face. I decide to tell him about what I walked in on this morning first and am delighted that he's as horrified as me.

"So then, after all the patients left I finally got brave enough to talk to him and you are mostly correct in your assumption," I tell him.

He has my favorite merlot and has poured me a glass. As he slides it to me he asks, "Did he worry about you leaving? I know that is a concern of yours, Molly, but you have to remember they survived for years without you, so they will manage again."

"No, that's not it. He suggested I go to medical school. Can you believe that?" I take a big gulp of my wine, trying to calm the racing feeling I have in my chest.

"That's a great idea! Why be a nurse when you could go the distance and be a doctor? Willmore has pre-med and a top-notch med school. I could put in a good word for you. Let's call tomorrow and get the application sent over. How cool would that be to go to college with your son?"

"Whoa, slow down there, Tom. I don't want to be a doctor!" I shake my head and smile at his enthusiasm. I watch his face fall and for a moment I think I've disappointed him.

"Shit, Molly, I'm sorry." He scrubs his hand over his face and says, "I hated that my parents didn't listen to me when I told them what I wanted to study in school, they jumped in and decided for me. I shouldn't have done that to you. If you want to be a nurse, then you should be a nurse. That's enough. That's important."

He holds my gaze and I'm sure he sees the tears I feel springing up. This man is so sweet. How will I get by when he's all the way in Connecticut?

I push that thought down yet again, and tell him, "Dr. Potter actually mentioned something I hadn't thought of. He suggested I become a nurse practitioner. I could see patients but would have a doctor to fall back on if a tough case came in. We had those at the first clinic I worked at. It never occurred to me to try for that."

"I think that sounds very interesting. If that's where your passion lies, then you should go for it." His eyes crinkle a little as he grins at me.

"Thank you, Tom. For everything. I really don't know if I would have ever gotten to this point if you hadn't come into my life. You have given me back something I lost at sixteen."

"I haven't done anything. You are an amazing woman."

"Let me finish." I take another drink of my wine and settle in my chair a little. "When I got pregnant, I lost myself. I was ashamed and scared, so I think I sort of shut down all thoughts of what I wanted out of life. My baby became my first priority, so I tolerated other people deciding things for me. I didn't have the confidence to stand up and say, I don't want that, or I think this would be better for me. I just went along with all of it because at the time it was easier. I didn't realize that I was losing myself."

"That's understandable, Molly."

"But now, for the first time since before I got pregnant, I'm in charge of what I want. It started when I went back to school and got my certificates, but that was an escape route. I didn't know how much I would love medicine, how right this career path would feel. Does that make sense?"

"Absolutely. I've always told my students to follow what makes their heart race. If going on digs sounds fun, then don't settle for anything less."

"I like that. I'm not going to settle for less ever again." I sigh and enjoy the rest of my wine and the evening.

"Time flies over us, but leaves its shadow behind." ~ Nathaniel Hawthorne

I HATED that quote the first time I heard it, but I get it now. The memories I have from this summer will stay with me for the rest of my life. I'm trying to be philosophical about all of this. Molly came into my life and showed me what strength, courage and beauty look like. That doesn't mean I get to keep her. I do get to keep the memories, even if the end of August came too damn soon.

She's sleeping on my shoulder, her thigh draped across my body, keeping me in bed. Not like there is anywhere else I would want to be. I trace my thumb over her soft skin and twist my face a little to kiss her forehead. She makes a contented noise and squeezes me with her arm and leg.

"How am I going to sleep without my Tom?" Her sleepy voice wraps around me and my heart clinches. Not in a medical way, but in a way that has taken over my whole world recently.

I swallow hard and clear my throat. "I don't know. I wish we didn't have to find out."

"Do you need to get up? It's a long drive to San Francisco. I don't want us to be late to the airport." She's got her hand over my heart, feeling it thump steadily along even if I fear it will stop once I am back in Connecticut and away from her.

"You really don't have to drive me. Lyle is okay with me taking his truck. We have a system—"

She cuts me off. "I want to drive you. I want to spend every second that I can with you. Stop trying to get rid of me, Tom!" She digs her finger in my rib, making me jump and laugh.

"Okay, okay. I'll let you drive."

Eventually we drag ourselves up, make a simple breakfast, then hit the road to the airport. The drive down takes less time than it ever has before and I'm wondering how I can stop this hurtling comet. I haven't felt this strongly about a woman ever, so why do I have the luck to meet someone like Molly who is ten states away from me? I actually looked at a map and counted the states between us. Ten. Ten stupid whole states keeping us apart.

We have plans to see each other, to talk on the phone, to write letters, and I know that I will cherish those. Once she finds a nursing program though, I fear that will fade. Her mind will be focused on more important things than me. I'm not trying to be pathetic, I swear.

I lift my suitcase out of the trunk and set it on the curb before I shoulder my other bag. We got lucky and found a spot in the hourly lot, so the walk to my gate isn't terribly long. Molly holds my hand and we talk in hushed tones about the week ahead of us. She will go back to work and I'll be teaching two first-year anthropology classes and an upper division class on the grant writing process. I already want to die of boredom and the semester hasn't even started.

"So no matter what, I'll see you in two weeks at the parent appreciation gala thingy, right?" Molly asks. She's trying to sound bright and positive.

"Yes. If you can get Friday off and fly in Thursday night we will have more time."

"I already got that figured out. I have Friday and Monday off." She smiles brightly at me and adds, "And I already have my flight booked. I put the information in your carry-on, along with a little something special."

"I love you, Molly." I lean in and let my lips gently rest on hers, attempting a sweet, chaste kiss, but she grabs my shirt and pulls me in for a deep soul-searching kiss instead.

"Tom," she breathes out as she pulls away, resting her forehead to mine. "Thomas Hemingway, I love you. We will make this work."

I nod a little and smile at her. "We will."

* * *

The first week back is always hard. Settling into early mornings, busy afternoons, and lonely nights. Fuck, I miss her. I miss her smile, her eyes, those beautiful, full lips. I miss talking to her, being able to walk down the street and knock on her door.

These thoughts are dancing around my mind when I pull into my garage late Friday afternoon. This time next week she will be here, and I am beyond excited to introduce her to my parents, and my sisters. Well, not Laura, who's back in New York and says she won't have a day off for the rest of her life. I believe her. The agency she works at is cutthroat and she wants to make partner, so even if they didn't say that to her, the self-imposed work schedule will not be adjusted to meet Molly.

I set my leather messenger bag on the chair by the door and walk to the fridge to grab a cold beer. The light flashing on my answering machine makes me smile. That has been a constant since I've been back, Molly keeping her promise to call me often. I lean against the counter and push the button while I pop the cap off my beer.

My machine says, "*You have five new messages, first message sent today at 10:00 a.m.*" There's a little click, then, "Hi Tom, it's me. Shoot, I was hoping to catch you, I really don't want to leave a message about this. I'll try later."

"*Next message sent today at 11:15 a.m.*"

Click.

"Hi Tom, me again. I can't remember your schedule for Fridays and I guess you're at work? Darn, okay I'll try again."

"*Next message sent today at 12:00 p.m.*"

Click.

"Tom? You're killing me here. I wish I had your number at work.

Okay, well, I have some news. It's good news. Mostly. Okay, I'm going to wait a little longer."

"*Next message sent today at 2:00 p.m.*"

Click.

"Tom! Damn it. Is this your long day? I know you told me but I'm just so frazzled, excited, nervous, and sad too. I can't think straight! I've got another hour so I'll try back then. I really hope I catch you."

"*Next message sent today at 3:00 p.m.*"

Click.

"Okay, I really tried. I was hoping to catch you so we could talk about this, but I have no choice, I guess. I got a call from Chico State today. They had two students no-show for the nursing program after getting in, and they confirmed they aren't coming. I got offered one of the spots! I'm leaving now to drive over and meet with a few people about housing. I'll try and call you this weekend, I need to hear your voice, hear you say to go for it. Okay, I have to go. I love you, Tom."

I blink a few times and look around the room for evidence of the train that just careened through here. I feel like I went on a wild roller coaster ride or something. I set the beer down and hold my hand over my heart waiting for the damn thing to slow down. I glance at my watch and curse. I missed her call by one hour. One hour spent in my office talking to a frazzled grad student who thinks he made a horrible decision by going for his doctorate in archeology.

If I had ignored him when he called after me in the hallway, I would have made it in time for that last call. I would have been here to tell her to go for it. I pick up the phone and dial her number to leave a message of my own, even though she won't get it until she gets back from her trip.

"Molly, I'm sure we will have talked by the time you hear this message, but I just listened to your messages and I wanted to say, go for it. Do it, and Molly, I'm so proud of you. I love you so much and I know you are going to do a great job in nursing school."

I hang up and call my parents' house to tell them I'll be over for dinner. I don't trust myself to stay here all night alone. The urge to buy a plane ticket to California is too great.

"Why so blue, son?" my father asks when he answers the door

wearing his typical outfit these days, jeans and a T-shirt and sneakers stained with green.

"I missed an important call. I'll be okay. How goes the lawn mowing?"

"I picked up two new clients this week!" He beams at me like he won some sort of prestigious award.

"That's great, Dad." I pat his arm as I walk past him to find the sane adult in this house. I don't expect him to follow me, but he does.

"Your mother had to run to the store to get more butter and sour cream. We're having a baked potato bar for dinner! Have you heard of this? It's incredible. You make a bunch of baked potatoes and then have all the fixings out in these little bowls." Dad picks up a white ceramic bowl that looks like it could only hold a few tablespoons of anything. "I like bacon and chives and, now this is going to surprise you," he pauses to make sure I'm listening. "Pineapple!"

I snap my head to look at him. "Pineapple? On a baked potato? Dad, what is wrong with you?"

"Don't knock it until you try it, it's better than it sounds. Especially when you add a big dollop of sour cream. The best combination of sweet and savory." He does a little motion with his hand, kissing his fingertips like a mobster.

I shake my head in disbelief. I'm not sure if this is grief or just the natural progression of a retired professor. I squint at him, wondering if I should schedule an appointment with the family doctor. His hair is freshly cut and his mustache is better kept than it was when he was teaching. His eyebrows have started to get a little crazy, but I think that's just genetics.

He takes a Tupperware container out of the fridge and sets it on the counter before leveling his gaze at me. "Now the big question is, do you want tomatoes or should I chop up some celery?"

"For the potato? God, no, Dad, neither of those things sound good."

"Suit yourself. Your mom says the celery adds a nice crunch. It's healthier than bacon, so maybe give it a try." He goes back to the fridge and pulls out more weird items for his potato bar. "How was the first week back?"

"About the same as always."

"Excited about the gala next week?" He sets a huge bowl on the counter as the oven timer goes off. I need to fix that damn thing, it sounds like an air raid siren. Dad chuckles as he jams his thumb on the button to silence it.

"Yeah, I am. Well, I'm looking forward to seeing Molly. She's coming out for—" I stop mid-sentence when it occurs to me she might have to cancel now. Damn.

Dad turns to me with two oven-mitt-covered hands holding a tray of six foil-wrapped potatoes. He raises a brow. "Your new friend Molly? Her son is here now, right?"

"Yeah, he just started. Molly might be coming, that was the call I missed. She got into a nursing program at a college in California. She was hoping to start in January, but they had a last-minute opening this semester."

"Oh well, that makes getting away a little more difficult, doesn't it." His voice is kind and he tilts his head a little, studying me. "You really care about this woman, don't you?"

"Yes," I manage. Dad and I don't have these kinds of conversations. This is Mom's wheelhouse. I know what to expect from her. Now? I couldn't even begin to guess what advice my father is about to bestow upon me.

"I've never seen you get serious with a woman, Tom." He sets the tray of potatoes on the stove top, then picks up two at a time, putting them in the large bowl. "I'm going to tell you a story, you may have heard this in some form or another over the years, but never from me. It's my story, really, but your mother loves to tell it."

I know immediately what he's talking about and a small smile forms on my lips. He's right, I've heard my mom tell this a hundred times, but I've never heard his side of the story.

"It was the end of our senior year in college and we had both applied to grad school. I applied to several, your mom applied to one."

"Willmore," we say together, and I laugh.

"She didn't want to leave the school she loved, or this area, but I was restless. I wanted to see the world, and my first choice was a school in

England. We talked about how we could make it work, and we also talked about ending things between us."

That is news to me. My parents met when they were freshmen at Willmore University and have been together ever since. I had no idea they almost broke up.

"I've surprised you, haven't I?" he asks with a smirk.

"Yes, I didn't know that. Mom always made it sound like you both wanted to stay here, she never mentioned you applied to schools overseas."

He shrugs and continues, "It really bothered her. She took my desire to see new places as slight against her. What she didn't understand was that I wanted to become a better person *for her*. I wanted to expand my horizons, but I knew I'd come back here. Do you know why?"

I shake my head, realizing that if he had left, I might not be standing here. Would he have come back? Couples grow apart, they meet new exciting people in those expanded horizons.

"Your mother had captivated me the first time I met her. I knew that there would never be a woman who could compare. Not in Connecticut, California, or a continent away. When you meet that person, you don't get over it. I knew that if I left for grad school I'd be back and I would marry her."

"But you didn't leave," I say.

"Oh, but I did." He levels his gaze at me and waits for this bombshell to detonate. I never knew this.

"What? Wait, I don't understand. You went to Willmore for undergrad and postgrad degrees. You must have come back right away?"

"I made it one week at Oxford." He grins at me, and I burst out laughing.

"A week? That's pretty funny, Dad. Why haven't we ever heard this story?"

"You have heard that I proposed during the first semester of grad school. Well, it was the second week of classes and I stormed into the lecture hall and—"

I cut him off. "Got down on one knee in front of everyone, demanding that she become your wife." I have heard that part of the story, but I had no idea it was after he had been away.

"I wasn't cut out for life without her, and it didn't take long for me to figure it out."

My mom comes in holding a small bag from the store up for my dad to see. "I got the butter and sour cream and a little surprise." She kisses my cheek as she passes me, then sets the bag on the counter.

"I'm glad you made it, Tom. You are going to love these." She beams at the odd assortment of condiments and potatoes.

I'm not so sure.

Molly

CHICO IS NICE. Chico State is beautiful, with the brick buildings, rose garden, and creek running through the campus. The people seem friendly and I'm currently having a burger at a very interesting restaurant right next to campus with a girl who has a room for rent.

"So did you like the house?" Dawn asks. She is nibbling on a curly French fry.

"I did, it's cute and not too far from campus. Do you think it will be a problem for me to take over the lease?"

"No, Sophia wants to get out of it so bad, she has already talked to the owner, and they understand. You should be able to slide right in."

I sigh in relief and nod. "Okay, I'll fill out all the paperwork today and get it to them. I need to go back home and get some more of my stuff, but I should be back Sunday night." I pause, knowing I have to ask this, but not sure how.

"That's awesome. To be honest, Sophia was really immature, I lived with her last year and I kinda knew she wasn't going to make it. I feel bad for her parents. They paid so much for her to be here and she was miserable. She missed her boyfriend. He goes to UC Santa Cruz. I bet she'll end up going there." She munches on another fry then adds, "I hate that, it's so lame."

"What?" I ask. I ordered a regular burger and fries too and am enjoying them so much.

"Women that can't survive without a man in their life. It's 1990, for fuck's sake." Dawn takes a huge bite of her burger. She ordered something called a Jiffy Burger that has peanut butter slathered all over it. I thought it sounded gross but she seems to be enjoying it.

I look down, then around the restaurant, not wanting to make eye contact with her, for fear that she will see how much I'm missing Tom. There are times that I want nothing more than to drop everything and move to Connecticut, but those moments fade.

I want this. I want to be a nurse, or maybe more. This opportunity is something I never knew I wanted and now that it's here, I can't pass it up.

"Can I ask you a question? Maybe I should have brought this up earlier, but I wasn't sure how to say it." I grab a curly fry and chew while she nods. "Do you throw lots of parties or are there a lot at your neighbors? I'm obviously older than you and desperate for a place to stay so I know I can't be too picky but—"

She cuts me off with a wave of her hand. "No. No parties and our street is pretty quiet. I think there are a lot of people in the neighborhood who work at the local hospital. It's just down the street."

I sink into the booth a little, relief washing over me. "Oh, that's good. Okay, then I am for sure taking the room."

Dawn and I go back to the house after lunch and I fill out the application to rent the room. I feel good about this. She is really nice and has been in the nursing program for a year already so she will be a huge help in navigating this.

With nothing left to do in Chico, I fill my gas tank up and head back up the hill to Mendocino. My mind is like a pinball game right now with all the things I need to do in just one day. The first thing I want to do when I get back home is call Tom, even if that's lame.

It's dark by the time I pull in front of my house. I'm so tired. I'm happy but so overwhelmed that I want to curl up in a ball and cry.

The first thing I see when I walk through my front door is the light flashing on my answering machine. My heart swells in anticipation of hearing Tom's voice. I push the button and frown when a woman's voice comes on,

"Hey Molly, this is Misty. I talked to Dr. Potter and he said you were going to rent your place. I wanted to let you know I'm very interested. Can you please call me before you put it in the paper?"

She leaves her number and I jot it down quickly, then wait for the next message to play, and my breath catches when I hear the deep rumbly voice of the man I have fallen hopelessly in love with.

"Molly, I'm sure we will have talked by the time you hear this message, but I just listened to your messages, and I wanted to say, go for it. Do it, and Molly, I'm so proud of you. I love you so much and I know you are going to do a great job in nursing school."

I glance at the clock and see it's past 10:00, so it's 1:00 a.m. in Connecticut. I dial the phone anyway, smiling when he picks up on the first ring.

"Hello?"

"Hi, Tom, sorry to call so late."

"Molly, don't apologize. I'm awake. Just reading a little, hoping you'd call."

My heart aches, trying to picture him in bed with his book open, now probably resting on his chest. He probably has his glasses on or they're also resting on his chest. I noticed he turns into an otter at night, storing all his important possessions there for easy access. I let my eyes drift closed and smile.

"I got your message and I want you to know, it means the world to me. No one has ever been in my corner before, and I'm realizing how much I needed that."

"Of course. We all need someone to cheer us on. I'm honored to be that person for you. Did you go to Chico?"

"Yes, I found a place right away, thankfully. One of the nursing students had just lost her roommate so I'm taking that room."

"You don't sound happy about that."

"I've never lived with anyone, well my mom, then Isaac's parents then him . . . but you know what I mean."

"I do. I think it's a rite of passage, a whole part of the college experience."

"I guess." I sigh then add, "I did miss that the first time. When I went to UC San Diego, I was living with Isaac's parents and I remember being so jealous of the girls who were living in the dorms or at a sorority. I always felt like I was living in an alternate reality. I had classes like them, but I had a baby at home."

"Then I am even more happy for you, everyone deserves to have college roommates. They are wonderfully awful," he says with a laugh.

"Great, thanks, Tom."

"In all seriousness Molly, you will be so busy with your studies, and clinicals, I doubt there will be much time to worry about who didn't do the dishes."

"I hope so. Dawn seemed to be neat and organized and she is in her last year, so I know she's taking it seriously. I'm sure it will be fine." I change the subject because talking about this makes my stomach hurt. "Did Grant stop by your office?"

"No, but the first week back is busy. I'm sure when he feels like he has the time, he will. Molly, can I assume you won't be coming to the gala next weekend?"

"Oh shit! God, I forgot about that. I don't know. I have labs on Friday. I don't know if I can miss them. I'll talk to the professor on Monday and let you know." I want to cry. I can't believe it didn't occur to me that I might have to cancel plans to see Tom and my son.

"Your classes are important, maybe I can fly out there soon?" Tom says softly. His kindness and support mean so much to me.

"Okay, I would love to see you." The last word comes out in a choking sob and just like that I'm bawling.

"Oh, my sweet girl. What's wrong? Please don't cry," Tom says, and of course this makes me cry harder. I draw in a few shuddering breaths and try to calm down.

He waits, quietly saying things like, "it's okay," and "we will get through this," and more importantly, "I'm so proud of you."

"Thank you, Tom, I really needed to hear that."

"Good. When you're up to it, I'd love to hear all about Chico State and your new roommate. I know this isn't how you planned on this going, but now you'll be done one semester sooner!"

I laugh at his optimism as I walk down the hall to my room. I want to climb into bed and talk to him until we both fall asleep.

* * *

We talked until 1:00 a.m. my time. So Tom didn't get to sleep until four. I'm up early regardless because I need to pack and get back down to Chico. My first class is at 8:00 a.m. on Monday. Tom tried to convince me to cancel my trip out there, but I want to at least try.

Once my bags are packed and loaded in the car, I call Misty and let her know she can rent my place. She comes over immediately to go over the details. I'm grateful that I didn't have to put an ad in the local paper, then field calls from out of town. I stand in my living room and spin slowly, taking in my little sanctuary. Misty and Jerald will take good care of her while I'm gone.

It occurs to me then: I might not move back here. I could go anywhere, maybe even Connecticut. As much as I love Tom, I can't picture that. I've tried but it's like when there's a storm and the TV channel cuts out. Maybe because I've never been out of California, maybe because I have a hard time believing Tom and I will last.

Maybe he came into my life to show me what love can be? I don't want that to be true, I want forever with him, but I won't change my dream again. I can't.

Tom

I STRAIGHTEN my bow tie and smooth my hair down, wishing Molly was here to be my date this evening. Grant called her and convinced her to stay in Chico and focus on her classes. He did the right thing, but hell, I hate going to these things alone.

All the professors are paired with a table of parents who have students in their department or similar disciplines. I'm never that lucky. I'd actually enjoy an evening talking to parents about the adventures of archeology and what a great program we have at Willmore. Tonight I will be seated with two very wealthy families so I can try to fundraise for the department. I don't recognize one of the names, but the second is impressive.

The Densworth family owns a large chain of hotels around the world and they have very deep pockets. The dean stopped by my office on Friday to make sure I was aware of all the good a sizable donation would do for the school.

No pressure.

My table is all the way in front, dead center, for the best visibility. Not of me, the sometime archeology professor or grant writing teacher, but for the wealthy families that will sit with me. I see two couples already at the table but as I approach one of the couples excuses themselves. I nod as they pass, and I glance quickly at the table for my name.

"Hello, I believe I get to share a table with you this evening. My name is Dr. Hemingway, and I'm a professor here." I extend my hand to the seated man, trying to ignore the fact that he doesn't stand to greet me.

"Mr. Densworth, and this is my girlfriend Candy Kane with a K, the last name, not the first." He motions to the blonde sitting to his right, who is using a butter knife to reapply her lipstick. I'm taking a moment to try and understand why he felt the need to tell me how her name is spelled when she looks up at him with wide blue eyes.

"Baby, is there any on my teeth?" she asks, then bares them for him to inspect.

"Nah, you're good. Better not let my mother see you doing that at the table. She's already in a mood," the man says. Both of them seem to be done with me so I return to my chair and sit. The lights dim, then come back up, signaling the speeches are about to start.

People begin finding their seats and I expect the other couple to return but instead I hear a woman say, "Take that napkin out of your shirt, son, for Pete's sake. I taught you better than that. And don't think I didn't see Miss Kane's disgusting display. Don't make me send you back to the hotel."

I straighten my spine and clear my throat before standing and turning to greet the newcomer. I hold out my hand and she takes it graciously. I smile and say, "Hello, I'm—"

"You are Dr. Thomas Hemingway, yes, I know. I requested that you be at my table. I am Vivian Densworth and I assume you met my son Isaac." She flicks her hand at him dismissively. "Oh, and his date Miss Kane."

I can feel the ice in her words and fight the urge to step back. This woman is terrifying. She is dressed in a long cream-colored gown and her dark hair, streaked with grey, is artfully done in a smooth blunt cut. The bracelets on her wrist probably cost more than my house. I swallow and shift my gaze to her icy green eyes which are narrowed at me with laser precision.

"You know my grandson, Grant. He speaks very highly of you. I have been looking forward to meeting you." Everything clicks into place, and I snap my head over to look at the man who introduced himself as Mr. Densworth. Isaac. Molly's ex. Grant's father. Holy shit. I'm instantly grateful Molly didn't come. Maybe that's why Grant called her, because he knew.

"Yes, I do. Grant is a fine young man." I stop short of saying that it's because his mother is an extraordinary woman. Instead I pull out a chair for Mrs. Densworth and steel myself for a long evening.

"So, you're like a doctor?" Candy asks once we are all seated again. I notice the two empty chairs next to her and wonder what happened to the couple that was there.

"I have my Ph.D. in archeology. I'm a professor here at Willmore," I explain, in case she didn't hear my earlier introduction.

"What part of the body is that?" she asks with her nose scrunched up.

"Baby, he's a teacher. It's different than like a doctor you go to for a cough."

"Or boobs? That kind of doctor is different too."

"Yes, baby." Isaac beams at her like she just solved world hunger.

I blink a few times and steal a glance at Vivian. She is pinching the bridge of her nose and taking deep measured breaths.

I try to think of a question for Candy that will maybe steer the conversation to safer territory. "What do you do, Miss Kane?"

"Oh!" she says, clapping her hands and bouncing in her seat a little. "I just started a company that will change the world."

"That's quite a claim! I'm excited to hear about it," I say, leaning forward a little.

"Well, I came up with this idea to print little sayings on paper, like motivational things you know? They will say, 'You can do it' or 'I believe you can.'"

I nod and smile, waiting for her to continue, but she doesn't. She seems to be distracted by a piece of hair that had flopped out of her updo. Next to me Vivian shakes her head and leans over whispering, "That's it. Don't expect there to be more to her idea."

I fight off a laugh, covering my mouth with my hand. When I feel composed, I ask, "So where will these motivational sayings be? Like in a cookie?"

Vivian snorts and Candy tips her head to the side, "You know? That's a really great idea. We could put them in a cookie and call them Bits of Happy, or better yet," she points a long red nail at me and says, "Cookie Confidence."

Vivian's foot nudges me under the table and I take a drink of water before saying, "That's a great idea."

"Her family owns Kane Kandy Kompany, all K's. So they can make that happen. Just you wait and see." Isaac is puffing out his chest like he is so proud of her. Jesus, Molly wasn't kidding when she said he wasn't very bright.

"I'm sure it will be amazing," I say with a smile.

The dean reaches the podium and begins the evening's speeches welcoming parents and touting all the accomplishments of Willmore University. I've never been so happy to listen to Dean Frank drone on about the college.

There are a few short presentations and then they start bringing out the food. Vivian has her eyes laser-focused on her son and his date now, so she hasn't spoken to me again. I am not going to lie, I'm okay with that. When the servers start to clear the plates, Isaac and Candy excuse themselves and I see Vivian relax a little.

"Grant seems to be settling in just fine here," I say. I didn't want to discuss Grant in front of Isaac, even though it's his son. I hate that he got to share that with Molly, I hate even more that he didn't appreciate it.

"He loves it here. He also seems to be quite fond of you." She glances over her shoulder then asks, "How is Molly? Grant tells me she got accepted into a nursing program?"

I am surprised by the kindness I hear in her voice. I don't want to betray Molly's trust, but if her son told his grandmother about it, I guess I can elaborate. "Yes, she called last night to tell me she's enjoying it so far."

"And you love her." It's a statement, not a question.

"Yes."

"God knows that girl deserves to find some happiness. I hope you can show her that she is worth all the good things coming her way." She takes her wineglass from the table and tips it back, emptying the whole thing in one gulp. "I wish that were whiskey. Wine isn't going to help me survive an evening with my dumbass son and his date."

Molly told me that her son knew a very different version of her ex-mother-in-law and I'm guessing this is who I'm sitting with tonight. "I take it you aren't a fan of Miss Kane?" I ask, leaning back and unbuttoning my jacket.

"Her parents named her Candy Kane. That poor girl never stood a chance. She's not bright but she seems nice enough." She waves her hand dismissively. "Isaac has never had good taste in women, with the exception of Grant's mother." She adds the last part quickly. "I so hoped he would rise to the occasion and be the man Molly deserved."

This surprises me, but I don't know what to say, so I nod.

"When he came home to tell me he had gotten a girl pregnant I admit I assumed the worst about her. We have a very recognizable name, you know. I just thought," she says, then pauses and taps her fingers on the table. "Well, it doesn't matter what I thought. I was wrong and it didn't take me long to figure out that Molly had been fooled by my boy. She had nothing, but she was smart, kind, and so beautiful. I am forever grateful that she is the mother of my only grandchild."

A server walks by and Mrs. Densworth waves him down. "Young man, is there any hard liquor in this place? I am in need of a highball."

"Yes ma'am, I can get that for you."

"Make it two." She looks at me and asks, "Dr. Hemingway, would you like anything to drink?"

I roll my lips to fight off the laugh I felt coming on and ask for a glass of merlot.

Once our drinks have arrived Vivian asks, "What are your intentions with my daughter?"

"You really cut to the chase, don't you?" I chuckle nervously and take a sip of the wine. I don't miss the way she claimed Molly as her own.

"I do. Pussyfooting around a topic will give you no real answers. Catching people off guard usually provides more honesty. That's how I knew right away that Molly was a good kid. She never lied to me, always worked hard and God, does she love her son. All admirable qualities. She deserves the best. Are you the best, Dr. Hemingway?"

I smile and nod. "I think I am a good person, a hard worker, and a loyal companion." I raise one eyebrow at her hoping she gets my meaning.

"So you won't cheat on Molly. My son can't seem to keep his dick in his pants or in one woman for very long. I'm sure he is seeing at least three other women right now. Candy is the only one dumb enough to attend an event with me."

That makes me laugh out loud. "Why, Mrs. Densworth, I find you utterly charming."

"You want a donation," she says, but it's with a slight smile.

"Yes, they do hope I will be able to secure a donation of some kind. I figured I had a fifty-fifty chance tonight since there were supposed to be two families for me to wine and dine, but the other couple never returned."

She glances around the room and spots them at another table. "Those two?"

"Yes, I guess they got lost and took the first open table?" I wonder aloud.

"No they spent ten minutes with Isaac and Candy and ran for the hills. I know them. They own a winery in the San Francisco area and supply us with some very fine sauvignon blanc for the hotels. They'll give whatever you ask for if they think they're topping my donation."

"Interesting. They are the competitive type then?"

"No, they are new money. They love to show it off. My grandfather started four successful companies before opening the first luxury hotel in San Diego. Jasper Inn quickly became the destination resort, and he knew that was where he would focus his efforts."

"Oh, forgive me, I assumed it was your husband's family that had started the chain."

"Most people do. I was already married when I inherited the empire, and I never liked the Jasper name. Sounds too hillbilly for a fine hotel." She twists in her chair and waves down the server again for more alcohol.

I had planned on making an excuse to leave as soon as I could, but I find Vivian's company very entertaining. I ask for another merlot and then stand to remove my jacket. Her gaze follows my movements and a smirk crosses her lips before it quickly fades.

"Now it is going to be your turn to forgive me, Dr. Hemingway, but you do not have the build of a professor. You are very fit. Do you go on a lot of digs? Those are the arms of someone who works hard."

I run my hand down my face and chuckle. "I have a hobby that keeps me pretty fit. In the summer I do some work for a friend in California." I stop myself from saying Mendocino, because Molly really didn't like the idea of her in-laws knowing where she was.

"Oh yes, that small town where Molly lived. Nice place. We looked at opening a hotel up there a few years ago."

The server returns with our drinks, and I take a moment before commenting on that statement. I let the wine calm my nerves before saying, "So you knew where she was?"

"Oh, yes. Do you really think I'd let any harm come to that sweet girl?" Vivian says then makes a sound similar to a hiccup, but she covers her mouth quickly with her fingers.

"I see. I don't think Molly felt that way, if I may be so bold."

"You may. Listen, Dr. Hemingway."

I interrupt her. "Tom, please."

"It's about time, your name is a mouthful. Listen, Tom, I may be a bitch, but I'm not a monster."

Before I can respond to that, Isaac returns without Candy, looking a bit disheveled. He attempts to straighten his tie and smooth out his jacket before his mother notices, but he is unsuccessful.

"Good Lord, were you having sex with that woman in a bathroom or something?!" she asks as she peers at him.

"What I do is my own business. I'm an adult and if I choose to find enjoyment at a mind dumbing event, then it's my prerogative." He tugs on his tie as he says this, making it a lot worse than it was.

"Mind-numbing, not dumbing, you absolute fool," she sneers.

"Did you already ask her for money? Might want to do it quick before she passes out. She's about three streets to the west," Isaac says. He tugs on his cuffs trying to get them back down.

This time I correct him. "Three sheets to the wind. It's an old nautical saying. A sheet is a rope, and if three are loose then the sail is out of control and flapping around. I guess that can be likened to a drunk person staggering as they walk, so—"

Vivian laughs, cutting off my explanation, then turns to me and says, "You are a very interesting man. No wonder Molly cares for you."

Isaac jerks his head up and stares at me. "You know Molly? How? Is she here? Did she come to see Grant?" He's now looking around the room like Molly might pop out from behind a potted plant.

"Go away, Isaac. Take the car and go back to the hotel. I simply cannot tolerate you for another minute." Vivian waves her hand in his general direction then places her elbow on the table and cradles her chin in her open palm. "Tell me, Tom, do you sail?"

Isaac obviously knows when to argue and when to leave, because he is gone without another word. I take a big drink of my wine and nod my head. "Yes, a little. My parents have a small sailboat and we all learned as kids."

"How many children are in your family?" she asks. Her eyes do seem a little out of focus but she's not slurring her words or swaying.

"Five," I say reflexively, then pause. This is the first time I've had to amend that. "Four now. We recently lost my brother."

"Oh, how terrible. I'm so very sorry for your loss. Was he ill?"

"Yes, so his death was not unexpected, but it is still painful."

"And how are your parents handling this?"

"As you would expect." I pause, then laugh a little. "Well, maybe not as you'd expect. My father has taken to mowing lawns and my mother is cooking very strange, yet trendy meals."

"I don't know what to make of that, but I bet they are doing the best they can?" she asks. I nod. "Good, and your other siblings? Do they live close?"

"Two of my sisters live here, and one lives in New York."

"Excellent. And you're close with them?"

"Yes, we are all very close. I still go to dinner at my parents' house once a week, and the girls come as often as they can."

She leans back in her chair and sighs. "I imagine it will be hard on you to go then?"

"I'm not sure I understand."

"Well, you can't let Molly go. If she's in school in California, you clearly need to move. I assume you can teach at any university?"

My breath escapes me in a forceful way as I stare at her. "Huh, you know, I think I can."

"Well, you should look into that. No one has ever fought for that girl, besides me, I mean. Her mother left her, my son was never going to give her what she needed or wanted, but you? I like you, Thomas. I like you for Molly. Come on. Walk me out and wait with me for a cab. I need to get to bed if I'm going to survive brunch with my son and grandson tomorrow. I think Grant is going to punch his father right in the nose. I want to be well rested to enjoy that." She stands and waits for me to grab my jacket then we walk towards the doors leading out to the lobby.

"Oh, one minute." She pulls me toward the couple who left our table. "Lindsey and Martin! So wonderful to see you. I thought we were seated at the same table?"

They both stand and nervously smile at her. I notice the wife wipe her hand on her dress before reaching for Vivian's. "Yes, so sorry, we ran into some old friends and got held up. I trust you had a lovely evening?" She glances at me then back at Mrs. Densworth.

"I had a lovely time. You missed out on the best stories. Dr. Hemingway really knows how to entertain. Do you know he is a professor of archeology and they are looking to go to Namibia in the summer?"

The woman raises her eyebrows and glances at me for confirmation. I have no idea what Vivian is talking about, but I nod along.

"Yes, they are looking for evidence of a lost tribe. This tribe, it is said, was close to discovering a cure for cancer! Can you believe that?"

"That is incredible, isn't it? I had heard of that expedition, but I thought it was another university," she says, her eyes flitting back and forth from me to Vivian.

"Dr. Hemingway is leading the charge. I am donating a half a million, but I know they need more." She shakes her head like she's sad about my lack of funds.

"Oh, we planned on giving a million, so hopefully that will fully fund the trip?" She looks at me when she says that and I swallow hard before nodding.

"Yes." I clear my throat. "Yes, that will just about do. Thank you. That's very generous."

"Wonderful! I look forward to tasting this year's offering at the wine expo. I'm coming myself, don't want that same mistake to happen." Vivian gives her a pointed look and I swear I can see sweat forming on the woman's brow.

"Of course. I will be there as well. Lovely seeing you again, Mrs. Densworth, and nice to meet you, Dr. Hemingway."

We both smile and nod before I lead Vivian out to the lobby. "I have no plans to go to Namibia," I say, holding out my arm for her to take.

"That woman couldn't find Namibia on a map if her life depended on it. I think you're safe. I hope, however, that you make plans very soon to go to Chico. Remember what I said, Tom. Fight for her. Show her the kind of love a real man is capable of." She reaches up and pats my cheek before walking off to the waiting taxi.

Molly

IT DOESN'T FEEL like the middle of October as I sit under a huge oak tree sweating and trying to memorize the facts for a pathophysiology class. I understand most of this, but there are some parts that have been tripping me up. I tip my head back and close my eyes repeating "Toxic insults can result in physical and biochemical alterations . . ." I lose the second half of that statement and groan.

I lower my head to find that passage again and see someone a few feet away. I blink a couple of times and shake my head because that man looks a lot like Tom. It can't be Tom. I blink again and set my book down on my lap.

The man is smiling at me now and walking straight towards me. My heartbeat speeds up as I scramble to stand. My textbook and papers fall to the ground as my brain catches up to what my heart knew right away.

Tom is here.

I run and throw myself at him, arms wrapping around him, kissing whatever I can touch. He picks me up and spins me, laughing and squeezing me. His lips find mine as his arms release me. I feel his big strong hands gently hold my face as he kisses my lips again and again.

I melt and not because of the ridiculous October heat wave, but because this wonderful man has come all this way to surprise me.

"Tom? What are you doing here?" I finally manage to ask after pulling myself off him.

"I had some things to attend to on campus. I didn't think I'd be so lucky as to find you sitting in the quad. How do I always seem to forget how beautiful you are? The pictures you sent me do not do justice to real live Molly."

That makes me laugh. "My hair is even longer than it was in that picture, I'm surprised you recognized me." I place my hand on his chest and smile up at him.

"I would know you, Molly, if you had not a hair on your head," he says with eyes crinkling in a delightful way. "May I take you to dinner? I have some news."

I glance at my watch and wince a little. "I have class in a few minutes, but then I'm all yours."

"You have no idea how wonderful it is to hear that," he says. He waits while I gather my things then walks me to class, holding my hand the whole way. I feel like I am floating and I keep glancing over at him to see if he's really here.

"I'll be right here when you're done," he says when I stop outside of Trinity Hall.

"It's an hour-long class, Tom. Are you just going to stand here and stare at the building?"

"Yes." He leans down and softly kisses my lips before stepping back.

He puts his hands in his pockets and rocks back on his heels. It registers for the first time that he's wearing a nice suit, but I can't be late for class, and if I ask any questions, I will be.

"Okay then, see you in an hour." I spin and walk into the building wondering how I will retain any information knowing Tom is outside.

I hurry in and grab my favorite seat, front row, dead center. Not like anyone else wants to sit here. This professor isn't very animated and reminds me of that teacher on *Ferris Bueller's Day Off*. A nice girl sits to my left every day and when she slides into her desk I hear her groan. I look up and see our professor walking down to the desk in front of the lecture hall.

She leans over and quietly says, "Shoot, I thought we had a substitute today."

I turn to her and whisper back, "Why?"

The professor begins to talk about the chapters we were assigned then announces we will be having a pop quiz. Most of the class grumbles, but I knew he would do this. If he assigns three or more chapters he won't test us, but if it's two, we have a quiz every time. I don't know how the other students haven't figured that out yet.

"There's a hot older man in a suit leaning against the wall outside. I was hoping he was here for us," she whispers back as she waggles her eyebrows.

I stifle a giggle as the tests are handed out. I'm sure Tom will love that he was called hot, though not so sure he'll be happy about the older part.

I flip the quiz over and get started as soon as we are allowed. I know most of the answers, so I fill those in, skipping the ones I'm unsure of. Once I am finished with all of them, I wait until someone else walks up to turn in their test. I learned pretty quickly that if you're first all the time, people get annoyed. The professor leans in and says something to the student, who smiles brightly. She turns and grabs her bag and leaves.

I gather my things and take my test to his desk. I place my it in the basket and he says, "You may go, have a wonderful weekend, Miss Sparrow."

"Thank you, sir," I say quietly. I wave at my friend but her head is down in concentration and she doesn't see me.

Tom straightens up and smiles at me as I push through the doors. I can't believe he's here. I'm shaking my head as I walk up to him. "I can't believe you came out here to surprise me. How long can you stay?"

"Well, that's something I hoped we could discuss over dinner. Do you have a place that you'd like to go?" he asks.

"Can I go back to my place and change first? You look so handsome in your suit and I'm in jean shorts and a T-shirt." I pluck at my shirt.

"I think you look lovely." Tom takes off his jacket and drapes it over his arm then he pulls on his tie to loosen it.

"Do you want a burger? There is a pretty neat place close by," I say.

"Do they have beer too? I would love a burger and an ice-cold beer."

I link my arm through his and say, "They do! The bartenders aren't as cute as the one at The Floppy Fish, but they can pour a beer."

"Perfect," he says as he leans over and kisses my cheek.

We wind through the campus toward downtown Chico. The Madison Bear Garden is a large red brick building that sits on a corner. From the outside it looks pretty plain, but inside? Like nothing I have ever seen. I jog up the steps and grab the door to hold it open for Tom so I can see his face when we walk in.

There is stuff everywhere, so it's hard to find a place to rest your gaze. There's an old-fashioned coach hanging from the ceiling and a giant antique red oil lamp that takes up space by the stairs right next to a large ceramic man holding a giant burger who leans out a little. The walls are decorated with paintings of women and Tarzan maybe? I've never been able to tell what that one picture is supposed to be.

There is already a line at the order window and a few people are gathered around the video game that sits to the left of the entrance. They're shouting encouragement to the student who seems to be beating Frogger at the moment. A crackle of a microphone cuts through the crowd noise and says, "Bobby, oh Bobby, where are you? Your burger is ready."

I spin and glance up at Tom who is looking all around like I did the first time I came here. I wait until he looks at me, then pull him over to the board listing the kinds of burgers they have. "I've tried almost all of them except the one with the chili pepper. That seems like too much."

"You tried the Jiffy Burger? Is it good?" Tom asks, squinting at me.

"I didn't like it. I get the Bear Burger. It comes with these amazing fries and a big crisp pickle spear. That's adventurous enough for me."

"Sounds perfect."

We order and give our name, then head to the bar, deciding to get a pitcher of beer to split. My plans for tonight included reading and trying to memorize a ton of pharmacology. This is so much better.

"Do you want to go back here? It's a little loud up front," Tom says, nodding his head to an archway.

"No. I can't eat by the horse. It grosses me out. We can go sit outside. It's quieter back there anyway."

"Horse?" Tom asks, confused.

I lead him through to the back room where a taxidermied horse hangs from the ceiling along with a carriage and a bomb. A deer wearing a party hat adorns the wall along with about a million smaller knickknacks and framed pictures. It's a lot to take in.

"Oh, yeah, I don't want to eat under the belly of a horse." Tom laughs and we turn to find a seat outside. There are a few students out here, but almost everyone stays inside where they can be seen. This is the happening spot for all the college kids. My roommate tried to get me to come out with her last weekend to see it packed, but the idea of getting beer spilled on me while shoving past a hundred drunk kids just didn't sound fun.

As soon as we sit Tom pours us each a beer. He takes a long drink and sighs. "That really hits the spot. It's been a long day."

"I bet, did you fly into Sacramento today?" I ask.

"Yes and no," he says.

I laugh. "What does that mean?"

"I flew into Sacramento yesterday. I needed to be well rested for a meeting I had today at Chico State." He raises an eyebrow at me like I am going to somehow understand what he's talking about.

"Why did you have a meeting? I wanted to ask that earlier but I knew if I did I wouldn't have made it to class on time. I'm so confused. Where did you stay last night? Wait, you called me last night! You were here?!"

"I was."

"So are you going to explain or—"

"Tom! Thomas, oh Tommy Boy, your burgers are ready, are you?" The voice over the loudspeaker cuts me off. Tom stands and holds up his finger signaling me to wait.

When he finally returns with our burgers, I am about ready to climb out of my skin. Thankfully as soon as he sits down, he explains.

"So, this morning I had an interview for a teaching position in the anthropology department." He says it in such a casual tone we might as well be talking about the color of the sky.

I haven't picked up my burger yet. I'm just staring at him trying to understand what he's talking about. "But you have a job, You teach at an Ivy league school. You want to teach here?" I ask.

He nods. "Yes, my classes have never been consistent at Willmore. I'd like to teach anthropology and archeology, not grant writing. They cut me back to only three classes this semester and were leaning heavily on me for fundraising and helping with a new project that quite frankly was a waste of money."

"So you'll teach here? What about your house? What about your parents, and your sisters?"

"I'm selling my house, and my parents are happy for me. My sisters will come around. Well, Lisa is on my side and she'll talk to Julie and Kimberly." He reaches for my hands then says, "I'm tired of living my life for them, Molly. I want to do this. I want to live for me."

Tears spring to my eyes instantly but I let them fall. I don't want to let go of him, even to wipe away my tears of joy. I blink a few times before asking, "So you're really moving here?"

"I am. I won't start teaching until next semester, so I have some time to find a place. Oh! And Lyle wants me to come over to help him with a few things so I won't be here all the time, bugging you while you're in classes."

"Tom, I don't know what to say." My throat feels tight and I feel more tears are coming.

"Are you upset I didn't discuss it with you first? I worried about that, but I wasn't sure if I'd be offered a job, and I didn't want to get your hopes up."

"No, Tom, God no. That's not it. No one has ever done anything like this for me. I would have never asked you to do this," I say, feeling a little panicked.

"I know. I did it for me too, Molly. There is this incredible woman here in California and that made Connecticut seem very, very drab. I don't like being ten states away from the woman I love."

"Ten?"

"I counted. Don't laugh," he says.

"Well, if I had known it was ten whole states I might have asked you to move closer."

"So this is a good thing? You're happy?"

"Very happy, Tom."

"Good, let's eat so I can take you back to my hotel and show you how much I've missed you." He winks at me then picks up his burger and takes a bite.

* * *

After dinner we stop at my house so I can grab an overnight bag and show Tom where I've been living. It's a cute little two-bedroom bungalow very close to campus. Dawn was overly optimistic about how quiet her neighborhood is, but it hasn't been too bad. She has been working night shift at the hospital doing her emergency room rotation, so she wasn't home when we stopped by. I was kind of relieved because I really want to get Tom alone and press every inch of my naked body against his. I need to feel his warm skin, and his hands all over me.

He wastes no time and is pulling off my shirt as soon as the door to his hotel room shuts. I grab at his shirt, unbuttoning quickly then peeling it off his strong broad shoulders. He unhooks my bra and presses himself to me, chest to chest.

He sighs and walks me backwards to the bed, never letting our connection break. "I have missed you so much, Molly." He kisses me, then gives me a gentle push.

I laugh and fall backward onto the bed. Before he climbs on top of me, he helps me out of my shorts and underwear. He steps back to take off his slacks. I expect him to come to me and wrap me in his arms, but he stands at the foot of the bed and stares at me.

"In all the world, I have never seen a woman like you. I will travel to every nook and cranny to find you if you ever decide to leave. I will prove to you that I am worthy." He smirks.

"Quoting Kent Price, are we?" I hold out my hand and he finally lowers himself to me, caging me in with his strong arms. I sigh contentedly when his body weight rests on mine. "We have so much to talk about. Book three was the best one yet. Do you really think Kent loves her?"

"I love you," Tom says, kissing me gently. "That is all I know."

"I love you too, Tom."

Epilogue

MOLLY

THE DAY before I am set to move out of Dawn's place, I'm walking to get her a small gift when I feel someone following me. Downtown Chico isn't that big and I'm only a few steps from The Golden Unicorn, so I duck inside. It's a small store, but carries fun gifts, T-shirts with silly sayings, and balloons. Lots of balloons.

I was planning on going to Zucchini and Vine, a little farther down, but the hairs on the back of my neck decided this store was best. I duck behind the rack of greeting cards and watch in horror as Vivian Densworth pushes through the door. She looks around and spots me immediately. Stupid wire rack.

"There is no reason to run, Molly. Good grief. I would have worn different shoes if I had known I was going to have to chase you down!"

I step out from my horrible hiding place and contemplate shoving the card rack over to block her path, but that feels dramatic. Instead I plaster on the fake smile that I hope she remembers from my teen years. "Why are you following me? Is there something you need?"

She bats at a ribbon that hangs inches from her face, only to have it replaced by another. They really do have a lot of balloons on the ceiling here, and I step away from a floating string just as the door opens, stirring them up again.

"Can we go somewhere to talk that isn't . . ." she pauses and bats at the ribbons dancing about her head, "quite so ridiculous?"

I fight a smile and nod. A lot of my anger has dissipated over the past year. From what Grant told me when he came out to visit, to Tom's experience at the gala, I've started to look at my past a little differently.

"Sure. There is a restaurant that serves bagels across the street, we could sit and have something to eat?" I see the look of surprise, then relief, cross her face.

"Yes, that sounds perfect."

We make our way over to Oy Vey Bagel Company and thankfully there are a lot of places to sit. Chico tends to turn into a bit of a ghost town when the students are gone, or at least down here by the college it does.

The waitress hands us menus and places water on the table and I notice Vivian's hand shaking a little as she reaches for her glass. She looks older, but still as polished as I remember. Her silk blouse with the bow tied close to her throat makes me feel overheated and claustrophobic. I try and picture her in a T-shirt and jeans and my mind can't even imagine such a thing. She sets her Louis Vuitton purse on the chair next to us and straightens up a little more.

I fold my hands in my lap and wait. While I'm not as angry at her, I also didn't follow *her* into a store. I have no reason to make this any easier than I already have.

"I see, well yes, I assume you are wondering why I am here?" she says, and I notice again the tremble in her hand as she reaches once more for the water. I cock my head at that and look closer at her face. Her lips are pressed into a thin line as she brings the glass to her mouth for a very tiny sip of water.

Holy shit. She's nervous.

I relax a little and say, "Yes. I am curious why you are following me. Why are you here, Mrs. Densworth?"

"Vivian, please, dear."

The term of endearment takes me by surprise and I don't bother hiding it. "Dear? Okay, is everything alright? You are clearly nervous and you just called me dear. Is something wrong with Isaac?" The possibility that she could be here to tell me Grant's father has passed away hits me. Is that what is going on, or is that wishful thinking on my part?

"Isaac? God no, he's fine. He's an idiot still, but he's fine. Probably in Aruba spending money on some hussy." She waves her hand dismissively. "No I came here to talk to you about your mother. Martha."

I lean forward, mouth agape, not able to picture any scenario in which Vivian and Martha would be in touch. "My mother? You spoke with her?"

"Yes. She contacts me regularly." She pauses and looks around then lowers her voice and says, "for money." She leans back after saying that and takes another gulp of her water.

"Have you had a chance to look at the menu?" The waitress appears over my shoulder and Vivian surprises me by ordering us both a turkey club on a plain bagel. She also asks for more water and I smile a little at that. Chico is showing off its heat wave today. It's barely noon and we are already at 100 degrees.

When we are alone again I narrow my eyes at Vivian and ask, "My mother calls you and asks for money? Like this is a regular thing?"

"Oh yes, has been since the day we met at the restaurant when you were sixteen." She sighs and looks around taking in the quaint little cafe with its small metal tables and bistro-style chairs. The board above the register boasts an impressive take-out menu and there are a few people in line.

"She told me she was thinking of moving up to Northern California. She has it in her head to come up here and, well I thought I should let you know."

"Martha is coming to Chico?" I say, unsure why she would move here of all places.

"Yes, well, actually she said a different town name but when I looked at the map, I thought it was too close for comfort. Apparently she has started seeing a man who runs nuts."

"Runs nuts?" I ask, completely confused.

"Yes, a long hauler, a truck driver. He drives nuts from here to all over. He runs them. Have you not heard that term before?" She cocks a perfectly sculpted eyebrow at me and I pinch my lips together so that I don't laugh.

"Sure, yeah, I guess I have. I didn't know what you meant at first. So she must be serious with this guy if she is moving up here to be with him."

"We can only hope. A nut runner makes decent money so I have my fingers crossed that she will finally stand on his feet if she can't stand on her own." I roll my lips to fight off a smile. I forgot about how she describes things.

"She has a job at the nut processing plant and everything. First time I've heard her be excited about anything to be honest. I didn't want her to come here and ruin your parade."

"Well, thank you for that. It would have been quite a surprise to run into her. You could have called or written or something," I say, assuming Grant has told her where I am.

"No, that wouldn't do. I wanted to see you for myself and know that you are okay." Her tone softens and for the first time in nineteen years I see the woman that my son loves.

"I'm okay. I am happy. I know you've met Tom, well, he lives here now, and I am taking classes to get my RN. Things are good."

She beams at me and I realize that I have only seen her smile a handful of times over the years. It's an expression that looks unfamiliar resting on her face, like she needs to practice it in a mirror or something.

"I'm glad to hear that. Nursing is a noble profession. UC San Diego has a wonderful program. If you had shown interest back then, we could have enrolled you for that. I imagine your communications degree really hasn't helped you at all?"

"Not really." I pause and look at her. "Do you mean that if I had shown an interest in something I could have picked my own major?"

"Well, of course, dear. You were so wishy-washy about your future. To be honest I think you were depressed, and who could blame you with my dolt of a son as a partner. I am sure you felt like there wasn't a point to it at all, that's why I pushed you for something simple."

I blink at her and think back to that conversation about college. Knowing she could see I was depressed hits me harder than the missed opportunity of picking my own classes. I don't think I ever admitted that to myself. I was depressed. We learned about postpartum depression in my OB-GYN classes and some of what they talked about felt very familiar. Adding in the fact that I was only sixteen and had been left by my mother to fend for myself with this new family, I guess it all makes sense.

"I guess I felt kind of hopeless back then," I admit.

"I can imagine. And how about now? Do you feel hopeful now?"

I don't even have to think about it before answering, "Yes. I do."

The waitress brings over the sandwiches and asks if we would like to pick a bag of chips to go along with our lunch. Vivian surprises me again by getting up to follow the waitress over to a rack holding the selection. When she returns she is using two long fingers to pull out a greasy salt-and-vinegar chip from the bag. "Grant says I am all that and a bag of chips! Did you know that?"

I laugh and say, "Yeah, he may have mentioned that to me."

Epilogue

THREE YEARS LATER

SITTING IN THE DARK AUDITORIUM, I crane my neck to see if the graduates have started to walk in. Grant is to my left and his grandparents are sitting to my right. Vivian looks incredibly out of place here surrounded by a hodgepodge of students and families who look like they might be going to grab a burger instead of a formal event, but she has a smile on her face.

"Do you see her yet?" she asks even though she can see the same empty aisle way that I can.

"No, they must still be getting ready." I hold out a folded fan I brought, but she waves her hand dismissing me.

"I'm fine. Is it always this warm here?" She adjusts her blouse a little and glances over at her husband, who insisted on wearing a three-piece suit. He looks miserable.

"Yes, we get a few months of cooler weather but for the most part we have summer and winter. The air conditioning unit must be broken. It's not usually this hot in here," I add helpfully.

She reaches for the fan and flips it open, fanning Mr. Densworth instead of herself. "I told you a nice shirt and slacks would have been sufficient, dear. You are simply melting!"

"I'm fine. I want to look nice for our daughter. It's a big day!" The warmth in his voice causes me to swallow hard. It wasn't easy to get to this point, but now that we are here, I am eternally grateful.

"Here they come!" Grant says, pointing to the line of nursing students filing into Laxson Auditorium. We stand, along with everyone else and clap as the graduates take their seats. Molly and two other students continue to sit on stage. She is graduating with honors and will be giving the commencement speech here at the pinning ceremony. She says she doesn't want to walk to get her second diploma, that this smaller ceremony is all that matters.

Once the dean has said a few words about the college and introduced the nursing program professors, he turns and beams at the students seated in the first few rows.

"Now I would like to call up a very special student. She joined us three years ago when we had an unexpected opening in the program. I am told by her peers and her teachers that it wouldn't have been the same without her. Please welcome Molly Kristen Sparrow, magna cum laude, nursing."

She stands and smooths down her robe. We're close enough to the stage for me to see she is nervous, and I watch her tuck her long curly hair behind her ear. Her white nurse's cap had to be pinned down, but even with the pins it sits a little crooked. It's okay; she is still the most beautiful woman ever to wear one.

"Thank you," Molly says. "I'm not like some of my classmates who knew from a young age that they wanted to be a nurse. My path here was a little longer. I won't bore you with the details, but I do want you to know that I made it because of the wonderful supportive people in my life. That is what being a nurse means to me. What drew me to further my education in the medical field, was the joy I got in helping others. Being a support system for someone who is sick, or afraid, or hurt is a calling like no other. Putting yourself in the path of those in need will always be worthwhile. You may have noticed I am older than most of my fellow graduates, but that doesn't mean I am wiser. I learned so much from them, and I saw firsthand what compassion for others can do. I hope that as we go forward into our careers, we can hold that in our hearts. Thank you."

A few more speeches and then the list of names as the students accept their pins. Once the last student is pinned and the dean congratulates them all for obtaining their nursing degree. Everyone claps and stands, attempting to get to their loved one.

"There you are! Goodness, I was about to send up a flare." Vivian has Molly's arm in her grasp and she pulls her in for a hug. I get a flashback to a year and a half ago when Vivian first tried to hug Molly. It did not go well. This hug, however, is fully appreciated. They rock back and forth both laughing a little as they embrace. It took Molly a while to wrap her head around what happened the day she and her mother met with the Densworths. What Molly thought to be true, that they bought her mother's silence since Isaac was over eighteen, was not at all the case.

The Densworths knew Molly's mother was struggling financially and was about to be kicked out of the mobile home park where they lived. They provided her with money to secure new housing where she and Molly and the baby would be safe. Martha decided instead of using the money for that, she would skip town. Vivian and Henry took legal custody of Molly to be able to provide her with the care and support she needed.

I think Vivian believed at the time that her son would rise to the occasion and be a good husband and father. The night of the gala she shared with me the deep disappointment she had over who Isaac turned out to be. She also confided that she bought him a Lamborghini in exchange for him getting a vasectomy. She said she didn't want Molly or Grant to suffer a string of half siblings.

"Can I get in there?" Henry nudges his wife aside and grabs Molly by the shoulder before planting a kiss on each cheek. "You will have to fly down to San Diego the minute I have any kind of health issue, is that understood?"

"Yes, sir," Molly says with a twinkle in her eye.

"I'm really proud of you, Mom," Grant says as he steps in for his turn.

"I can't wait to attend your graduation next year. I can't believe my baby boy is going to be a journalist." Molly hugs Grant as I wait patiently.

The first year I was here teaching Molly lived with Dawn. I wanted her to have her own space, her freedom and her college experience. For the past two years we have lived in my modest home that sits on a beautiful street behind the campus. We have made it ours with paint and wallpaper and love.

Later tonight when I have Molly Kristen Sparrow all to myself, I'm going to ask if she's done traveling now, if maybe she can be a bird I cannot tame as Mrs. Molly Hemingway.

As I step into her arms and kiss her, I know of all the places I could go, there is no place I'd rather be.

www.ingramcontent.com/pod-product-compliance
Lightning Source LLC
Chambersburg PA
CBHW060300310726
48976CB00007B/2141